ISBN-13: 978-1-952412-05-9

Cover design: Christopher Doll
Published By: Vagabond Publishing
Printed in the United States of America

Waterloo

Magdalena Richtaus, Mags to anyone who didn't enjoy being punched, was sitting at a console in Engineering. She was scrolling through reports from everyone who reported to her, waiting impatiently for the first battle with the Syndicate fleet to begin. She had served aboard Coalition frigates for almost twenty years, working her way up to senior lieutenant, and this would be only the second real clash of her career.

The first, a short skirmish over Earth, hadn't gone so well for her. She kept tightening the fist of her bioprosthetic left arm, a reminder of that day. Mags was trying to get accustomed to the feel of the artificial nerves running into her shoulder. After a few weeks of therapy, she'd been so sick of sitting around the medical bay that she told the doctors to put her back on duty. If not for the impending confrontation, she felt sure they would have argued and kept her in their care for another week or two.

A report came up on the screen, sent from Ensign Avila on the bridge. Mags couldn't stop a proud smile from flashing across her face. When her young protégé had received the field promotion, it had felt as if years of her own work were being validated with approval from the captain. Knowing Natalia was posted to the bridge for the duration of the fleet battle gave her a sense of strong pride, and also a relief at knowing one of the best was keeping a watch over things up there.

"Lieutenant?" a tinny voice said over the comms earpiece she wore.

"Go ahead."

"Chief wants someone to check on railgun emplacement three. Looks like the controls are a little sticky over there."

"Copy, I'll send a couple of people over." She ran a finger down the duty roster and found two familiar names. "Nunes and Cho, hustle to railgun three. It sounds like we have some controls that aren't responding as needed."

"Yes, lieutenant," a pair of voices said. Mags had no doubts that the two had found some dark corner somewhere out of the way. It was a poorly hidden secret in Engineering that they'd been getting closer than the brass liked coworkers to be. She'd have to adjust the shift schedules, keep them apart during work hours as much as she could. It was hard to deny that the pair worked very well together, though.

While waiting for the next request or update to come in, she pulled up camera feeds from the bow of the *Waterloo*. Since the frigate was carrying the Fleet Admiral, they were at the vanguard of the Coalition fleet. Her view was unobstructed, filled with thousands of stars as they traveled farther from Earth. The only items out of place in the picture were the seven rapidly growing ships.

The Syndicate cruiser, *Indomitable*, made the frigates surrounding it look like freight shuttles. It was still hard for her to wrap her mind around the fact that the corporate leaders of the Syndicate had built something so massive. On top of that, they had managed to hide the existence of the behemoth for more than seven years, constructing it in untraveled portions of the asteroid belt.

Mags had a chuckle as she thought of the reprimands and lectures the boys and girls in Intelligence had to be suffering through. When the Navy first saw the message from a Transport Guild captain warning of the existence of the cruiser, Intelligence had immediately responded with internal memos to all senior officers denying the possibility of such a thing.

Captain Andrews had shown her the communiqué during one of their shared meals. After serving on the same ships for two thirds of her career, the two had become close friends. The captain had been hesitant to question the denial of the cruiser's existence, but Mags had known too many Intelligence officers to put stock in something that was released so quickly. Her bullshit meter had been telling her not to believe this memo, especially.

Now they were staring down the barrel, with the cruiser half an hour away from the *Waterloo*, and Intelligence had long since tried to cover up their snafu. The current battle plan had been created with their input, and the Fleet Admiral seemed to accept every suggestion that had come from the so-called experts in Geneva.

A chime on the comms broke into her thoughts, and she pressed a button on her console to answer the request. "Richtaus."

"Lieutenant, I think we found the problem with number three." Nunes sounded uncertain as she spoke. "An actuator is reporting all kinds of errors, and Cho thinks we'll have to head outside if we want to attempt repairs."

Mags sighed and looked again at the enemy ships. They were close enough now that she could make out individual details on the cruiser. There were lumps and bumps on the hull that she felt sure were weapon emplacements. Many more than were on her frigate.

"It'll have to wait until after the battle, Nunes. Make sure you do everything possible from inside the ship to get that railgun working as best you can. Then head back to your stations."

4

"Got it, lieutenant."

The comm chimed once to tell her the call had disconnected. Just in time, since her new arm was starting to tingle. The doctors had warned her the nerves would go through periods of numbness and tingling as her body adapted. She walked around the room for a bit, swinging the bioprosthetic and stretching it out. She looked at the display on her console each time she passed by, to make sure she didn't miss any incoming requests.

On the fifth trip around the room, she saw a message come in from Ensign Avila on the bridge. Mags dropped back into the chair and pulled it forward on the rail to look at the display. She frowned as she read the message, her teeth hurting from how hard she was clenching them by the end.

Intruders on bridge, take control. Three dead. Getting ship out of battlefield. Can't let guns on friendly targets.

Mags realized that she was gripping the edge of the desk with her prosthetic, and looked down to see the plastic surface dented under the silvery gray fingers. She forced herself to release the grip, and started to type at the keyboard implanted in the console. Years of military discipline told her to get confirmation from above first.

But she knew Natalia, had worked beside the woman for years and trained her. The only person she trusted more on the *Waterloo* was the captain himself. She sent a connection request to Captain Andrews, and waited for fifteen seconds. The request refused to go through, which only confirmed Natalia's message in her mind. Andrews had never turned off his comms in all the years they had served together. He especially wouldn't have done so right before the largest fleet confrontation in history.

Mags pulled up the Engineering menus, looking through the commands that had been sent through from the bridge before Natalia's message went out. The deck beneath her feet had already started to thrum with increased intensity as the frigate's engines flared. Natalia obviously didn't want to risk injury to the crew, but needed to get the ship away from the battle quickly. Ramping up to a four G acceleration burn would have them passing through the enemy fleet within minutes, away from where they could cause harm to the other Coalition frigates.

The Chief was storming over moments after the ship started to speed up. "Richtaus, what the hell is going on in here? Someone just initiated a hard burn."

Mags was waving him over to look at the message Natalia had sent when four soldiers in matte black armor burst into the room from the corridor beyond. The suits flowed over their bodies like bumpy organic skins, leading to sleek helmets that gave them an alien appearance. It struck a chord of fear when she saw them turn in her direction.

"You will cease acceleration now," the lead soldier said in a grating electronically altered voice, deadly weapon pointing at the chief engineer.

"Okay, I'm doing it," he spluttered, stepping quickly to Mags' terminal. He tapped at the screen for several seconds, cycling through menus. Multiple attempts to abort the commands sent from the bridge resulted in flashing red screens and cursing. "What the hell is going on here?" he breathed just loud enough for the lieutenant to hear him.

A quiet hiss was the only warning, and Mags felt blood splatter across her face as the Chief yelled out in pain and slumped to the ground. He was holding an arm over his stomach, blood welling up from under the cobalt uniform.

Mags turned in anger to see four weapons all pointed in her direction now.

"Stop the engines," the modulated voice said.

"I can't! The commands were initiated on the bridge. It'll take the captain's command codes to override them while the systems are locked down."

The soldier's helmet turned a few inches to the side, and Mags guessed that the intruders were talking to each other. She dropped from her chair to kneel beside the chief engineer, trying to get a look at the bullet wound. The man's face was pale, and he was sweating intensely. His eyes were staring up at her, not focusing as they should. She hoped he was just in shock.

A hand grabbed her good arm, yanking her away. "Take us to the engine room, and tell everyone to do as we tell them. Otherwise, there will be more people like him." The weapon motioned toward the man slumped on the floor.

Mags felt rage boiling up from within, but worked hard to keep it contained as she led the black-clad soldiers through her domain and into the main engine room. A dozen people were racing around the room, yelling out questions to each other as they tried to figure out why the ship was still accelerating away from the battle. She could feel herself growing heavier with each step, and years of experience told her that the *Waterloo* was passing two G's already.

One of the engineering crew turned to see her, and his face lit up thinking that an officer had come to tell them what to do. A moment later he saw the soldiers, and his face went slack. The second person to see them reacted differently, screaming out in surprised fear and drawing the attention of everyone else.

Mags raised her hands, and shouted out to be heard. "These Syndicate bastards shot the Chief. Do what they say, or they'll kill us all." As she spoke, she was examining the enemy soldiers. They were well trained, and had spread out immediately after entering the large engine room. With their placement, they could keep every person in the room covered by at least two weapons, while being too far apart for an effective counterattack.

The crew were all herded into one corner of the room, forced to sit with their backs against a curving bulkhead. Two of the intruders kept weapons trained on them, while the other two walked around the room placing explosives in nooks and crannies. Mags could tell from the placement that these soldiers had received at least a rudimentary engineering education. The charges were set where they would do a significant amount of damage. If all of them were set off, she felt sure the reactor would go critical and tear the frigate apart.

"What do we do, lieutenant?" a quiet voice asked beside her.

Mags turned her head slightly to see a man she recognized from the many times she had been in the engine room to talk with the chief engineer. "We wait. I signaled the Marines as soon as I saw these bastards. They should be on the way down already."

The frigate was approaching three G's as she spoke. Mags could feel the increased weight pushing down on her. She couldn't figure out how the Syndicate soldiers were still moving so freely, but she doubted that the ship's Marines would be able to move as swiftly. If help didn't arrive soon, the entire frigate would be at the mercy of the menacing intruders.

Two

"Charges are set, corporal. This reactor is a bit different from what we trained with, but I'm confident we can still do the necessary damage."

Lopez couldn't stop a smirk every time she heard her new title, even as she berated herself for taking her mind from the mission. "Detonation program A is disable, and B is destroy?"

"Yes, corporal."

She used eye movements to tell her suit computer to create icons for each option on her main HUD, ensuring that she could trigger the explosives with a quick retinal or verbal command. Aside from the frigate's increasing speed, her mission had gone exactly as planned.

She opened a channel with the Group One leader. "Lieutenant, engine room is secured and charges are set."

"Excellent, corporal." Davis sounded more strained than usual, but anyone who hadn't worked with the man for most of a year wouldn't recognize the undertones in his calm voice. "We've had a bit of unexpected difficulty on the bridge. It seems that some Coalition officers have the kind of resolve I'm used to seeing in our own ranks."

"Is that why the engines are pushing hard, sir?"

"Yes. An ensign here initiated the acceleration and locked us out of the system. She won't be a problem any longer, but the captain and admiral are still refusing to give up their codes." The channel issued an almost silent static sound that told her the line had been muted.

While she waited, Lopez cast her eyes over the ship's engineering crew. Her gaze was drawn to the officer they had encountered in the previous room. One of the woman's hands was silvery gray, a new kind of bioprosthetic that she'd heard about but not seen. She was tempted to force the woman to pull up her long sleeve, to find out how much of her arm had been replaced.

Davis broke into her thoughts as the line went active again. "Lopez, we've passed by the *Indomitable*. Even if we could stop the engines now, we'd be too far away to rejoin the battle. Hold your team there, and maintain control of the engine room."

"Yes, sir," she said.

Two of her group were ordered to keep watch over the prisoners, while the third was detailed to be on lookout from the previous room. She knew the ship's Marines would attempt a rescue before the acceleration forces were too strong to resist. The officer probably thought she'd been furtive in signaling them when her group burst in, but she'd recognized the movement.

Their assault suits were built with special stabilizer frames that enabled the squad to move easily under increased gravity forces. Even though her body weighed more than twice as much at this point, Lopez could walk easily and felt little of it. Her team wouldn't begin to feel the strain until the ship surpassed three G's. Marine squads aboard the frigate wouldn't have that advantage, and would have to move quickly if they were going to have any chance of fighting back.

While they waited, Lopez walked around the engine room. She looked into every dark hollow between bulkheads and equipment, searching for anything that might be different from the Syndicate ship plans that she had trained with. It still amazed her how two entities that had grown from different ideologies could build ships that were so functionally similar to each other. Perhaps her instructors had been right, and humanity always recognized the most efficient designs.

"Corporal, I have movement." The lookout sent his helmet feeds over, showing two full squads of Marines advancing down a corridor. She snickered as she watched their laborious movements. The Marines had taken too long to respond to the request for help. It was just another proof that Coalition forces were inferior to their Syndicate counterparts.

"Gage, with me. Howell, shoot any of these crew if they try to make a move against you."

She hurried across the engine room, followed by the soldier she'd called for. They took up position to either side of the wide aperture between the two Engineering sections. Lopez pulled up the menu for the recon drones she carried. There were six of them stored in small depressions in her armor. Each was no larger than a fingernail, capable of flight for up to ten minutes before their miniscule batteries were expended.

Two of the drones detached from her suit, filament wings moving so quickly they were almost invisible. The only sound of their passing was a small whisper in the air, impossible to notice under the sound of the engines. A couple of small windows opened on Lopez's HUD to show the view from the drones as they sped out of the engineering section and along the corridor.

The Marine squads were spread out raggedly, some better able to handle the increasing gravity than others. She sent the drones along branching corridors to ensure that other squads weren't approaching from another direction. Once she was certain they were facing only two squads, she recalled the drones. By the time they were attached to her suit once more, the computer marked them as expended. Their batteries would need to be recharged before she could use them again.

"Purdy, two squads confirmed. Can you find a place where you won't be visible to them?"

"Already done, corporal," the woman said in a whisper. "I'll ambush them from the rear when you give the word."

Lopez grinned, feeling the surge of adrenaline that always came with the anticipation of fighting. They may have missed out on springing a trap against the Coalition forces in the naval battle, but they would still get a chance to take a few of the enemy down.

Her suit display was showing only a few ticks away from four G's as the first of the Marines entered the engineering substation between the corridor and main engine room. The view from Purdy's helmet camera showed the cobalt armored Marines sweeping the room with their weapons while struggling to traverse it. Their steps were slow and looked almost painful, as each boot could only slide across the deck plates. The first one to reach the body on the floor stooped to check for a pulse, shaking his head as he struggled to stand and continue moving forward.

Twelve of the sixteen Marines had entered the substation when Lopez knew she couldn't wait any longer. She gave the order, rolling out from behind the bulkhead to raise her flechette rifle and fire at the nearest soldiers. Gage followed her lead, and three of the enemy were down with their first few shots.

Purdy had hidden within some piping high on a wall, and she dropped gleefully with a heavy thump to fire rounds into the backs of the nearest Marines. She took two of them down before those nearest recognized the source of the rounds and turned to fire at her. The recon armor had protective plating sewn into the material, but a lucky shot hit her right between the chest plates. The round pierced her sternum, shattering as it went through the bone to spread metal shards through her chest cavity.

Lopez cursed when she saw the indicators go red for her squad mate, pushing that anger into her attacks. She stepped forward to pick out Marines and fire at them until they dropped to the ground, and then moved on to the next target. Gage was beside her, only a few steps away, firing just as fiercely. Each of them had been hit a few times, but the rounds were stopped by armor plating. Only seven of the Coalition Marines remained, and Lopez felt an exultation as she felt sure they were going to wipe out both squads sent against them. A sudden chiming surprised her, and she saw Howell's indicators turn red. She tried to pull up the feed from his helmet cam, but saw only a dark bulkhead.

"Gage, keep these grunts occupied while I check on Howell." The man acknowledged, and after a few more shots she turned to move as quickly as she could back to the engine room. She froze halfway across the room, sweeping the area with her weapon. Their prisoners were no longer against the curving bulkhead.

Howell was crumpled up near where she'd last seen him standing. She rushed over to check on the soldier, and grimaced as she saw the armor around the back of his neck dented. It looked as if someone had punched the man in the same spot repeatedly, driving the plating against his spine until his vertebra were cracked and spine severed. A violent display, and not what she'd expected from crew members working in Engineering.

Lopez scanned the room again, but she couldn't see any sign of the prisoners. She thought about the minor differences she had noticed between this engine room and those on Syndicate ships, and wondered if she had missed some other entry. Perhaps Marines had gotten behind them, but if so why wouldn't they attack her and Gage?

"Corporal, I need some help here!" Gage's voice was strained, and she knew she'd have to worry about the missing prisoners once the immediate threat was gone. Her group was down two members now, and she couldn't lose another.

She'd taken two steps toward the substation chamber, when a heavy weight dropped onto her shoulders. With the frigate accelerating at four G's, the extra weight was more than her suit's support structure could take. She dropped to her knees, and the flechette rifle clattered on the deck plating as it slid from her grasp.

A heavy blow on her back made Lopez cry out. Her elbows gave way, dropping her to lie flat on the deck plates with her face slamming against the front of her helmet. A hand wrapped around her shoulder, flipping her over with relative ease. The officer they first encountered was staring down at her, a dreadful grin on her face.

"It's ironic," the woman said. "You Syndicate bastards are responsible for giving me this new arm, and now it's going to help me stop you." The silvery gray hand was flexing as she spoke. The woman batted away Lopez's attempt to push her away, and then the bioprosthetic hand wrapped around the soldier's throat and started to squeeze.

Lopez could feel the armor plating around her neck begin to crumple under the strain, the edges of the steel digging into her skin. She was struggling for breath, feeling the heavy weight and powerful grip crushing her windpipe. Her attempts to hit the woman seemed feeble. Lopez was unable to get much power into arms that now weighed

14

almost five times as much as they should. As the edges of her vision started to go black, she heard Gage fearfully calling for help again. His suit indicators went red a moment later.

Knowing that her own time was awfully short, Lopez moved her eyes across the HUD. Finding what she was looking for, she blinked rapidly three times to signal the system. The indicated icon started to flash red, hard to see through the haze that was beginning to obscure her vision. As the first explosive detonated, her last thought was disappointment that she had failed the Syndicate.

THREE

Rinde Brighton watched buildings slide by through the darkly tinted windows of the government car. Geneva was quiet in the early morning hours, the sidewalks and awnings covered in a light dusting of snow. It was the first time in five years that the city had received snowfall, and he couldn't help but think it had picked the perfect day. He was on the way to the temporary headquarters of the Coalition government, an old building on the outskirts of the city that had been hastily prepared after the bombings several months before. Two of the four buildings in the main government complex had been heavily damaged in the explosion, and the prime minister had decided to transfer his ministers and senior staff to a different area away from the crowded city interior.

Security forces had worked for a week on the disused building, installing detection and monitoring systems. The walls of the building were strengthened to reduce damage in the event of another bombing, and the streets around the new headquarters were blocked off to any motorized traffic. It was now the safest part of the capital, and also the dreariest neighborhood Rinde had ever seen.

At the beginning of the year, he had been a typical member of the Coalition Parliament. One of four members for Lagos, with his fourteen years in Parliament making him the most senior member from the city. Since the beginning of the current term, he'd served as Chair of the Defense and Military Affairs committee. It was an important position, especially during the long stagnation of the cold war years.

When the war with the Syndicate had started to heat up, it had given his position even more prestige.

When the Defense Minister died in the bombings, along with a handful of other senior cabinet members, the prime minister had reached out and asked Rinde to take the job. It had been an honor to accept, but he knew it would be a grueling experience. He'd been among those pushing for the government to take a stronger stance against the Syndicate aggression. The prime minister still resisted most of the measures they called for, but the man had finally buckled under the pressure to send the fleet to meet the cruiser.

As the car came to a stop near one of the checkpoints, an aide rushed forward to pull the door open as Rinde exited the car. "Good morning, sir," the attractive dark-skinned woman said. Uju Tyjani had been with him since his earliest days in Lagos, when he'd served in the regional government. Without her, Rinde knew he'd be hard pressed to keep up with rapidly evolving events.

"Uju, I'll never understand how you can get the call after I do and still show up before me."

"You're assuming I ever leave the office," she said, her eyes sparkling.

"I sometimes wonder if you do. Keep being so efficient, and the prime minister will be asking you to replace me."

"Sir, I wouldn't take your job if they offered me twice your salary. Far too much stress for me."

"Where were you to tell me this before I accepted?" Rinde said with a laugh. They were hurrying through the empty streets, entering the government building as quickly as possible. "Please tell me I'm not the last to arrive?"

"No, several other ministers still haven't checked in yet."

They paused at a security desk, two armored Marines running scanners over them to verify no weapons were present. Rinde put a thumb on the scanner to authenticate his identity, and then stepped through the gate that snapped open when he was recognized. "Good morning, Minister Brighton," the artificial voice said as he stepped through.

An elevator was already being held open for them at the end of the row, and Rinde half jogged into it. He nodded in appreciation just before the doors closed, separating them from the building security guard who had held the doors.. As the elevator began to descend, Uju passed him a tablet that had the meeting agenda displayed.

"The prime minister wants you to speak first, sir. The aide I spoke with made it sound like he's not very happy at the moment."

"No, I imagine not." Rinde scanned the list and was dismayed to see that the recent conflict between the fleets was the only item on the hastily crafted agenda. The elevator dinged, and the doors slid open. Rinde stepped out into a dank corridor, buried a hundred meters below the building. It was originally used for maintenance and electrical generators that kept the building running during blackouts. Two decades before, such occurrences had been far too common as the government suffered through the first war with the corporate committees that ruled the Syndicate.

A uniformed guard led them along the hallway, pointing out areas where taller people needed to duck below piping and conduits passing overhead. Soon they were standing in front of a thick titanium alloy door, a keypad beside it with a DNA scanner attached. Rinde typed in the twelve digit code he had been given a month earlier, and then pressed a fingertip against the scanner. A microscopic needle pricked his skin to take a blood sample, comparing it against a massive database of every citizen in the Coalition. Millions of Syndicate citizens were in that database, as well, samples taken any time someone crossed the borders.

A loud buzzing announced that his entry had been approved, and they stepped back as the door slowly opened on heavy hinges. Loud conversation from within the chamber filtered out as soon as the airtight seal of the door was broken. Rinde could hear several voices he recognized, ministers and high ranking members of the Houses. It seemed as if more people had been invited to the urgent gathering than he'd expected.

Once the opening was wide enough, he stepped through with his aide on his heels. The security guard remained behind, ready to escort the next arrivals once the secure door was closed again. Rinde saw the Naval Minister, and beelined for the woman. She was older, her white hair pulled into a tight bun on the back of her head. The uniform she wore stood out from the suits and dresses of most others in the room. Juliette Rinova was still an active duty admiral in the fleet. The prime minister had insisted that she retain her rank when he asked her to join the cabinet, feeling that someone with ties to the fleet would serve the government better.

"Rinde," she greeted him, turning away from the Parliament members she had been speaking quietly with. "Are you ready to break the news to all these people?"

He pressed her hand gently as he nodded. "It is my unfortunate responsibility. I'd gladly let you do so, if you wish." Although he technically only had authority over the Marines and planet-based security forces, the Naval Ministry had always been seen as a subsection of the Defense Ministry.

She smiled and shook her head once. "I'm sure I'll have to run through it for quite a few people after the meeting. Not many of you bureaucrats understand fleet matters."

"I've learned more about it than I ever expected." Rinde pulled out his tablet and was about to ask her opinion on the next steps in the war effort when a trilling whistle filled the room. All eyes were drawn to a door at the side of the room. The prime minister entered with half a dozen others in tow. Answering the signal, everyone in the room hurried to take their places. Rinde found his chair at the oval table in the center of the room, folding his hands on the surface in front of him.

Once everyone was seated, the prime minister waved for Rinde to present his briefing. Standing and staring around at colleagues, some of whom he'd worked alongside for years, he spoke. "Our fleet met the Syndicate ships in a brief clash. The *Waterloo* suffered a malfunction before the battle and accelerated away unexpectedly, and our other frigates have been unable to raise communications with them. The Syndicate fleet did not slow after the initial pass. One of their vessels was destroyed, and the rest appear to be damaged to varying extents, but the cruiser and remaining support frigates continue their advance on Earth."

There was murmuring around the room, so he had to raise his voice. "We have eight days before the *Indomitable* arrives in orbit."

"What about our ships?" a voice called out. "Are they pursuing?"

"They are, but because of the acceleration to meet the Syndicate fleet they will be far behind by the time they can change momentum."

Juliette stood beside him, raising her hands at the shouts of dismay and accusation. "It's simple physics, people. You can't stop forward motion and turn in the other direction at the drop of a hat. Especially in the vacuum of space, where there's no air friction to help slow your progress."

"What do we do?" another voice called. Rinde had to hold back a smile when he saw it was Uju, shouting the question he had been hoping someone would ask.

"The Syndicate ships were damaged enough in the short attack that they are accelerating at a slower rate than before. If our frigates push their engines beyond safe limits, they will still intercept a few hours from Earth orbit. Our only hope is that they manage to damage the Syndicate ships enough to prevent them from turning weapons on our citics."

"That's not our only hope," a quiet voice said, cutting through the others in the room. Everyone turned to look at a man in his early thirties, leaning against a wall far from the powerful people in the center of the room. His exposed forearms were covered in tattoos, but his clean shaven face could have fit into any crowd on the planet. His looks were the very definition of average.

"Ladies and gentlemen," the prime minister said, patting the air with his hands to tell everyone to take their seats. Rinde followed the command, unable to look away from the unknown man as he stepped forward through the crowd to stand beside the prime minister's chair. "I suppose there is no better time than the present to introduce all of you to my Propaganda Minister. Theodore Poul."

"When did we vote to approve a new ministerial position?" Juliette whispered.

"Mr. Poul has been working with me over the last several months to craft a campaign to generate support for the war. Our citizens have grown complacent over the last few decades, convinced that war with the Syndicate wasn't necessary. We have to show them otherwise, that the status quo can't be maintained."

Poul spoke to everyone at the table, seeming to ignore the others in the room. "The wave of bombings made people angry. It was that anger that allowed Parliament to pass the legislation that finally set the fleet in motion. We need to keep that momentum going, so the people will continue supporting the prime minister as he works to keep us all safe and secure."

Rinde narrowed his eyes, staring at the speaking man. To his ears, it sounded as if this new minister was more concerned with the popular opinion of the prime minister than that of the war. He seemed to almost believe the bombings that killed thousands of Coalition citizens were a good thing.

"My office is going to be releasing a series of posters and targeted videos over the coming week," Poul continued. "Our aim is to show the people that their prime minister is working hard to protect them. We also want to show them how large a threat the Syndicate represents. They need to know all the degradations that will be heaped upon them if we lose this war. The people must fight for the Coalition, no matter what it takes."

"He's one of *those*," Juliette sighed. "He won't last long."

22

Rinde was looking at the way the prime minister seemed to hang on the man's every word, a faint smile on his face. "I'm not so sure."

FOUR

It had been a while since the voice on the other side of the wall had first spoken. Sometimes it felt like days, and other times it felt like months. When you were locked in a cell with no access to the world outside, it was hard to keep the mind focused. All that really mattered was that the voice had responded, and they had agreed to work together. It was a small hope, but the first felt in a long time.

The prisoner could hear the woman in the other cell grunting as he pressed his ear to the small vent. Grunting and straining, as she worked to strengthen her body. She'd whispered to him about her cybernetic implants being removed, an operation that left her muscles weak and wasted after years of relying on the artificial enhancement. Something about the words made him picture a face, but he couldn't remember why it was important or who it could be. He only knew he had to wait for her to be well enough to go through with the plan, and he chafed under the weight of all the seconds draining away.

There'd been a brief period when the ship shuddered and groaned around them. The woman whispered about a battle between fleets, but it felt like no more than a micro meteor storm to him. The deck had vibrated half a dozen times, what felt like heavy railguns firing magnetically accelerated rounds into space. But no more than that. Surely not enough for a battle.

Lying on the cold metal floor, he tried to remember everything that had happened since then. Had the ship shuddered just that morning? No, it had to be longer. He had used the bare toilet six times since then. No! It had been seven times. Food trays had been pushed through a slot at the bottom of the door three times. But he didn't put much stock in those anymore, after the guards had tricked him early on in his imprisonment.

Was he still sane? It was a question that seemed to occur to him less frequently than it had in the beginning. Or perhaps it occurred more often and it only seemed like the time between was longer than it truly was. Could he even say that he had been locked in the room longer than a week? No, the voice on the other side of the vent had told him it was at least five months that he had been locked away in this featureless room. He didn't ask how she knew such a thing. He just accepted it, as he accepted the idea that had come to him of how to escape this prison and be free once more.

The noises from the other room stopped, and he heard the woman breathing heavily. The sound of her breath grew louder as she dropped to the floor and got close to the vent. He closed his eyes, wondering how it would feel to have that breath on his skin instead of in his ear.

"Hello," the whisper came, always the same word. It was a word that made his heart beat faster.

"I'm here," he told her, pressing his lips against the slits in the vent. "Are you ready?"

There was breathing for a few seconds, and he felt the anticipation preceding her response. He always asked the question, waiting for the instance she would say it was time to set his plan into motion. Today wasn't that day.

"No, I'm not strong enough. I was able to stand for a count of two thousand today, but after that my legs were shaking and I couldn't stay up. I need more time."

Time. Always more time. He was obsessed with time, how you always wanted more of it and at the same time wished it would go faster. What would the world be

25

like without time? Would the stars stand still? Would planets stop turning? Could people still live and grow without it?

"Are you there?" Her voice was urgent, and he realized that he must have gotten lost in the flow of his thoughts.

"Yes. More time. Keep working."

"I will."

They were quiet for a while. He was thinking about how it would feel to share a room with another person again. It had been ages since his guards had been more than fingers pushing and pulling trays of food into or out of his cell. A harsh voice now and then reprimanding him if the tray wasn't ready to be pulled away when they came for it. He could hear the hatred in their voices, the derision that came naturally for one such as he.

"I want to tell you my name."

This again? Always she wanted to tell him her name. "No! It's not safe. I don't want to know your name, and you don't want to know mine. Not until we're free." *What is my name?* he thought.

"Okay," she said. He could hear resignation in her voice. There was a rustle as she pushed away from the wall. He almost cried out to make her stay near him longer.

"Tell me your name!" It was on his lips, but he refused to speak the words. He couldn't give in. He had to be strong. It was the only way to survive and escape.

"Am I still sane?" the prisoner asked instead, whispering the words that the woman couldn't hear.

FIVE

Mags stared down at the bodies of the four soldiers who had stormed Engineering and held her prisoner. Stripped of their fancy armor and menacing helmets, they looked like nothing more than kids. But then, everyone under twenty five started to look too young when you reached her age. The joy and triumph she had felt at killing two of the intruders and freeing the captured crew members had faded when she discovered the chief engineer had died from his wounds before the Marines could arrive.

The frigate's engines had been disabled in the detonation triggered by the last of the intruders. Luck and bad placement were the only things that saved the ship from being torn apart by a reactor explosion. Part of the blast had been funneled away from the engines by a bulkhead, leaving the ship whole but without the ability to change course or speed.

Waterloo was still heading for the outer system. It would take days to repair the engines, and even then she wasn't sure how much use they could get from the ion thrusters. Repair teams would have to do tethered checks outside the ship to see how much damage was done beyond the engine room. Mags couldn't help but feel that they used up all their luck when the reactor hadn't been touched by the bombs.

When the Marines left after clearing Engineering, she requested someone be left behind. She wanted to have someone nearby to keep her updated on what the teams approaching the bridge found. With the Chief dead, Mags was effectively in charge of the section until the captain or admiral could select a replacement. Worse, with every naval officer more senior than her on the bridge before the confrontation with the Syndicate fleet, she was now the officer in charge of the ship if it was determined that the bridge was compromised.

Dozens of people were swarming over the engines, off duty shifts called in to help with the urgent repairs. Mags yelled out an order now and then, or answered shouted questions, but for the most part she kept an ear turned toward the Marine standing nearby. Sergeant Yates was a young woman, mid to late twenties at best guess, and had the rigid posture of someone wishing they were in the action instead of just listening to it over comms.

"Is something happening, sergeant?"

"The squads are getting close to the bridge, lieutenant. My CO is going to try his override codes to force an entry."

"Keep me updated." Mags turned her attention back to the hive of activity in front of her. With the engines dead, everyone was having to work in zero gravity conditions. It was such a rare occurrence that many of the crew in the room were still growing accustomed to the feeling. For someone used to working with at least a quarter of a full G, it was easy to forget and send yourself spinning across the room with an errant push or pull.

Sighing, Mags pushed herself off the wall she was braced against. She caught the latest victim of zero gravity, using her momentum to bring them both to a stop near the center of the engine room. The man nodded his thanks, looking a little queasy as he grabbed the nearest projection and pulled himself back to where he was working.

The Marine joined Mags above the room, an urgent expression on her face. "Lieutenant, the bridge refuses to accept override codes. CO said that means it's locked down from inside with the captain's command protocols."

"Shit," Mags spat. "Still no response to communication attempts?"

"No, ma'am. The major is setting up barricades around the three entries to the bridge, in case anyone comes out."

Mags rubbed her forehead, feeling a massive headache building. On top of that, her arm was still aching where the bioprosthetic melded with skin. Her maneuver to drop on the enemy soldier from above in more than three G's had put much more strain on the artificial limb than it was supposed to bear while still healing. She knew she needed to get to the medical bay to have it checked out, but there wasn't time.

"Rafferty!"

A middle aged man with short sandy hair that only covered half of his head turned and pushed off to float up to where she was anchored. "Yes, lieutenant?"

"I'm putting you in charge down here. Make sure everyone keeps working on those engines. I want this ship ready to return to Earth in five days, tops."

"Okay," he said, warily looking around at the mess left behind after the explosions. She appreciated that he didn't point out how crazily optimistic that timeline was.

"Find some maintenance crews to check the ion jets outside the ship, too. I want that done and a report submitted no later than eleven hundred tomorrow."

"Yeah, sure. I'll get it done, lieutenant."

Mags patted him on the shoulder, giving him a gentle push back down to the mayhem below. With a wave for the Marine to follow, she pushed off and floated toward the wide doorway that led into the substation where she usually worked. Thinking about a normal workday of dispatching and monitoring teams working on various requests throughout the ship made her feel nostalgic.

They continued into the corridor, and she could feel the Marine wanting to ask their destination. The young woman held back, respecting a senior officer to know what they were doing. After a few twists and turns along the corridors, they entered a lift. Mags pressed the button for deck two on the pad beside the door.

"Sergeant, I know you want to be in on the action. So do I."

"Yes, ma'am." Yates said hesitantly.

"Save your speeches about how senior officers shouldn't put themselves into dangerous situations. If we can't regain control of the bridge, this entire ship is the most dangerous situation any of us have ever been in."

"Yes, ma'am."

The lift dinged, and the doors opened. Two Marines were stationed by the doors, turning to watch them exit into the corridor. "This deck is restricted," one of the Marines said, reaching out to prevent them from moving forward.

"Seeing as I'm the senior officer in charge of the ship until we can determine what's happening on the bridge, I'd say I'm authorized." Mags didn't look back as she pushed off from the lift doors and propelled herself ahead. She could hear Yates say something quietly to the Marines before following her.

Around an intersection, they found the first Marine barricade. It was set up only ten meters from one of the two main doors onto the bridge. A full squad of Marines were crouched behind the interlocking steel plates that were magnetically attached to the decking. One of them, with rank bars marking him as a lieutenant, waved them down behind cover.

"What are you two doing here? This deck needs to remain clear of all personnel."

Mags shook her head. It was obvious that the Marines lived in their own little world, not aware of the rank structure of the Navy personnel onboard the frigate. But then, she couldn't say she knew where this Marine lieutenant fit into their own command, or even what his name might be.

"I'm Lieutenant Richtaus, the most senior officer not trapped in there." She pointed at the doors down the corridor. "What's the plan for getting everyone out?"

The Marine officer looked at Sergeant Yates, and she nodded in confirmation. Mags could almost feel his resigned sigh as he faced forward again. "My captain is checking on our options for breaching the bridge. It won't be easy, since it was built to resist any attempts like this."

Grunting, Mags turned to look back the way they'd come. "You always have Marine guards on the lift?"

"Yes, and on the stairwells. Doubled up when we're anticipating action, as we were today."

"None of them saw anything, right? No one was knocked out or killed by enemy intruders?"

"Of course not," the Marine lieutenant said. He seemed almost offended at the suggestion that his soldiers could have been victims of a surprise attack.

"Okay, so how did *they* get in there?" Mags looked at the man with raised brows, and saw understanding bloom on his face. The Marine officer turned away, and she could hear him talking into his comms. Mags shared a look with Yates, glad to see the sergeant smiling approvingly. After fifteen minutes of listening to one side of a long conversation, the Marine lieutenant raised his voice.

"Our EVA team found the entry point. Looks like the Syndicate troops cut through the hull above the admiral's quarters. Captain Farrow has authorized entry, so we're on alert in case the enemy try to exit the bridge."

Mags looked around, and leaned back. "Sergeant, I'd really love to have a weapon right now. Any chance of that?"

Yates looked at the Marine officer, and saw a slight nod. Motioning, she led Mags down the corridor, into a small armory where the Marines performing guard duty around the bridge would gather armor and weapons before and after shifts. The locker with the flechette rifles was still secured, but the cage with stun pistols was standing open. Yates passed one of the pistols over, and pulled a weapon to slide into the empty holster attacked to her own thigh plate.

"No lethal weapons?" Mags asked, staring at the locker.

"We can't risk it, ma'am. The rifles have a good deal of recoil, which is too dangerous in zero gravity. Stun weapons have less of a kick, which means less momentum pushing back at us each time the trigger is pulled."

"Oh." She looked at the pistol, making sure she understood the mechanics of the weapon. Naval officers were required to go through weapons training, but it had been years since her last course. "Are these bolts going to penetrate that special armor, if they're wearing the same thing as the group that was in Engineering?"

Yates nodded, reaching over to show her how to dial up the amperage. "Keep that setting high. That much juice should short circuit those fancy suits, and hopefully jump into the person wearing it. It'd probably be lethal if it hit flesh, so make sure you don't fire wildly and hit a friendly."

Armed and feeling more confident, they returned to the barricades to crouch and wait. Mags was wishing she was patched into the Marine channels so she could hear what was happening on the hull of the ship. She was turning to ask about getting one of their comm systems when the Marine lieutenant grinned. "They're in. Squads three and seven found the holes on the inner hull where the enemy cut through, and they are in the ready room just off the command deck. Breaching the bridge in two minutes."

The Marines visibly tensed up, waiting for any indication of how things progressed behind the doors they kept their weapons trained on. Mags shared their anticipation, wishing she could've been among the party storming the attackers on the bridge.

A hand touched her shoulder, and she turned back to see Yates leaning forward. Holding their heads together, Mags could faintly hear the voices over the Marine comms.

"Breaching door in," a voice said, starting a countdown. "Three... two... one."

There was a loud squealing sound, the door from the admiral's cabin onto the bridge being forced opened. Magnetic boots thumped against the deck as the Marines rushed through onto the command deck. Mags closed her eyes, trying to imagine how the two squads would file out and search the area for enemy soldiers before descending to the main bridge.

A jarring stutter issued on the comms, followed by the sound of someone dropping to the deck. "Return fire," someone shouted.

"Two contacts on command deck, and shots from bridge below."

"I see two targets on bridge. Make that three. We have five total!"

For half a minute, the channel was filled with the sound of heavy breathing and weapons firing. The flechette rifles gave off a quiet noise that was hard to hear over the comm lines. Grunts or groans came through the comm now and then, and Mags could only hope it wasn't their own people getting hit by the lethal rounds.

"Command deck clear," a deep voice called out, raising a ragged cheer from the Marines behind the barricades outside the bridge. "Squads advance to lower deck."

A voice broke into the line, and she recognized the captain of the Marines on board the frigate. "Are the captain and admiral accounted for?"

"The captain is injured but awake, sir. No visual on the admiral at this time."

"Get medics at the ready outside the command deck. Squad seven, advance and clear the bridge. Squad three, maintain control on command deck and assist from above." Mags wondered how the Marine captain could know which squads to give the jobs to, and then realized he must have access to their helmet cams. She grumbled to herself for not thinking of it sooner and heading to his office instead of crouching behind the barricade uselessly.

"Seven is advancing. Three enemy targets, two taking cover behind bridge stations and the other no longer in visual."

"Fire when you have a clear target."

Silence again for several seconds before the sounds of weapon fire filled the channel. Yates had her teeth bared as they listened, the muscles in her neck corded with the desire to be part of the action on the bridge.

"Two more down, bridge is clear."

"Where the hell is that other bastard?"

"Anyone have eyes on the admiral?" the Marine captain called out urgently.

"Negative, sir. No visual on Admiral Holgerson."

Mags thought furiously, trying to recall the exact layout of the bridge. She'd been there only a handful of times over the last year, usually to report to Captain Andrews on the status of the *Waterloo*'s upgrades and retrofitting. The command deck was wide open, with a large console against the back wall divided into six stations and a rail at the front where senior officers could look down on the people working the bridge below.

The main bridge was filled with five rows of terminals, sixteen total, forming a rough inverted V shape from rear to front. There was a walkway around the terminals so the junior officers overseeing multiple stations could move easily between them. And at the back of the room...

"Yates, tell them there's a room under the command deck. It's a small area for the officers and crew to grab food and drink without having to leave the bridge. The door is flush with the wall, so it's invisible unless you know it's there."

The sergeant relayed the information through the Marine channel, and Captain Farrow cursed. "That's labelled as dead space on our schematics. Squad seven, get into that room."

"Copy, sir. Advancing on rear wall now. How do we open the door?"

Mags relayed the information through Yates. "Second panel from the left, press against the seam about three feet up from the ground. It'll slide open."

"Copy," the voice said, speaking quietly. Everyone on the channel waited breathlessly, and Mags jumped when she heard a grating modulated voice call out for everyone to stand away. It was the same sound the soldiers in Engineering had made when they spoke, their voices scrambled by the suit's computers.

"Captain, one enemy combatant. He has a weapon on the admiral, shielding himself behind."

"If you get a shot on that Syndicate bastard without hitting the admiral, you take it."

"Copy. Enemy is backing toward port exit from bridge. Be advised that it looks like he's going to exit."

Mags grinned, grateful now that she'd ended up behind the barricades. The door they were facing was the port entry for the bridge. She raised her stun pistol and kept it trained on the space where the enemy soldier should appear. "Come on," she whispered. "Come to mama."

Seconds flew by with no movement from the doors, and then they swished open to show the back of a soldier in matte black armor. Mags gritted her teeth, reminded of the intruders who killed the Chief. She raised her pistol to point it at the soldier's back, seeing the Marines around her do the same thing.

"Drop your weapon!" the Marine lieutenant nearby called out. The enemy soldier's helmet turned slightly, looking over their shoulder. "Drop it now!"

Admiral Holgerson was completely motionless in the grasp of his captor, and Mags couldn't help but admire his nerve. She whispered to Sergeant Yates, telling the woman about the strengths and weaknesses of the Syndicate armor that she had seen during the hostage situation earlier. That information was passed along through the Marine communication channels. She could see weapons shifting slightly as Marines sought out better targets on the soldier's back.

36

"If you shoot me, your admiral dies," the Syndicate soldier said, their voice modulated into harsh tones by the suit's computers.

"You'll die, too," Holgerson said, loudly enough for them all to hear. "Shoot him."

The enemy soldier's arm tightened around the admiral's chest, their weapon raising to his head. Without a second of hesitation, the marines around Mags began to fire. She joined in, getting off a shot with her stun pistol before the soldier's arm drooped and their weapon fell from nerveless fingers. The Marines on the bridge had been firing lethal rounds, and she could see blood dripping from several wounds as the enemy soldier crumpled to the ground. Admiral Holgerson extracted himself, pulling his uniform straight and nodding in gratitude to those behind the barricade.

"Squads, medics are seconds out," the Marine captain said over the channel. "Give me status on bridge staff."

"Admiral Holgerson is uninjured, sir. The rest of the bridge crew are deceased."

"Captain Andrews is injured, looks like a shot only centimeters from the femoral. There's a lot of blood but he's awake and talking. All other officers on command deck are dead, sir."

"No!" Mags cried out. She didn't realize until that moment how much hope she'd been holding onto that Natalia Avila would still be alive. It was a relief that the captain she had served with for so long would make it, but it felt like a hollow victory with so many others dead.

SIX

Erik Frost was starting to hate the high gravity compression suit. After days of being stuck in the bulky garment, feeling water and air coursing along tubes tight against his skin to keep blood flowing, he was craving the freedom of wearing only a ship's jumpsuit again. Not to mention getting out of the command chair where he spent most of his days, as they continued to push the *Vagabond* as hard as possible to reach Earth.

"What's the status?" he asked.

"*Indomitable* is slowing, five hours from Earth. Thirty one hours for us." Mira sounded as exhausted as he felt, and Erik felt a little guilty for pushing his crew so hard.

"When do we need to start the braking burns?"

"Soon." Mira's screens started to change, and he knew she was whispering voice commands to the system. "Now, really, unless you want to skim the atmosphere and have to circle the planet."

Erik thought about the maneuver. The friction from the atmosphere would slow the ship quickly, but the heat generated would put a great deal of strain on their new hull. He wasn't sure how long they could stand that kind of pressure, and didn't want to bother Fynn with it. "Go ahead."

The engines cut out almost immediately, and he felt his body sliding forward as the gel of his command chair released him from its protective grip. The straps pulled tight as his body floated in the sudden zero G. *Vagabond* was still shooting across space at an incredible rate of speed, but inside the fragile steel skin there were no physical forces on their bodies. It was almost peaceful, and he felt a strong temptation to release his restraints so he could float free through the corridors of the freighter.

Without warning, the engines fired once again and he was pushed deep into the gel. Mira had flipped the ship around, so that the powerful ion engine at the rear of the vessel could exert more power than the small thrusters on the bow of the ship. They would slow faster, but have to suffer through being trapped in crash couches and high gravity suits until it was done.

He voiced commands to his display to flip through reports until he verified that the rest of the small crew had handled the brief maneuver well. The four of them were still strapped in, enduring the same confinement that he had for most of the week.

Isaac was in the technology hub, still working with the computer systems to improve their functionality. He'd tried to get his captain to load up another AI during the refit on Luna, but Erik had been firm in his desire to run the ship without one for now. He wasn't sure if he could ever trust another artificial intelligence system again after Aurora had gone crazy and almost killed them all.

Jen was in the compact medical bay, with the monitor showing that she was deeply asleep. He couldn't help but wonder how she was adjusting to being aboard a freighter again after seven years trapped aboard the *Indomitable*. She seemed overjoyed to be able to use her medical training again, instead of being stuck as a basic orderly.

Fynn and Tom were in Engineering. The two had become good friends after their escape from the Syndicate cruiser. Fynn had helped the other man through some rough patches, times when Tom was feeling crushed by the betrayal of their old crewmate. Even though Tom had worked as a simple cargo hauler on the old *Telemachus*, he had taken to the engine room like a natural gear head.

Erik still felt a deep sense of grief every time he realized Tuya was no longer on board the freighter. He realized with a shock that he'd not thought of her since the second battle, when the Syndicate frigates were disabled or destroyed. He hoped that she was still safe on the *Indomitable*, and that she'd managed to find her brother, Altan, captured during the escape attempt many months before.

A chime from the terminal drew Erik's attention, and he gave the verbal command to accept the connection request. A face appeared on the screen that sent his heart soaring, and brought a wide smile to his face.

"Heya, handsome. Are you guys getting close to home?" Dexterity Avila was grinning just as widely as he was, her even teeth white against her brown skin. Amber eyes flashed at him in the picture, partially hidden by long, curly black hair that could never be contained.

"Hi, beautiful. We're about thirty hours out, according to Mira." Erik had been infatuated with the Transport Guild representative for years, ever since he took command of the ship after his father died. Imprisonment and escape from the *Indomitable* had given him the resolve to finally voice his feelings, and he'd been stunned to find that she felt the same for him. They'd had only three days together on Luna, but made the most of them.

"Good. I can't wait to see you again. You did such a great job executing the plan, dropping the debris in the path of those ships."

"Not sure if I did it well enough, though, since that cruiser is still around and threatening Earth." The plan

40

hatched by the Guild president had destroyed one of the enemy frigates, but only dealt moderate amounts of damage to the rest of the Syndicate fleet. It had been more than they'd expected, but less than he'd hoped. "Have you had any news about the *Waterloo?* Your sister is on that ship, isn't she?"

Her eyes flitted away from the screen and then back, her smile fading. "Natalia. Yes, she's serving on board. I haven't heard anything from her since a few days after they left Earth orbit. My mom hasn't gotten any messages, either. But from what I'm hearing, no one has heard anything from the ship since it started accelerating away from the first battle."

"Sorry to hear that, Dex. I'm sure she's okay. That frigate looked fine, so I bet it was just an engine malfunction." Erik knew his words weren't as reassuring as he hoped.

"I actually called you about something else, though. Did you hear about the riots in Aldrin?"

Aldrin Dome, the Coalition counterpart to the Syndicate Armstrong Dome, had been hit twice by bombings. The first destroyed the landing pads and docking facility minutes after the *Vagabond* departed them, and the second had killed two of the three Marine squads stationed at the checkpoint in the tunnel that connected the domes. In the wake of that attack, Aldrin administrators had pulled the Marines in to protect their building.

The dome's citizens felt betrayed by the act, gathering in the central square to demand answers. The crowds had grown every day, and eventually the resentment boiled over causing a bottle to be thrown from the crowd. A Marine hit by the projectile overreacted, firing into the crowd of civilians. By the end, eight of the protestors were dead and the dome administration was still refusing to speak about their plans for the future.

The Transport Guild was now the only entity providing for the citizens of the dome. Using freighters that had been unable to have guns mounted after the docking facilities were destroyed, President Meyers had food and supplies brought up from Earth. He also brought in people willing to work in the dome that the admiral in charge of the *Indomitable* had threatened to demolish. Before the protesters were killed, he'd managed to get a new landing pad and docking tube installed, allowing for quicker access to the dome.

After the shootings in the square, the people of Aldrin had gone wild. Many tried to leave the dome, but seats to get off Luna were limited with only Guild freighters running supplies. Others took their frustration and anger out on anyone around them. Homes and businesses were broken into and looted, people were attacked and left in the streets, and some maniac had even started a fire in the home the dome administrator had not been to in weeks.

"Yeah, that's a strange situation. I never thought I'd see people turn on their own so easily."

"They feel like the government has abandoned them, and I don't know that they're wrong. The dome administrator refuses to speak, the Coalition government on Earth never mentions Luna, and if not for our freighters the people would be struggling to get the food and supplies that they need to survive."

"Are you staying safe? I don't want to get a message that some wackjob attacked you in the streets on the way home."

Dex held up a stun pistol, filling the screen with the weapon. "Meyers insists that I carry it all times these days.

Two of the militia guards walk me home the rare times that I don't sleep in the Guildhall, too."

"Wait, militia? When did that happen?"

She grinned, leaning forward to get closer to the camera. "That's one of the things we need to talk about. President Meyers is changing things up, and he needs the advice of people with experience. When you reach Luna, he wants you to land at the dock and meet him here."

"But the cruiser will be over Earth. I can't just ignore it while they do whatever they want to the people below. They could even turn their guns on Aldrin, as they originally planned."

Her curly hair flew as she shook her head sharply. "I'm watching the *Indomitable* approach now on another screen. They're aiming for orbit over Hong Kong. With all their frigates gone, I think the Executive Committee is freaking out a little bit and feeling unprotected."

"They should," Erik said. "Three Coalition frigates are hard on their heels."

"Exactly. They have to be wary of each other right now, until one feels comfortable attacking the other." A cute little smirk spread across her lips, making Erik wish he were sitting in front of her and could kiss those lips. "The Defense Minister in Geneva is even trying to get in contact with us again. After more than a week of total silence, convinced they didn't need the Transport Guild ships any longer, they're calling to beg us to work with them."

"Will we? I wouldn't mind joining forces with the frigates again and sending a few railgun rounds through that cruiser."

"Get here as fast as you can, and you can talk to Meyers about it. See me first, though."

"I plan on it, Dex. We'll divert to Luna instead of entering orbit around Earth."

After the call ended, Erik was feeling better than he had in a week. Just getting to chat with Dex over a link with no delay was enough to make him feel slightly giddy. He liked the idea of the Guild forming a militia, too. It felt like they were taking action, instead of sitting back and letting the adults decide what scraps they could have from the table.

SEVEN

The bridge of the *Indomitable* was silent as the cruiser approached a home world that many of the original crew hadn't seen in a long time. Admiral Yumata hadn't been this close to Earth in more than eight years, since the day he left the planet on a specially modified shuttle to find the perfect location to build a devastatingly powerful ship in secret. He shared the awe and wonder felt by his crew as they looked upon the blue and green planet on the large screens.

In all those years, he'd worked autonomously with only occasional reports sent to and from the ruling committees. Now, he received almost hourly requests to speak with some committee member or another. At first, it had been refreshing to speak with people he only knew through highly encrypted video files that were often weeks out of date by the time he received them from relays in the asteroid belt. Within a few days, it had become an onerous chore to have to explain yet again why he failed to crush the Coalition fleet to some pampered ass sitting in a cushy office.

A mechanical whine followed by heavy footsteps alerted him to a new presence on the command deck. When he'd selected his first officer, he failed to consider how much tension their opposing ideas could cause over the long years. "Admiral," Captain Guildersen said as he stepped up to the rail to look out over the bridge below. The man had somehow grown even more insufferable since receiving his promotion directly from the Military Committee several days before. "It's good to be home again. Will you transfer to the planet as soon as we are in orbit?"

Yumata raised an eyebrow, one of his few visible signs of emotion. "This ship is my home, captain. I will not leave her until the Coalition is defeated and there's no one left to stand in the way of Syndicate progress." He saw a grimace on the fat man's face from the corner of his eye, and smiled inside. Guildersen had tried to hide his desire to take command, but his feelings were too obvious.

"It's a shame that your Lieutenant Davis couldn't be here to share the moment," the captain said, a gloating tone in his voice. "I suppose we placed too much faith in the man and his team of so-called elite soldiers."

"Ghost Squad succeeded in their mission, captain. The *Waterloo* was removed from the fight, and will not trouble us again."

"Then why haven't there been any communications from the assault squad, sir? It's been more than a week since they infiltrated the frigate."

"There are too many possibilities to dwell upon it." Yumata turned and strode across the command deck to stand over the bank of stations at the rear. The lieutenant in charge of communications was speaking with someone on the ground, while the lieutenant commander in charge of the cruiser's weapons was trying to request a shipment of replacement railguns.

When six of the Syndicate frigates had rushed out from Earth to meet the cruiser during its advance into the system, they'd brought along enough of the large weapons to fill twelve emplacements. With their eighteen railguns and four torpedo bays filled with sleek and deadly ammunition, they had felt ready to face anything the Coalition sent against them. A feeling that drained away when the cruiser

46

passed through the long trail of debris dropped by several freighters in the first confrontation. Yumata still kept the extent of the damage from anyone outside of his senior staff and the Military Committee, but most of their weaponry had been damaged or destroyed when the chunks of rock and ore had smashed against the ship. He could count on perhaps four railguns, and only the two torpedo tubes at the rear of the ship.

He'd urged the Military Committee to let him rain destruction on Aldrin Dome with the operational weapons, but they refused the request and told him to take up a protective orbit over the Syndicate capital. With three of the Coalition frigates only hours behind, they wanted to make sure their own coddled carcasses were covered. Yumata had felt a wave of disdain for his supposed superiors at that moment, but still followed their orders.

"*Indomitable* has attained steady orbit, admiral." The navigational officer looked up as he spoke.

"Excellent work. How long until resupply shuttles will arrive from the surface?"

The communications and weapons officers shared a chagrined look, before the first turned to deliver the bad news. "Resupply hasn't been authorized, sir. The Military Committee is asking that you travel to Hong Kong to meet with them and discuss strategy."

"Yes, that sounds like an excellent idea." Guildersen had snuck up behind him while his attention was diverted, something the large man should never have been able to do. "Prepare the admiral's shuttle. I'll take care of the ship while you're away, sir."

Yumata turned and frowned slightly at Guildersen. "I think you should come along, captain. Dealing with the committee is more your thing than mine, so I will welcome your input."

Guildersen turned a sneer into an ingratiating smile. "Of course, admiral. I'm always happy to be of service, however I can."

Half an hour later, a Marine shuttle was lifting from the deck in Bay Three. It would take ten minutes for them to reach the ground, and the craft was already cleared for a landing on top of the towering skyscraper that housed the committees that ruled and regulated Syndicate territory. Yumata was smiling as they entered the atmosphere, quite pleased that he had thwarted Guildersen's attempt to have them depart the cruiser in the sleek and luxurious shuttle constructed for his personal use. He preferred the dangerous looking assault ship, which would give the impression he wanted.

As the ramp on the side of the shuttle hissed open after landing, Yumata led the way down the short set of steps. There were three people waiting near the landing pad, one in an expensively cut suit and the other two wearing the shiny black armor of Syndicate Marines. The one in the fancy suit hurried over with an oily smile and clammy handshake. He looked to be in his early thirties, with a pale clean-shaven face below long brown hair that was slicked back against his scalp.

"It's an honor to have you back on Earth, Admiral Yumata. I'm Morris Abernathy, junior member of the Military Committee."

"Pleasure to meet you," Yumata lied, eying the Marines with approval at their sharp appearance. He vaguely wondered which conglomerate the man owned a piece of to get a position on one of the most important committees. His training told him he should show such a man respect, but eight years of having no superiors made it extremely difficult to do.

Guildersen was more effusive with his greetings, praising the recent performance of the committee member's company. *He would know,* Yumata mused. *The captain has always been too concerned with matters outside the fleet.* Before the two men could finish trading their false praises, he marched forward. The Marines fell into step just behind, with the junior committee member hurrying to walk at his side as they entered the building.

After descending a dozen levels, they arrived outside a set of double doors in a marbled hallway. The suited man waved the admiral toward a row of plush leather chairs, and an attendant hurried over to ask if they should like something to drink. "The Military Committee is in session at the moment," Abernathy said. "I'll let them know you're here, and someone will come out to escort you in when we're ready. Shouldn't be more than an hour or two." He disappeared through the doors, squeezing through without allowing a view within.

Yumata fumed as he sat stiffly in the overly plush chair. The committee had summoned him, so they should have already been waiting for his arrival. He was being forcibly reminded of the petty gestures of those in power, as they showed him that even the commander of the most powerful ship in the system could be made to wait.

Guildersen spent the time admiring expensive paintings hung along the hall, sipping at spring water in a glass filled with perfectly square ice cubes. The fat man was almost purring at being so close to the seats of power, and Yumata began to wonder if forcing him to come along had been a mistake.

It took precisely seventy three minutes for the double doors to open wide, and emit a crisply attired woman who called for Yumata. He rose from the leather chair and pulled his uniform tightly to get rid of wrinkles. Stepping forward, he held up a hand. "I'll meet the committee alone, captain. Please wait here until we're done."

Guildersen's face went red with anger at the obvious snub. "Of course, admiral," he said through clenched teeth.

The committee chamber was dominated by a curving table facing the doors. Seven people sat at the table, with one empty chair at the far end. The attendant led him to a small table, pulling back the single chair as he sat to face the members of the committee. As she retreated to stand against the wall of the room, Abernathy introduced him to each member of the committee as if he hadn't already been sharing messages with these people for months.

"Admiral Yumata," a woman near the center of the table said. "Welcome to the committee chamber. I'd like to start out by saying that we're all impressed with the ship you designed and shepherded through construction. The *Indomitable* is truly an awe-inspiring sight, one that assures the world that Syndicate power can't be ignored."

"Thank you, madame chairwoman." Selene Onassis was CEO of the company that produced most of the weapons and hardware in his ship, so Yumata was very familiar with her influence on the committee. "It has been an immense honor and privilege to be put in charge of such a vessel."

"That's what we wanted to discuss today," another member of the committee said, leaning forward as Yumata turned his attention upon him. "This committee feels, and the Executive Committee agrees, that an officer of your skill and standing deserves a better command than a single ship."

"Especially now that the rest of the fleet is gone," Abernathy chimed in, earning a sharp look of reproach from the chairwoman.

"Be that as it may," the man speaking to Yumata said loudly, "we feel that you've earned a posting on the planet." He waved toward the empty seat at one end of the table. "Admiral Yumata, your service has earned you a significant number of shares in multiple corporations. In recognition of that, we are honored to invite you to join the Military Committee."

"Thank you," Yumata said. "I am honored by the offer, but I must decline. I prefer to stay with my ship."

Met with a stony expression where they'd expected joyful acceptance, the committee shared dismayed looks. The chairwoman took over. "Admiral, you'll still have oversight on how the *Indomitable* is put to use. As you know, this committee determines the strategy and targets of our ships and soldiers. As one of us, you will have greater access and control than you possibly could on a single ship."

"I feel that my skills are more valuable on the bridge of the *Indomitable*, madam chairwoman. There is no one else I would trust with her command."

There was a bit of mumbling between the people at the curving table. The chairwoman tried once more. "Admiral, it's my understanding we just promoted your chosen first officer. Captain Guildersen has an exemplary record, and we're quite confident that he can take command of the cruiser in your place. He will oversee repairs and rearmament. You belong here, admiral, where you can help us with the larger decisions."

Yumata clenched his hands, the only outward sign of the roiling feelings that were seething within. Guildersen had outplayed him, somehow. There was no other answer for why the committee would be trying so hard to get him to leave his ship. He knew there was discontent about the outcomes of the two brief battles with the Coalition frigates, but that shouldn't have been enough to cause his removal from the cruiser.

They were careful to couch it in terms of offering him an honorable position, but he knew accepting a seat on the Military Committee would make him unable to affect change or direct operations. His voice would be a minor one at the table, always outvoted and overruled by those who controlled larger stakes in the corporations that ruled the Syndicate.

He also knew that he had no choice. If he continued to decline the offer, there would be other reasons to keep him on the planet. This battle was lost, but there were still many more ahead. He would have to make the smart moves, and keep his eyes open for a chance to take an advantage.

Admiral Yumata rose, and bowed deeply to the seven people sitting before. "It is a privilege to accept your offer, madam chairwoman. I hope that I can prove to be a valued member of the Military Committee."

EIGHT

Erik watched the *Indomitable* enter a high orbit over the Syndicate capital with relief, but also a great deal of confusion. For several hours, the cruiser could have done as it liked to the planet below. He couldn't understand the reasoning for holding back, even while he appreciated that it had happened.

When the three surviving Coalition frigates straggled in and took up orbits over Coalition space, he became frustrated. It appeared as if the Earth powers were going to retreat back into the tense standoff that had existed for two decades. He couldn't understand the Coalition thinking if that were the case, since they were only giving the Syndicate time to repair any damage suffered by the massive cruiser.

The *Vagabond* arrived a day later, entering a brief orbit around Luna before they received clearance to land at Aldrin's functional docking pad. As the freighter descended, he could see workers clearing away the remaining wreckage from the explosion. There was already a row of thick metal pylons driven into the gray dust where a second pad would shortly be constructed.

As soon as the ship had settled on her landing struts, he unstrapped from the command chair and hurried to his quarters. He could hear Mira's chuckles as he left the room, but ignored her. He'd stripped out of the high gravity suit as soon as they entered orbit, and now he took a quick spritzing shower and ran a razor over several days of stubble.

Once he felt clean and presentable, he pulled on denim pants and a nylon shirt. He preferred a jumpsuit while on board the ship, but liked to wear civilian clothes when he entered a colony or lunar dome. It helped him blend in and feel more normal. It also made him feel more attractive, which was most important in this instance.

Tom and Jen were already waiting in the airlock antechamber as he entered. He pretended not to see their sly glances as he stepped up to the console and initiated the procedure to cycle the lock. The trio stepped inside as soon as the door opened and waited patiently for the atmosphere to match that in the docking tube. It was all he could do to keep himself from running forward once the airlock opened and he could enter the rigid tube. The hard surface felt strange under his feet after years of the modern flexible docking tubes.

The airlock on the other side of the tube stood open, and a familiar figure was already inside. Erik rushed forward and wrapped his arms around Dexterity, lifting her in a tight hug as their lips met. A whistle from behind made him lower her to the ground, and sent a blush across his face.

"Get a room, you two," Jen said through a broad grin. "Preferably not one I'm sharing."

Dex patted him on the cheek and then extricated herself to step forward and greet Jen and Tom. She had only met them briefly while the *Vagabond* was in port for a quick refit, but Erik knew they all seemed to like each other. Dex had been too young to be working in the Guild office when the other two served aboard the *Telemachus* more than seven years earlier.

"I'm glad both of you were able to come," she said. "President Meyers is hoping to meet with each of you after he talks with Erik. There's a lot of pressing business to get through."

Tom shrugged, and tossed his small bag over his shoulder. "I'm not sure why the president of the Guild wants to meet with me, but it's the least I can do after you've all been so good to us. Promise me he isn't going to keep us from getting back up there to join the fight when the rest of the Guild ships arrive."

"I can assure you that President Meyers has no intention of keeping you from the fight, Tom." Dex smiled at him, and then turned to lead the group out of the airlock chamber. The Aldrin docking facility was still under construction, being rebuilt after the bombing that mangled it into uselessness.

"Wow," Erik said as he looked around. "They decided to take the opportunity to make it larger, huh?"

"Yes, we did." Dex continued walking a few steps ahead of the group, so he couldn't see her face as she spoke.

"We? Is the Guild working with the dome administrator now?" That came as a surprise, based on how badly the administration had been handling the situation since the bombing that killed two thirds of the dome's Marines.

"Sort of?" Dex turned and shrugged. "Meyers will explain it better than I can."

He quickened his pace to draw even with her, matching her stride. "You're being very secretive all of a sudden. I hope you'll at least tell me if I get to see you tonight when I'm done at the Guildhall."

Her warm laughter sent shivers down his spine, and he felt anticipation flood through him. "You're mine as soon as that meeting is done, mister. I already told Mira not to expect you back on the ship tonight."

"Uh huh, conspiring with my crew now?" He grinned over, leaning in to nudge her shoulder. "I'll have to talk to them about mutiny when I get back on board."

"You won't even remember it when I'm through with you."

"Promises, promises." He was feeling elated as they approached the dome's central square. As soon as they exited the walkway, however, he came to a standstill. The pleasant airy space that he was used to was filled with men and women carrying weapons. There were two Marines in Coalition armor standing near the administration building on the far side, while closer to the Guildhall were more than a dozen people in gray uniforms running through drills. "What's going on?"

"That's part of our new militia," Dex said, pulling his arm to get him walking again.

"Part of? There are more than that? Isn't this kind of thing against the rules of our charter with Earth?"

"Patience, Erik. You'll get all your answers soon."

Inside the Guildhall, he found the same even rows of desks with low walls surrounding them that he was familiar with. But there were twice as many, and the people sitting at them were less raucous and free spirited than normal. It was also a shock to see two people with dull metallic armor plating over gray uniforms standing to either side of the door, stun pistols and batons hanging from their belts.

Dex led them to a small area outside the president's office, getting Jen and Tom settled into chairs before ushering Erik into the office. That space had also changed almost beyond recognition from the last time he'd been inside. The glass-topped desk Meyers used was still in place, but another had been added to the opposite side of the room along with several strong safes and a secure server cabinet.

Meyers himself looked to have aged a few years in the weeks since Erik left the dome. His thick brown hair had much more gray in it, and the dark circles under his eyes looked to be spreading. The president still had a bright politician's smile, though, as he rose to shake hands and greet the returning captain.

"Erik, great work out there with *Montford* and *Cambier*. I think it's safe to say the three of you made the largest contribution to that first skirmish."

"Thank you, sir. I just wish we could have ended everything there."

"We all do, son. You work with the cards you're dealt, though. I still have sources on the ground in both territories. I'm hearing that the guns on that behemoth bore the brunt of the damage. My guess is that they kept running because of it."

"Why haven't the Coalition frigates moved against it, then?"

"Political wrangling, of course. Have you seen those ads the prime minister is putting out?"

Erik groaned. "I saw a few in the newscasts on the way in. Seems like fearmongering to me. 'Vote for me, or we'll lose the war' kind of stuff."

Meyers chuckled. He opened a drawer and pulled out a data chip, which he slid into the slot next to his desk's display. Waving Erik over to view the screen, he pressed the button to play the ad. "This is the latest one from Geneva. It doesn't go live until tomorrow."

On the display, the image panned across an idyllic landscape of green rolling hills with farmhouses dotted across the countryside. When the image came to a stop, they could see a small town with old-fashioned buildings and children playing football in the street. A gentle female voice began to speak over the images, talking about how the peace and security of the Coalition was under threat. Suddenly, soldiers in exaggerated black armor with large weapons rushed into the picture. Shots were fired, children left dead in the streets, and the soldiers smashed through doors into houses.

"Our prime minister needs your support to keep this from happening where *you* live. Send a message to your member of Parliament, and tell them to support the prime minister. We must act now, or all will be lost."

A soldier burst from a nearby doorway, turning his gun on the camera and firing a shot just before the screen went black.

"What in the hell was that?" Erik asked incredulously. "Are they trying to scare people into doing whatever the government tells them to?"

President Meyers sat back in his cushioned chair, clasping his hands on the desk as Erik sat across from him again. "It certainly appears that way. Which brings us to the changes I'm making in the Guild."

"Like those militia guards doing exercises in the square and guarding the door?"

"Yes. After the unwarranted Marine reaction to the protests, and the riots that followed, it is clear to me that Aldrin needs a firm hand at the rudder again. The dome administrator either will not or cannot step in, so there's no other choice but for us to do so. Our militia has forty members already, with the newest recruits being those you saw in the square."

"Do you think the Coalition is just going to let you take over their dome? They've been in charge of Aldrin for thirty years."

"They still would be, if they'd taken responsibility for the citizens. By retreating into the administration building and refusing to even speak with anyone else, they've effectively resigned their position as protectors of our colony."

Meyers leaned forward, an intensity on his face that Erik couldn't remember seeing before. "I'm not taking this course because I wanted to, Erik. I'm doing it because we have to. If events continue as they have for the last three weeks, Aldrin will fall into total chaos and burn itself down. Literally and figuratively."

"So what's your plan?"

"First, we have to show the people that the Guild is here to serve their interests. I've had shipments coming up from Earth for weeks now with food and supplies, and several shops across the dome have signed partnerships to sell those goods. Prices will stay at their pre-war levels, and our shops will never price gouge.

"At the same time, our militia will begin patrolling the streets. They'll serve the same role as security forces on Earth, protecting the people and investigating crimes that happen. We'll also be starting the process to clear the rubble from the tunnel that connected us to Armstrong. It's vitally important that we reestablish communication with them to find out what's happening there."

"Send some people across the surface to their docking facility. Surely that wouldn't be too difficult a journey."

"We tried it," Dex said behind him.

"Syndicate Marines thought it was an invasion attempt," Meyers said through a sigh. "We got lucky the warning shots didn't hit anyone, and our people retreated quickly. I've been trying to establish communications over the network, but either they're only monitoring the government channels or don't take us seriously. For all I know, the Coalition administrator has told their counterpart that we're an uprising."

Erik couldn't stop a grin. "Well, it kind of sounds that way. It's one I agree with, though. What do you need from me?"

"I need to borrow a few people from your crew. I'd like your ship's doctor to give some first aid training to our militia, so they're able to provide basic medical assistance when needed. And Dex tells me that Tom has years of experience with the Marines. We need that experience in our training."

Erik chewed on his lip as he thought it over for a bit. It was going to be hard to run the *Vagabond* without Jen and Tom, but hopefully their absence would be short. "If they agree to help out, I won't object. I'd like your assistance getting a few more people for my crew, though. Not to replace them, because I want Jen and Tom back, but to help out with all the tasks we have to do without a ship's AI."

Meyers smiled, his eyes darting to Dex. "There are two people you'll need to take onto the ship."

"You remember all that data you sent me from the researcher on Interamnia?" Dex asked, making him turn to look at her.

"Robert Silva? Yeah, last time I asked you said they were making good progress on it."

"Excellent progress," she said. "In fact, we have a full scale prototype reactor that's passed every test they've subjected it to. It's time for a real world test."

"That's great news! You want me to take it somewhere to be tested?"

Dex chuckled, shaking her head. "We want the *Vagabond* to be the test."

Meyers slid a tablet across his desk, and Erik caught it before it fell to the floor. He looked at the data on the screen, flipping through a few pages of schematics and technical notes. Most of it was gibberish to him, but he could grasp the basic concepts.

"You want to replace our nuclear reactor with this prototype fusion reactor? Fynn is going to kill me if I say yes to this. That's months of work, getting all the ship's systems changed over to work with a new power source."

"The team in Berlin assures me it will take their own engineer and physicist no more than a week for the switch. They're already on the way up from Earth to join your ship and start the work."

Erik couldn't believe what he was hearing. "Is this really the right time to be doing this? What if those ships over Earth start firing at each other and you need help protecting Luna?"

"If that happens, Captain Frost, I don't know that our small fleet of lightly armed freighters will mean much. However, if we get this reactor loaded up and it works as I've been told it will, then we have a chance of improving our odds."

He kept reading through the schematics, remembering how excited Robert had been on Interamnia so many months ago. The researcher had been sure that fantastic new inventions would be possible with his proposed fusion reactor. If it was even remotely possible...

"Okay, I'll break the news to Fynn and Isaac while you chat with Jen and Tom about working with the militia. I can't deny I'm very curious to see what this new power source will be capable of."

NINE

The bare steel wall was so cool against his hot skin. It had taken hours to find the one perfect spot in the cell that felt so right. He could stand there for hours with his face mashed against the bulkhead.

But his toes quickly tired of holding up his body to reach the point high on the wall. The thin mattress on his small bed always slid forward when he was straining upwards, too, making him have to constantly reset his position.

The ship had been quieter than normal for what felt like weeks. The humming of the deck plates was barely noticeable, telling him that the engines were running low enough to give the ship a small amount of gravity but not enough to be traveling. The prisoner wondered if they were back at Earth, a planet he hadn't seen in years. Or was it decades? Sometimes he wondered if such a place existed anywhere but his imagination.

Metal squealed as the small flap in the door was raised and a meal tray was pushed into the cell. He sat slowly on the bed, looking at the sparse food spread across the beige plastic. This wasn't the lumpy brown slop he was used to eating. There was green and yellow and red. Colors! He couldn't remember the last time he'd seen anything but brown slop and gray metal walls. Even the crinkly prisoner clothing they gave him was a dull brown color.

He dropped to the floor and crawled over to look down at the rainbow of food. The smell of it was so different, so foreign. It triggered memories of when he had eaten food like this before, but that felt like it had been another lifetime.

With shaking fingers, he reached out and touched a green sprout with dozens of leaves curling in on each other to form a ball. It felt warm and wet. It also felt safe, so he picked it up and held it to his nose to breathe in the strange odor of it. He popped the green ball into his mouth, holding it on his tongue to savor the new flavor. It was slightly bitter, but that was so different from his usual meals that he enjoyed it immensely. When he finally bit into the sprout it almost disintegrated because it was so mushy.

The short, wide cup on the tray that was normally filled with a watery broth contained brown liquid. He dipped a finger in, swirled it around, and then brought the digit to his mouth. So sweet! Had he ever tasted sweet before? He liked sweet.

The cup was empty in moments, and he looked into the barren depths with sadness. He felt rage, then, hot and sudden. He threw the cup against the door, and it banged loudly before dropping to clatter and roll on the floor. The lip of it was cracked.

"Hey!" a voice shouted as a fist banged against the other side of the door. "You break anything in there, and you'll regret it."

The prisoner stared at the cracked plastic cup, wondering why he'd thrown it. Had he thrown it? Maybe there was someone else in the cell. Someone that he couldn't see. Couldn't hear.

His body went still as he tried to listen hard, his eyes darting around without moving his head. Yes, he could feel it now. Someone else was trapped in the room with him. Had been trapped there from the beginning, taunting him and torturing him.

A scratching sound made him jump, but he quickly recognized it as the sound that meant the woman wanted to talk.

"What?" the prisoner asked curtly as he bent next to the vent. He kept his eyes moving across the room, searching for the Other. "What?"

"Are you okay? What was that noise?"

"It was nothing. Everything is fine." He knew his words didn't sound very convincing, but he just wanted her to shut up. The Other was getting closer, and there was a prickling along this spine.

"I can't believe they gave us fresh vegetables and fruit today. Something big must be happening."

"Yes, something big." He knew her words were important, that he should give her more attention. But the Other was behind him now. He could feel it creeping ever closer, waited for the moment to whirl and catch it.

"I'm feeling stronger. I'll be ready soon. Is the plan still in place?"

There! He whirled and swung his arms together through the empty air. Nothing! The Other had eluded him. He howled with frustration, banging his fists against the wall.

The tray drew his attention, the brightly colored food that was so different. The Other must have come in with this strange food. It was the only answer. Gleefully, he smashed a fist down on a red ball, feeling it squish beneath his fingers as wetness sprayed across his face. He raised his fist and slammed it down again and again.

He was laughing, unable to stop. Curled into a ball and covered in sticky juice. How long had he been there?

The cell door made clicking noises before it was thrown open. The guard standing there was snarling with

64

rage as she looked down at the pulverized food on the broken tray. It was the first face he had seen in living memory. His laughter stopped, as he stared open mouthed at this stranger in shiny black hardness. Was that the creature's skin?

"You absolute shit!" the guard yelled, pounding over to swing the back of her hand across his mouth. "I don't know why they tried to do something nice for a traitor. Filth like you should be fed filth." Her snarl turned into a nasty grin, and she leaned in to breathe her words on his face. "I'll make sure you get what you deserve, and you'll eat all of it."

The prisoner watched as the frightening creature bent to pick up the shattered remnants of the food tray. The green and red and yellow mess remained on the floor as she left the cell and the door slammed behind her. He started at it fearfully, knowing that the Other was still in the room. How could he rid himself of that presence?

TEN

Mags entered the command deck and stiffened as much as possible in the zero gravity. Her eyes were drawn to the place on the deck where she had seen the body of her protégé. She felt she could still see the blood staining the ground. It had to be her imagination, since the bridge had been spotlessly cleaned after the massacre that had occurred.

"Reporting as ordered, sir."

Captain Andrews turned and waved for her to relax. His right arm was still in a sling. The man refused nanobot repairs for the muscles and tendons shredded by the flechette round fired near his shoulder. Instead, he endured painful regrowth stimulants in daily visits the medical bay, asking the doctor to save the nanobots for more urgent needs. "At ease, Mags. Thanks for coming up."

"No problem at all, captain. It's good to see you at the rail again."

He smiled faintly, reaching out to pat the railing with his good hand before grabbing it to keep from floating away. "It feels like coming home. I wanted to get your report on the engine room repairs."

"Progress is slower than I'd like, but we're getting close. The teams on the hull got the ion thruster nozzles replaced in the overnight shift. If all goes well with the final repairs, we should have rudimentary engine controls within thirty six hours."

"Excellent. I know I speak for everyone when I say that I'm ready to feel the deck under my feet again. The admiral, especially, is finding it hard to operate without gravity."

Mags chuckled, her eyes darting around to make sure the superior officer didn't witness it. "Where is the admiral, sir?"

"He's been working with the communications techs. The system wasn't tampered with as far as we can tell, but for some reason we're not getting any responses to messages we send out to Geneva."

"Very odd. I'll have a couple of people from Engineering head down to assist as soon as the engines are working."

"Thanks, Mags. So, how did you enjoy your brief stint in command of a frigate?" Andrews grinned at her as he spoke.

"Frankly, sir, I was glad when it was over. That was a terrible time to get a first taste of command."

"Indeed." The captain turned to look down at the bridge below. The enemy soldiers had killed so many of his best, but the crew and officers from other shifts were hard at work on training replacements pulled from other departments across the ship. By the time they were able to get back to Earth and rejoin the fleet, those new people would be proficient at the stations. "Mags, we lost a lot of our senior staff during that assault. My first and second officers were killed, as you know."

"Yes, sir." She closed her eyes, dreading what was coming.

"I know the loss of the Chief has been a big blow to Engineering, but the loss suffered on the bridge was greater. We need someone to step in and help take up the slack. There's no one I'd trust to do that more than you, Mags." Andrews turned back to meet her gaze. "Will you be my first officer?"

"Captain, it would be an honor. I just don't know if I can leave my people without leadership right now."

"I figured you would say something like that." Andrews bent over and motioned for someone below. Several seconds later an ensign appeared, pulling himself along the stairway railing. "Ensign Graves studied engine mechanics and reactor physics in the academy. He's agreed to transfer into Engineering from the bridge crew until we can get back to Earth."

Mags saw the captain's lips twitching, and felt herself outmaneuvered. "In that case, sir, I'm happy to accept your offer."

"Excellent!" He waved the ensign away, and pushed off gently to float closer to the lieutenant. "I'm pleased to tell you that the Fleet Admiral has approved your promotion to lieutenant commander. Effective immediately."

A small box with a circular pip was presented. One side of the pip was black, the other white. Andrews pulled it free and attached it to her uniform beside the two white pips that she'd worn since becoming a senior lieutenant. Once that was done, they traded salutes.

"Congratulations, Commander Richtaus. Take the ensign down to the engine room to introduce him around. I expect you to report for your first shift on the bridge tomorrow morning at zero eight hundred."

Mags pulled her uniform tunic tight as she floated onto the bridge to begin her second shift on the command deck. The captain and admiral were already at the rail, eager for the first test of the newly repaired engines.

"Everything looks good down in Engineering, sirs."

Andrews turned a smirk on her. "You couldn't resist checking in before your shift, could you?"

"No, sir," Mags said with a grin. She gripped the railing, looking out over the stations below. The crew manning each terminal were strapped in, and the junior officers had retreated to crash couches that lined one wall. "We should probably strap in, sirs. I told Ensign Graves to start slow, but you never know what a recently repaired engine is going to do."

Fleet Admiral Holgerson nodded, pushing off the rail to join the two officers manning stations at the rear of the command deck. Captain Andrews followed, and Mags was close behind. Once they were all strapped in, she swiveled her chair to face the station in front of her. Chimes sounded over the ship-wide comm system, and Andrews announced that the engine test would begin shortly.

A row of small displays was above head height, with three larger screens at eye level. She pulled up the camera views from Engineering, along with the engine stats and reports. She watched with tight lips as the ensign several decks below and half the length of the ship away gave the orders to initiate feeding power into the ion engines.

The deck shuddered once, barely perceptible to anyone not attuned to the feeling after ten years spent working in and near engine rooms across multiple naval vessels. Mags allowed herself a small smile as she watched the power indicators rise at a painstaking pace.

"Bow thrusters firing," she said, loudly enough for the officers nearby to hear. The frigate was speeding through space, on track to pass through the mid-system asteroid belt in less than two months. She felt a shift to their weightlessness as the forward thrusters fired to flip the ship, pointing her bow toward the inner system and their home world.

"Flip successful." She could hear the triumph in her tone, trying to keep her elation down with the most important test still to come.

"Initiate main engines," the admiral instructed.

Mags relayed the order to the engine room, and turned her attention to the four large ion thrusters at the rear of the frigate. After more than a week, the large 0 that filled each power percentage display flipped over to .001. The numbers kept increasing as she watched, and she realized that her prosthetic hand was tightly gripping the armrest of her crash couch. She forced it to unclench before the power in the bioprosthetic limb could cause damage.

"Main thrusters are at point zero five percent power," she announced. There was a noticeable amount of gravity now, perhaps a hundredth of Earth's gravity pressing down on them. As more power was fed into the ion engines, the intensity grew.

"Holding steady at five percent power," Mags said after fifteen minutes. "So far, all readings are in the green, and I'm not seeing any errors in the readouts." She looked through all the screens, ensuring that she didn't miss one vital error that could lead to failure. The ensign in charge of Engineering concurred that everything appeared to be working as expected.

"Requesting permission to increase to ten percent."

"Do it, commander." The admiral sounded pleased with the results, eager to start reversing their outer system course.

She sent the command along, and watched as the power was dialed up. They were feeding energy into the engines faster now, taking no more than a minute for each percentage increase. The indicators showing the frigate's speed started to slow at a greater rate.

"We're at ten percent power." A small cheer rose from the bridge below, where the crew were listening in. *Waterloo* was feeling a twentieth of a G now, enough force to cause weightless objects to begin a gentle drift to the ground. She hoped that everyone had considered that when preparing their departments and cabins for the tests. "Readings are holding steady, sirs."

"Commander, how much power could we feed into the engines with the repairs in effect?" Captain Andrews had an audible grin.

"I'd be comfortable with thirty percent, captain. Forty, if you really feel like pushing it."

"Let's go for thirty, commander. We can re-evaluate after a few hours at that speed and see what we all feel comfortable with."

"Aye, captain." Mags sent the message down to Engineering joyfully. For the next hour, the power to the engines was ramped up through five percent chunks, pausing each time to ensure there were no reported errors. By the end, the ship's thrusters were firing with enough force to keep them at a fifth of Earth's gravity.

"Engines at thirty percent and holding steady," Mags said happily. "Projections show that we should bleed off our momentum in seventy nine minutes."

"Excellent work, commander." The admiral passed his congratulations down to all of the crew members in Engineering, as well. He gave the order to hold the steady speed, and everyone unstrapped from crash couches to resume normal duties. "My God, it feels good to put my feet on the deck again," the captain said as Mags rejoined him at the railing. "Even if it makes my shoulder ache with the strain on the wound."

Mags unconsciously reached up to rub the area where prosthetic met real flesh. "You get used to it, sir. I don't think I even felt anything until you mentioned it."

"Sorry, commander. I already forget about your arm. You're so good with the new one that it's like a natural limb."

She smiled, holding up the silvery gray hand to clench and unclench her fingers. "It's a little bit better than a natural limb. Not that I'd say no to a little time travel and a push out of the way of the railgun round that clipped me."

"What kind of timeline are we looking at if we maintain this speed?"

Mags considered it, running numbers in her head. "It'll take a little less than four weeks. We could cut it down to three if we increase power a bit, but I wouldn't want to put much more strain than that on our repairs."

"It'll be good enough," Andrews said. "The admiral is still trying to get some kind of response from Geneva. They sent a message out to the belt last night, and the colony on Hygeia responded. So we know our transmitters are working."

"Very strange," she murmured. "Do you think Earth is getting the messages but not responding? Maybe they think we're under enemy influence."

"I didn't have time to warn them we were boarded, so they shouldn't have known anything about that until the admiral told them we had regained control of the bridge."

"Well, sir, I guess we'll get an answer in three or four weeks. Worst case."

ELEVEN

Rinde stood at the small window, staring out on the darkness of the city. It had been a long day, but he knew it would be several more hours before he'd be able to leave his office and head home for some rest. Uju entered the room, carrying a tray with bottles of water and a plate filled with fruit and ham sandwiches. He would have preferred a big bowl of spicy tomato stew, like his mother used to make, but the late night offerings were few. To be fair, those not in his exalted position would have had to settle for bland protein bars and pouches of vitamin laced fluids.

"Come eat, sir. You've been working too hard."

"Someone has to do the job," he muttered, turning his eyes to where he knew the prime minister's windows would be dark. It was hard for him to see how cavalier the man's attitude about their situation could be. "Why won't he let me send our frigates to end the threat of that cruiser, Uju? Our intelligence reports show they're shipping up weaponry, which means they have to be most vulnerable at this moment."

"Perhaps he's afraid of a backlash from the people? It could be seen as warmongering to pursue an enemy that's stopped attacking."

Rinde scoffed. "History has shown us time and again that you can't let someone attack you and then pull back without following them to finish the job. How many wars has this planet seen because the previous war wasn't brought to a final conclusion?" His aide deposited a plate of the food on his desk, forcing him to sit and turn his attention to sustenance. He wouldn't admit it, but this was the first time he could remember eating since breakfast before dawn.

"I've spoken with the Minister of Foreign Affairs," he continued. "We still have no ambassadors in Syndicate territory. As far as she knows, the prime minister won't even try to reopen communication with the Executive Committee."

"There could be unofficial talks," his aide said gently. "Perhaps he doesn't want to announce anything until he's sure of a positive result."

"If so, his cabinet should at least be told." Rinde chewed on a tough bit of ham. The substandard sandwich filling only reminded him of another recent aggravation. "Have you heard anything from the North American region about the food shipments?"

Uju shook her head as she swallowed a bite of melon. "The only contact that responded said they shipped out three percent more than the same period last year. They can't explain why we're seeing food shortages here."

Rinde looked at the tray of food before them. The melon was as juicy, but the two apples looked more withered than usual. "I tell you, something strange is going on lately. It's not just all these ads that Propaganda Minister keeps running. I haven't found the proof yet, but I feel that he's manipulating events to stay in power."

"Sir, the Coalition constitution is firm on a prime minister serving no more than three terms. He can't run again in next year's elections."

"Laws can be changed. It's happened before."

Uju leaned forward and placed her cool hand on his arm. "I think you are working yourself too hard, and the stress is making you see patterns in random things."

Rinde sighed and wiped a hand across his face. "Maybe, Uju, but the more I think about it the more I feel my instincts are correct."

The aide rose and put his half empty plate back on the tray. She left one of the apples sitting on his desk as she prepared to leave the office. "Do you need anything else, sir?"

"No. Go home, Uju. I'm sure I'll have thought of a dozen things for you to do by the morning."

"Good night, sir."

The door closed with a quiet click, and he looked at the papers strewn across his desk. Rinde couldn't explain even to himself why he had requested the old files, records of cabinet meetings and sessions in the three Houses going back a dozen years. He'd been looking through them for days, when he had time between other duties, but had found nothing out of the ordinary.

In the two weeks since the emergency cabinet meeting when the two fleets first met in a shorter than expected battle, he'd felt increasingly uncomfortable about the direction events were going. The propaganda being released that painted the prime minister as their only savior was the first in a series of questionable policy changes. The citizens of the Coalition had breathed a sigh of relief when the *Indomitable* fell into orbit without attacking them, but then seemed perplexed when the remnants of their own fleet failed to press the attack when they arrived at Earth.

There had been two cabinet meetings since then, but Rinde had only been invited to the first. He and Juliette, the Minister of the Navy, had urged action while they were in a strong position. The prime minister only waved away their concerns and pointed at the two new frigates under construction in the shipyard around the Coalition orbital station.

"As soon as those ships are complete, we can reassess where we stand and decide if military action is still warranted."

Rinde had been flabbergasted at the words, and thought perhaps bad information had been given to the leadership. "Sir, it will be another seven months before the first new frigate is complete. Even then, there will be a month of tests before the ship will be ready to join the others in our fleet."

"You worry too much, Rinde! I'm sure the Syndicate leadership will be amenable to peace talks if we give them time to consider their position."

He'd wanted to ask why there were so many ads being put out about how dangerous the Syndicate was if the prime minister was considering peace talks. But he hadn't had the opportunity as the man moved to the next item on the agenda as if the war were nothing to be concerned about.

The next meeting Rinde hadn't known about until it was over. Juliette had also been left out of the discussions. They heard afterwards that the prime minister had proposed sending two of their three frigates back to the location of the second fleet battle to check on the heavily damaged frigate that had been left behind. A proposal that was only narrowly voted against.

"But they haven't sent any communications, have they?" he asked.

"None," the Minister of the Navy said. "We tried to reach them for weeks, but there was only silence. The Guild freighters that stopped to assist said the frigate was so badly damaged that they couldn't even gain entry. Frankly, from the images I've seen I doubt anyone survived."

"Why send two thirds of our defense away?" Rinde couldn't understand it, or why such a thing would be discussed without the two ministers in charge of the fleet in attendance. "What about the *Waterloo?* Have we heard anything from them yet?"

"Nothing." Juliette's lips tightened. "Rinde, my office is being blocked from the frequencies the fleet uses to communicate. I tried to send off messages myself, but they get intercepted and returned as unapproved."

"What? No one has the ability to block either of us from using those channels!"

"The prime minister does. I can't figure out why, but he doesn't want us talking with the frigates."

That had been the moment that his investigation coalesced into a detailed search of the records. He'd thought there had to be some records to show why recent decisions would be made. Until a year ago, the prime minister had been no more than a normal politician trying to pass regular legislation while deriving some small benefit from his office. Just like thousands of other politicians throughout history.

The first sign of a change happened in a cabinet meeting several weeks before the existence of the *Indomitable* came from the asteroid belt. They'd been discussing new sanctions against the Syndicate in response to a Coalition cargo ship being boarded and seized in the Pacific Ocean. Forty thousand containers had been unloaded in a Syndicate port, and they claimed the ship had strayed into their coastal territory with contraband. Increased tariffs on imported goods had been the consensus, but the prime minister had overruled the decision. He claimed to have information that couldn't be revealed, proof that the seized container ship really had been carrying contraband being smuggled into Syndicate territory.

From that moment on, Rinde found many examples of inexplicable decisions against punishing Syndicate transgressions. At the same time, the prime minister was harping on the danger of their old enemy in public speeches. It was a dichotomy of opinion that had been constant through the opening stages of the new war, with the prime minister fighting against internal calls for a military response while calling for strong measures against Syndicate aggression in public speeches.

Rinde pushed the papers together, bouncing them on the desk a few times to square up the edges. Perhaps he should put it away for now and look at it again in a few days with fresh eyes. His aide could be right, that he was letting the stress of events make him see connections that weren't there. The door opened suddenly, and Rinde looked up in surprise. "Uju, I thought you went home long ago."

Her face was pale, and he could see the hand on the door shaking. "Syndicate troops just crossed the border. Five divisions of soldiers, and they're pushing hard in our direction."

Rinde shot to his feet, sending his chair toppling over. "Get Juliette on the line. And get us a connection with General DuPont. We need to get our military activated as quickly as possible."

She nodded and stepped out of his office as he hit the button to turn on the displays lining the wall across the office from his desk. Half a dozen news programs appeared, and his eyes scanned them. There were no reports yet about the incursion, and he felt minor relief that there was time to mount a defense.

"Sir," Uju called. He leaned out to look at her desk near his office. "Minister Rinova isn't on Earth. Her office says she boarded a shuttle several hours ago, and they were told she was visiting the *Yorktown* in orbit."

Rinde frowned at the news. He and Juliette had been trying to arrange a visit to the frigates for days. He couldn't think of a reason why she would leave without informing him when she was finally able to make the trip. "What about DuPont?"

"I've put in a communications request, but no response as of yet."

"Keep trying. Contact the next general in line, and the one after that if you have to. I need to speak with someone in charge before it's too late."

He returned to his office, and felt the air leave his lungs as he saw the six screens. Each of the programs was showing the red border of urgent news, with text scrolls across the bottom of the screen announcing the invasion by Syndicate forces. One of the networks had even managed to launch a camera drone that captured images of the soldiers from several miles away before it was shot down.

Rinde slumped into a chair, watching his worst fears play out across the displays. Several of the networks were replaying recent ads from the prime minister, threatening that just such an event could happen. One so-called expert was shouting into the screen about how only the prime minister could save the Coalition now. General DuPont appeared on one screen, stepping up to a podium. Rinde fumbled with the controls, unmuting that display as Uju stepped into the office.

"The security forces are denying my communication requests, sir." Rinde waved her to silence, his eyes riveted on the display where the general was staring into the camera with a steely gaze.

"Good evening," the general said, his voice serious but relaxed. "I know there have been reports of an incursion into our territory by Syndicate forces. I wanted to come before you this evening to assure you that the security forces have been alerted and we are mobilizing our troops. At this time, we will keep our focus on protecting the capital while the prime minister works on negotiations with the Syndicate leadership."

The scattering of reporters seated before the general were muttering and shifting, wanting to shout out questions. General DuPont didn't give them the chance. "The cabinet is meeting as we speak to discuss our strategy going forward. As soon as they have relayed their wishes to me, I will put those commands into action. A press release will be issued at that time. Good night."

He strode from the podium, ignoring the shouted questions from reporters as confused by the statement as the viewers.

Rinde turned to his aide. "Were we informed of a cabinet meeting?"

"No, sir," Uju said, shaking her head. "I'll see what I can find out."

"Don't bother. Get me a link with Aldrin dome, instead. I want to speak with President Meyers of the Transport Guild."

TWELVE

Yumata sat stiffly, his face impassive as he listened to yet another mid-ranking officer of the planet based Defense Forces drone on. The Military Committee had been in session for three full days, first listening to status reports and tactics discussions before the invasion and now listening to status reports and tactics discussions after the invasion.

He tried to imagine commanding a ship in this fashion, and his brain couldn't even conceive it being possible. Nothing would ever get done, and the ship would be stuck in space as officers debated the same points over and over again. Yumata spent half a day trying to remember if he had experienced this much bureaucracy before departing to begin his posting on the *Indomitable*. While he could think of many meetings, none seemed as interminable as his short tenure on the Military Committee had been.

"Thank you, major," the chairwoman said, snapping him from his thoughts. "Your report has been very enlightening, and we appreciate your input."

The man sitting at the small table facing them rose and saluted the committee. It was a breach of military etiquette since Yumata was the only person at the table to ever serve in any branch, and only naval personnel should salute him. The rest of the committee treated it as an expected gesture, however, to his chagrin.

One of the attendants always standing against the wall hurried forward to escort the officer from the room. A woman in uniform was shown in next. Yumata was still refreshing his memory of the ground based rank designations, but she wore the same number of red slashes on her sleeve as a colonel who had briefed the committee earlier in the day about supply shipments.

"Colonel Johannson, thank you for coming." The chairwoman always managed to sound genuinely pleased each time she said the words. He felt as if he'd heard them a thousand times over the last few days. "Please tell us which matters you're here to discuss."

"Thank you, madam chairwoman. I'm with the Fifteenth Armored Division. We are being held in reserve for the next push into Coalition territory. I'm here today to brief you on the plans we've come up with for quick strike tactics, to cover the most ground with the fewest casualties." Yumata sighed inwardly as he prepared to listen to another hour of the same "innovative" strategies that a dozen people before the colonel had already discussed.

He thought of his younger years, when he was fresh from the naval academy and joining a frigate to begin his first posting. It had been only months after the brief flare up of activity between the two Earth powers. The Syndicate had struck first, launching dozens of missiles against high value targets in Coalition territory. In retaliation, the Coalition fleet had performed a couple of quick attack runs against their counterparts. The ship Yumata started his career on had been badly damaged in those strikes, and witnessing the repair process had strengthened his determination to see the Syndicate emerge victorious.

A stagnant cold war had been the last thing he'd expected, but by the time he was promoted to lieutenant commander and was posted to his third ship he had known that the Navy would be his life. The company shares he began to receive as annual bonuses once he achieved the higher ranks were an excellent inducement, as well. It had been a stroke of genius for the early Syndicate leadership to realize that a feeling of ownership vested their officers with a greater commitment to see their nation succeed.

When he'd been approached with the plan for building a supership in the asteroid belt, he had been intrigued by the project immediately. At the time, the autonomy of such a project hadn't crossed his mind. He'd just been ready for the challenge of achieving something never done before. In that elation, he had allowed the Military Committee to suggest candidates for his senior staff. Guildersen had seemed a harmless but necessary evil back then, a paper pusher who would make sure that all the rules were being followed and tedious tasks completed so that Yumata himself could focus on the real work.

Now he realized the error of his thinking. Guildersen commanded the ship in orbit, while he was stuck with the tarnished honor of sitting through excruciatingly boring meetings. His last actions as a serving officer had been to run from fights with the Coalition fleet. Twice. All because of Guildersen himself, constantly goading to put the ship to use and convincing the Executive Committee it was ready for action before Yumata felt that way.

As the colonel left the chamber after providing only a few seconds of information that hadn't already been spewed forth from those who came before, the chairwoman formally called the day's session to a close. Yumata strode from the chamber, glad to be out of the room. Sitting in his inconsequential spot at the table felt constricting.

"Admiral," the chairwoman called as she entered the short hallway behind him. Each committee member had a small office there, close to the center of their power. "Would you join me for a moment?"

Yumata bowed, and turned to follow to the largest of the offices. Her words may have been phrased as a request, but he knew a command when he heard it. He wondered if he would receive another polite lecture about treating his position with the respect that it deserved.

The chairwoman's office was a richly appointed space. Walls covered in dark wood panels gave it an old world feel, while the large windows looking out across the city could allow in enough natural light to keep the room from feeling dim. There was no desk in the room, only comfortably cushioned chairs and a wall covered in displays.

"Would you like a drink, admiral? I just received a crate of whiskey from North America that is absolutely divine."

"No, thank you."

She waved him to a seat as she opened a cabinet and poured a drink for herself. The clink of the ice cubes falling into the glass was a sound that always made his skin crawl, though he'd never understood why. Once the liquor was poured, she sat in a chair nearby. Both of them had unconsciously sat in the perfect location to look out at Hong Kong spread far below. The light was turning orange with the approaching sunset, hiding all the imperfections of the city below.

He waited, listening to the ice cubes rattling against the sides of the glass with every sip the chairwoman took. They sat in silence for several minutes, watching the daylight slowly fade through the windows.

"What do you think about the progress of the war?"

It was not what he had expected, and Yumata turned his head to look at her. "How do you mean, madam chairwoman?"

"We're not in meetings. You can call me Selene."

"Very well. How do you mean, Selene?"

84

"You've heard the same reports I have these last three days. When you're not lost in thought, of course." She turned to smirk at him. "Do you feel that our defense forces are acting efficiently?"

Yumata met her gaze, considering how to respond. "Do you want my true feelings, Selene? Or do you wish to hear a Military Committee response?"

She laughed, an unexpectedly pleasant sound. "If I wanted someone to tell me what I want to hear, I'd have asked Abernathy. Or gone into my company's offices where the board falls all over themselves trying to please me. I want your true opinion."

"In that case, if the officers we've seen the last several days are any indication, I doubt this war is going to go well for us." Yumata gripped the arms of the chair, raising his chin as he spoke. "We had surprise on our side last night when our troops crossed the border. That allowed us to take a large swathe of territory into our control. Once the Coalition security forces gather their troops, the response will be a heavy blow."

"Hmm," she said, draining the whiskey. "I'm not privy to all of the Executive Committee's information, but from what I hear we're not expecting a quick response from Geneva."

"Then we should be sending more of our own troops forward to secure our hold on what we've taken. Within a day, we could push forward again. Each foot of land conquered is a blow to the morale of the Coalition people."

"It may surprise you, Hiro, but I agree. The officers we listen to in there," she waved the empty glass behind her, "are the paper pushers and middle management types. They don't have the spine to go into the real action, so they like to sit around and talk about how it should be done."

Yumata grunted. "I never would have thought you felt that way, watching how you hang on their every word."

"It's a talent you pick up after a lifetime of meetings. Look as if you're listening, but catch only the important points." She tapped her cheek under the blue haze that covered her left eye, and he knew that she had been spending most of the day doing other work while half listening to the officers speaking to them.

They were silent again for a while, enjoying the spectacle of thousands of lights appearing through the encroaching darkness. When Yumata spoke, his words were quiet. "Why was I removed from my post, Selene?"

"You were the victim of a man who spent eight years building support among those who hold the real power, while you focused on the temporary power of your command."

"Thank you for being honest." It was Guildersen, of course. He'd known it from the moment he was offered the chair on the committee, but had never expected someone would confirm it.

"Since we're being honest," she said, "the Executive Committee may have forced you on us, but I'm glad to have you. We need someone on this committee with real experience out there. Too many of those people we share a table with believe every word the mouthpiece majors and colonels spit out."

"I'd like to visit the front," Yumata said suddenly. He hadn't even realized he was going to say it until the words were leaving his mouth.

"Why would you want to do something as stupid as that?" the chairwoman asked in astonishment.

"You said you need someone with my experience. I need to see what's really happening out there to put that experience to use. Give me a shuttle tomorrow. I'm quite certain I won't miss anything important here." He offered a dry smile.

She shook her head as she chuckled, rising to place the empty glass on the cabinet she had gotten the drink from. "I'll agree to it, but on one condition."

"Name it."

"You take Abernathy. That boy needs some real world experience. I don't think he's even been outside Hong Kong."

Yumata blinked slowly, then nodded. "Very well. Perhaps he can learn something on the trip."

"The shuttle will be ready for you at dawn. I'll have an aide get the message to Abernathy to meet you on the roof then."

Sensing that the meeting was concluded, Yumata rose and bowed more deeply than he had at the invitation to speak privately. Surprisingly, he felt better about his role on the Military Committee after their conversation. He did wonder how much of what she'd said was true, and how much was crafted just for such an effect.

THIRTEEN

Shifting his bulk, Guildersen sneered at the handful of men and women clustered on the other side of his desk. "What do you mean, the crew refuses to work on repairs? You're the officers in charge of Construction and Maintenance. Tell them to get to work!"

"We've tried, captain," one man said quietly, seeming to shrink as baleful eyes turned on him. "They won't do the work."

"Why the hell not?" He could feel his jowls shaking at he screamed the words, and tucked his chin down against his chest. Guildersen wondered again if he should stop eating so much, but the discomfort of hunger was a feeling he detested. "Throw a few out the airlocks. The rest of the scum will do their jobs after that."

His first officer, Commander Vegley, stepped forward to stand in front of the others. The woman had arrived on the ship with the infusion of crew brought out by the frigates, and he had loathed her from the moment he saw how well she and Yumata clicked. There had been a brief fear that the woman would be promoted above him, but his contacts on the Executive and Military Committees had proved to be useful in securing another rank slash on his uniform.

"Captain, you've been pushing our crew too hard. You demand that they work twelve hour shifts, you schedule six days of work in each week, and then you hand out demotions to those who can't keep up under the grueling load. It's not the proper way to run a ship."

Guildersen placed his hands on the desk and pushed his large body out of the wide chair. He could feel the heat that was suffusing his face, and knew from the blurriness of his vision that he was losing control of his emotions. "This ship is filled with useless idlers, Vegley. If any one of you had the makings of even a half decent officer, you'd have recognized their lack of quality and I wouldn't have to be telling you what to do. Push them harder!"

He lumbered around the desk, raising a hand to poke the air as he stalked toward the group of officers. All but his XO took unconscious steps back. "I want this ship back in pristine condition! Do you hear me? I'm giving you one week to get the work done, or I'll find officers who can. We'll see how you useless fools handle being ensigns again. Now get out of my office!"

Vegley glared at him as the other officers fought to leave the room. He held her gaze for half a minute before the woman turned away and strolled from the room. Guildersen grinned at her back, proud once again that he had proved his superiority over the lesser officers who served under him. Not one of them had a single contact on the ruling committees. He couldn't understand how they had been promoted to lead departments, much less become officers in the first place.

He was breathing heavily as he returned to his desk, and felt sweat rolling down his face. In spite of that, he felt better after venting his rage. It reminded him of all the times he'd called Lieutenant Davis in so he could yell at the man. Dressing down the admiral's favorite had been a soothing balm against whatever cares or worries he might be facing on a given day. As much as he enjoyed the lieutenant's obvious failure, he still missed having that outlet available.

Seated behind the desk once more, Guildersen pressed a button to open communications with the colonel in charge of the *Indomitable*'s Marines. He drummed his fingers on the desk impatiently, beginning to fume once more as he waited for the man to answer the call.

"Captain Guildersen, how can I help you?"

"Colonel Rozier, I'm having a problem that I need your assistance with. My officers are proving to be incompetent nitwits, and they can't manage to make their departments do the necessary work. I want you to post squads of Marines across the ship, and arrest any man or woman shirking their duty."

There was silence on the line for a few moments before the colonel spoke again. "I will do as you command, captain, of course. But are you sure that's the wisest course of action?"

"Rozier, I didn't contact you for your opinion. Do your job. If a day or two in a cell won't get our people working, then I'll toss them all off the ship and bring in people who will do what they're paid for."

"Yes, captain. I'll send the orders to my squad leaders now."

Guildersen nodded in smug satisfaction. An idea blossomed, and he almost purred at the thought. "Colonel, keep a close eye on Commander Vegley, as well. The moment that bitch steps out of line, I want to know about it. I'd love to be the one to toss her out of the service. Let's see how she handles begging for food on the streets somewhere."

"Yes, sir." The man's tone was hesitant, but Guildersen knew he would obey the orders. The leader of the cruiser's Marines was a man who knew which side would be triumphant. He could be counted on to do whatever was needed.

A fat finger closed the connection, and Guildersen leaned back to lay his hands on his belly. He daydreamed about tossing each of his pathetic officers from an airlock, watching their panicked expressions as their bodies froze in the cold of space and their lungs struggled to find air. Perhaps he really should get rid of a few, to set an example to the rest of the crew. If they didn't work harder after that, he'd be very surprised.

His body quivering with a rolling chuckle, Guildersen leaned forward to press the button for communications again. "Ensign Lucas, meet me in Bay Two. Now!"

Guildersen struggled to his feet, cursing the ship's laundry service for shrinking his uniforms yet again. No matter how often he called the manager of the department to his office to berate the man for ineptitude, he continued to get uniforms that were tighter than the last time he'd worn them. The idiot had the nerve to suggest the captain's eating habits were to blame! He stopped, turned back to his desk, and sent a command for the laundry service manager to meet him in Bay Two, as well. Might as well kill two birds with one stone.

FOURTEEN

Fynn was surprisingly chipper when Erik glided into the engine room. The *Vagabond* had spent six days sitting on the bare lunar surface, freeing the docking platform for other traffic. The crew could leave the ship only after stuffing themselves into bulky pressure suits and making a laborious trek across the gray dust. At the end, they had to suffer through an hour of decontamination procedures before they could enter Aldrin. Needless to say, few of them had opted to make the trip more than once.

The physicist and engineer from Berlin had been on board since shortly before the freighter moved off the docking platform. It had taken half a day to get all of the gear loaded that they'd brought along. A large crate sealed with several layers of encryption had contained the new fusion reactor. After complaining and protesting about all the work that would be required, Fynn and Isaac had been quite happy to marvel at the new technology once it was unveiled.

Erik had been informed an hour before that the new reactor was finally installed and fully connected to his ship's systems. The pair of Earth researchers had submitted a list of tests they wanted to run, and he'd been shocked to find a document longer than most of the instruction manuals that he never read after buying new products.

"How's it looking, Fynn? Is our girl playing nice with the new tech?"

Fynn was grinning wider than he had in almost a year. He looked just like a kid who'd opened a Christmas present and found the one thing he'd secretly been hoping to get. "Erik, you're not going to believe how well this new reactor works. We've had it hooked into all our systems for four hours now, and the efficiency ratings on the power generation are ten times better than our old reactor ever was."

"That's great. So you're happy to start all the testing."

"We already started," the engineer said. He waved his captain over to look at the display on his central console in the engine room. Half a dozen items already had green checkmarks next to them. "Everything has been passing with flying colors, so far."

The early items on the list had been fairly simple. Enabling as many internal systems as possible to check the power usage spike. Sending an overload signal through the programs to test that the reactor would stop sending power to those components. Switching to the backup systems to ensure that power flowed correctly. Now it was time for the first real test, thruster burns. Erik returned to the control center and gave a warning over the ship comms. "Sixty seconds to first thruster test. Everybody get strapped in, because we don't know what's going to happen."

"Are you ready to do this?" he asked after closing the comms.

"Born ready, cap." Mira had been bouncing with impatience for days, eager to see what she'd be able to do with the increased power from a fusion reactor.

Erik had readouts from the engine room up on the main display, so he and the pilot could watch for any sudden spikes or warnings. He checked the exterior cameras to be sure the area around them was clear. "Okay, take her up."

"Woo!" Mira yelled out, finger sliding along her terminal's keypad as she fed power into the main ion thrusters. The *Vagabond*'s ascent was smooth, and faster than he was accustomed to.

"Holy hells, cap. I'm getting way more power than I usually do at this setting."

"Keep an eye on it, and take it easy. The last thing I need is to be making an unexpected trip through Earth's atmosphere."

Mira laughed, and turned her head just enough for him to see her tongue sticking out. He smiled and checked the camera feeds again. They were already several kilometers above Luna, and would be passing through the orbital paths soon. This area had been cleared for the tests, the other Guild ships clustered on the far side of the moon.

"We just passed half a dozen more items on the checklist," Fynn said over the comms. "Dr. Francks says the reactor is purring and ready for more."

Erik shook his head and laughed. "Let's do a trip around the planet, and see what happens when you open up the engines a little."

"You got it," the pilot said, punching the power forward.

He was pushed back into the gel layer as the *Vagabond* shot forward. A glance showed him that the freighter had just jumped to a full G within seconds, when it would have taken minutes of acceleration to reach the speed with the old fission reactor.

"Careful with the power!" he called.

"No worries, cap. Our baby can handle what I'm giving her."

Mira piloted them deftly into an extremely high orbit of the home world, nearly five thousand kilometers above the surface. He watched the landmasses and oceans pass underneath as the *Vagabond* completed the circuit. Mira

94

adroitly killed power to the main thruster and channeled the power into the forward thrusters.

"Testing deceleration," she said. He could hear the gleeful undertones that said she was enjoying the process much more than she probably should be.

"Fynn, how much juice did we use with that long burn?"

"Amazingly little," the engineer said, before another voice broke in.

"Captain Frost, the benefit of a fusion reactor is that it uses much less fuel than the standard fission model. What you could do with a single fuel rod before will do no more than skim the surface of your available energy now." Amelia Houghton was the engineer sent up with the physicist. Erik had been sure there would be friction between her and the old Norwegian who had cared for the ship for more than a dozen years, but they had gotten on extremely well.

"Amelia's right, Erik. With this reactor, we could make several trips out to the belt and back and not even worry about running out of power. This new technology is going to revolutionize space travel." Fynn's approving tone told Erik that he was looking at the frazzle-haired Berlin interloper as he spoke.

"You won't believe it, cap," Mira said, breaking into the conversation. "We just reversed our momentum in two thirds of our typical time."

"Okay, that is impressive." Erik looked at the long checklist, seeing several more items with green marks next to them. "Let's keep running the list and see how far we get before something goes wrong."

Five hours later, they were dropping down to the recently completed second docking pad for Aldrin. Erik looked over at the empty docking pads outside of Armstrong as they descended, wondering what was happening in the other dome. He hadn't seen any activity there since returning from the fleet battles. The *Vagabond* had passed over the dome on landing, but the material was built to be opaque from outside and transparent from within.

Meyers and Dex were waiting when he passed through the airlocks, to give him a strong handshake and a congratulatory hug. It was Erik's first time back since being asked to test the new reactor technology, and he was stunned by the changes. Two of the militia members were guarding the docking facility, standing at opposite ends. Instead of the bare metallic armor he had seen a week before, these soldiers wore armor that was ash gray. Standing out over their hearts was the red bow and arrow symbol of the old *Telemachus*.

"I see there's been a bit of an upgrade."

President Meyers laughed, nodding at the nearest militia soldier as they passed. "Captain Fitz has given quite a few suggestions for improving our forces. He said that giving them a color and symbol would give them a pride of belonging to a group, while bare metal felt rough and unorganized. He was correct."

"*Captain* Fitz? Tom has really taken to the job, hasn't he?"

"Yes, I dare say he seems more alive now than he did when I first met him. I don't know that you're going to get him back, Erik."

Passing professional looking militia soldiers as they strolled along the Aldrin streets, he wasn't sure Tom would be coming back to the *Vagabond*, either. He was impressed at how well the man had managed to improve the Guild's small security force in so short a time. "How is Jen doing? Don't tell me I'll have to find a new doctor, too."

Meyers laughed and slapped him on the back. "No chance of that. She's an excellent doctor, but I've seen her watching every freighter that flies over the dome. I've no doubts that Jen is ready to get back to the *Vagabond*."

Erik felt fingers against his palm, and spread his own to let Dex interlace their hands. He smiled over at her, fighting the urge to lean in for a kiss. *Work first,* he told himself, *then you can have time for pleasure.* Her amber eyes promised a lot of pleasure.

Another surprise awaited as they entered the central square. The barricades that had surround the administration building were moved closer, giving only a few feet of space between them and the walls of the building. The Marine guards were nowhere to be seen, replaced by Guild militia who stood near the entrance to the structure.

"We've moved into phase two of the plan," Meyers said, noticing his gaze. "Now that people know there is still someone who will provide safety and comfort, they're quite willing to have us replace the old administration."

"What will you do about the Coalition people in there?" Erik asked, motioning at the building.

"Not many are left. We offered them transport to Earth at any time, and most of them accepted on the first day. The Marines were all on the first shuttle for the planet, interestingly enough." The Guild president pushed open the doors of the Guildhall and led the way inside. "Perhaps they knew what was coming, and wanted to get back."

"Huh? What was coming?"

Dex poked him in the ribs, grinning as he tried to fight her finger away. "You never think to check on the newsfeeds when you're wrapped up in a project, do you?"

"I figure if it's important someone else will see it and tell me."

Once they were ensconced in the office, Meyers hit a button on his desk to activate a large wall display. A twenty four hour news program was showing a panel of half a dozen people, a few wearing uniforms of the Coalition planetary security forces.

"Two nights ago, the Syndicate sent armed troops into Coalition territory." Meyers pulled up a map in a smaller picture on the display. It showed Coalition territory in blue and Syndicate territory in red, with a large section of the blue striped in red. "Yesterday, the invading forces held firm. It looked like they were waiting on a counter response that never materialized. This afternoon, they've begun pushing deeper into Coalition territory."

"My God," Erik said, leaning forward to stare at the screen. "This must be their fallback plan after the *Indomitable* failed to overwhelm the fleet."

"Most likely it was their plan all along. Those soldiers were too prepared for it to be a hastily assembled force."

"What's the Coalition doing in response?"

Meyers leaned back, sighing deeply. "Absolutely nothing so far, and I can't understand it. These people," waving at the people talking on the screen "keep saying that the full security force is being mustered and equipped. But not one of them will give a timeline on when troops will actually head into the fight to try and push back the invaders.

"I've had a few conversations with the Defense Minister in Geneva, Rinde Brighton. He's just as confused

98

about what's going on down there. I'm sure you'll be as alarmed as I was when I tell you that he's been excluded from every cabinet meeting for the last several days."

Erik shook his head in dismay. He'd seen a lot of nonsensical moves from the Coalition government over the last year, but this one was so preposterous that he couldn't wrap his head around it. "It's almost like they *want* the Syndicate to take over."

Dex coughed, and he saw her faintly nod as he looked over.

"That's been our conclusion, as well," Meyers said grimly. "Minister Brighton is quite convinced, since no one in the Navy or security forces will respond to his requests for information or updates. Worse, the Minister of the Navy has gone missing. She was last known to have boarded a shuttle that would take her up to the *Yorktown*. There hasn't been a peep from her since."

"Has there been any movement from the frigates? Maybe she was trying to get them to attack the Syndicate cruiser."

"No movement aside from light shuttle traffic between them. Minister Brighton has spent most of yesterday and today trying to talk with as many Parliament members as possible. He's hoping to organize a vote of no confidence against the prime minister, so they can replace the man. That is supposed to be happening in a few hours."

"I hope he succeeds." Erik leaned back and ran a hand through his hair. "What can we do in the meantime?"

Meyers shrugged. "Not much, I'm afraid. Keep testing that protype reactor. If it passes all the tests, we can begin building another to retrofit one of our other freighters. For now, I'm keeping all of them in a scattered orbit over Luna, in case that cruiser does make a move against us."

"Eleven freighters with light rail guns against a ship ten times our size. And I'm sure they're rearming it again while we sit here and watch it happen."

"Erik, I share your frustration and your desire to do more. Trust me, I'd send all our ships against the *Indomitable* this very moment if I could. But that would just stir the hornet's nest and we'd have to fight off those Coalition frigates right after, when they declared us a terrorist organization. I've already received threats of that happening after we started asserting our control of Aldrin."

Erik nodded in reluctant understanding. "I guess I can see your point of view. On another subject, what's happening in Armstrong? I noticed again that there's no activity on their docking pads."

Dex spoke, drawing his attention. "When the people from the administration building finally came out, they told us they've had no contact since the day of the bombing in the tunnel. There were fragments of reports of explosions there, as well, so we think the bomber hit both domes."

"Why wouldn't they work with us, then? They have to need our help, since the Syndicate seems to have abandoned them just as the Coalition did with Aldrin."

"They probably assume that the Coalition ordered the attack," she told him. "Just like we all assume the Syndicate ordered it. Tom… sorry, Captain Fitz is prepping a couple of his troops to attempt another entry into Armstrong to discover what's going on in there."

"By the time you finish testing that reactor," Meyers said, "we should know something."

FIFTEEN

"Why were you acting so crazy?" the woman asked. Her voice was insistent through the vent the prisoner had his ear pressed tightly against. "Did they do something to you?"

"No," he whispered. "It wasn't me, it was the Other. But he's gone now."

There was a long silence, and he almost forgot the conversation and drifted away from the vent. It was getting so much harder to think. He was sure it had been easier, in the before. That lifetime long ago when he wasn't trapped in a small room.

"Are you still able to go through with the plan?"

Plan? Oh yes, that plan. It seemed days since he had even spared a thought for it. "Of course, of course. As soon as you're ready, we can do it."

"Tell me again," the woman said, her voice hoarse with urgency. "How do we escape?"

"I have a weapon." Where had he left it? Was it under his mattress? No! It was shoved behind the small basin that served as a sink on top of the toilet. A shard of broken food tray from when he was first put in the room.

"I will draw the guard in, yell and scream at them until they want to punish me. Then I'll attack! I'll stab and punch until they're dead." He bared his teeth at the thought, playing it out in his head as his hand moved through the air.

"What then?" the woman asked insistently.

"Then I go to the security console. I know where they keep the codes, so I can open your door. And then we can be together." He could touch her skin, taste her and know that he wasn't alone in the universe.

"The guard at the other end of the corridor. What will you do to them?"

He thought, furrowing his brows as he tried to remember. Was there more than one guard? He felt sure that the entire universe existed of himself, the guard that gave him food before taking it away, and the voice of the woman. There wasn't room for anything else. The universe was so tiny.

"You'll raise the ion barrier, remember?"

"Yes, yes, I'll raise the barrier. What else would I do?" How did he raise the barrier? It felt like something he should know, something he had known. In the before. "Then we'll disappear into the tunnels. I like the tunnels. So dark and silent. Smaller than here, but big enough for us."

"Yeah, I know the tunnels." The woman's voice sounded different than it had before. She sounded less certain. Did she doubt him? Did she think he was lying about the tunnels?

Or did she know about the Other? Maybe the Other waited outside the door right now, wanting him to try escaping. The woman must know that, but would feed him to the Other to save herself. Well, maybe the woman would be surprised about who became the meal.

"We'll do it soon," he whispered, almost laughing at the secret he held inside. "A day, maybe two. Then you can be free." Free to keep the Other occupied while he could escape.

Am I still sane? It was a tiny voice, far in the back of his mind. Too small to hear. Too small to notice.

SIXTEEN

Rinde tugged on the knot of his tie as he walked along the hallway. He needed to look his best when he stood up in front of the Sector One House and proposed his bill of no confidence. Urgent and sometimes whispered calls had convinced him he'd have the votes he needed for the first and second Houses. He felt less sure about the Sector Three House, with members from the same regions that the prime minister came from. But surely they would vote his way if the first two Houses passed the resolution.

There was already a milling throng outside the House chamber as he approached, hundreds of people waiting to get inside or talk with members after the session completed. Only a few hundred of the thousand members were in Geneva, but most of the others would attend via video feeds. He needed a two third majority of their votes for his attempt to succeed.

"Defense Minister!" a voice called, and Rinde sighed. He turned, thinking that an errant reporter had managed to get word of what he was about to do and wanted to bombard him with questions.

Instead, he found four uniformed soldiers surrounding a harried looking man in a poorly cut suit. He knew the man, one of the prime minister's junior aides. Someone from a poor family, trying his best to fight for a better position in life.

"What can I do for you? I don't have much time before the House session begins."

"The prime minister would like to speak with you, sir. It's an urgent matter."

Rinde stared at the aide with a raised eyebrow. "Yes, I'm sure it is. You'll have to tell him that I'm too busy at the moment. Perhaps we can meet after the House session is complete."

The aide had the grace to look embarrassed as the soldiers jogged forward to surround Rinde. "I'm sorry, minister, but it wasn't really a request. I was told to bring you no matter how it needed to happen. I'd much rather you cooperated, sir."

"So, this is how far he has fallen? Stooping to armed coercion to prevent a legal measure that could well go against him?"

"I'm sure the prime minister has an excellent reason for this summons, sir." The aide turned and started to walk along the wide hallway, and one of the soldiers poked Rinde in the back to tell him to follow. He did so reluctantly, looking around at everyone gawking at the spectacle. Why was no one protesting something so obviously illegal? But he knew that if he were one of those people standing on the sidelines, he wouldn't protest. He would just assume the person being escorted away had been accused of some crime or offence. Most likely, these people would turn back to their business and forget having seen him within minutes.

Rinde thought about trying to get away from the soldiers. He could dart down a side corridor, or turn and bolt for the House chamber where they'd have to make too much of a scene trying to grab him. A look at one of the soldiers told him he wouldn't succeed. The woman behind him had her eyes on him the entire time, one hand resting on the butt of her stun pistol.

They came to a halt near the bank of elevators, five on either side of the hallway. The other people waiting for one edged away, glancing uncomfortably at the group until a familiar ding told them a car had arrived. One of the soldiers waved everyone out of the elevator, telling them they could get another one, and then ushered Rinde and his guards in.

As the doors slid closed, Rinde could only look imploringly at everyone staring at him. He'd hoped to see something in their eyes to tell him they knew he was being wrongly detained, but instead he saw only inquisitiveness and a scattering of disgust. *How quickly people can turn against you when they think you've done wrong*, he thought wryly.

"What is this all about?" he asked. It was intriguing that the elevator was going down instead of up to the prime minister's office on the highest floor. The aide was standing in front of the panel, so Rinde couldn't see which button had been selected.

"The prime minister will discuss it with you," was all the man would say.

When Rinde opened his mouth to press for an answer, one of the security force soldiers put a hand on his shoulder. As a quiet way to tell him to shut his mouth, it was very effective. He closed his eyes and said a prayer, asking for guidance in the strange situation.

The elevator doors opened onto the spacious lobby. There was a crowd of people standing just outside the doors, waiting to shove their way in to travel to whichever floor they needed to be on. Two of the soldiers pushed everyone back, creating a barricade as the other two led Rinde toward the revolving exit doors. He looked back to see more bewildered looks, but already people were turning away to crowd into the open elevator.

A long black car was waiting at the curb, with an immaculately dressed driver standing beside the rear door. The aide led the group straight for the vehicle, and the driver opened the door once Rinde was a few steps away. Recognizing the invitation, he ducked and slid onto the soft leather seat. The door closed behind him.

The interior of the car was dim. It smelled of real leather, a rare luxury, with a faint acrid smell of cigar smoke. On top of it all was an aftershave that he knew too well.

"Prime minister, why have you pulled me away from a House session?"

A light flared, showing a familiar tanned face under thick black hair. The prime minister puffed on his cigar, holding it to the flame until the tip was burning. With a flip, the lighter was extinguished and the car was filled with murky darkness again.

"Rinde, my boy, you've disappointed me. I picked you for a seat on my cabinet when your predecessor died in the bombs. You should be loyal to me above all else."

"I am loyal to my government and our people, not to one man temporarily filling the top position." Rinde could feel the vehicle moving, the swish of the tires on wet streets. The snow that had survived for many days was starting to melt as temperatures warmed.

"I *am* the government. That's what you should see when you look at me, the will of the people. They elected me three times, and soon they'll make it four."

"You can't run again," Rinde said steadfastly. "The constitution forbids any person from holding one office for more than three terms."

"Rules were made to be broken," the man replied. Rinde could almost see the negligent hand gesture the prime minister always made when someone objected to one of his ideas. "Name one person you'd want handling our government right now. You can't, because we're in the most dangerous fight of our lives. The Syndicate have a ship with overwhelming strength in orbit, and now the military they've been building up for years has crossed the border and threatens us with annihilation."

"That overwhelming ship could have been handled when our frigates returned to Earth, sir, and you know it. Minister Rinova and I have been telling you that for days, and if you hadn't excluded us from your cabinet meetings..."

"You would have continued to bore the rest of us to tears with your adamant claims that we could win a fight. Yes, yes. I've heard it before, Rinde, and I don't need to hear it again."

"And as for this invasion," Rinde continued, talking over the prime minister's objections, "the Syndicate military never should have been allowed to grow to these levels. My predecessor and I have both pointed out the intelligence received about their defense force receiving larger and larger supply shipments. Our ambassadors should have called for a halt to that accumulation of strength two years ago!"

His words stopped, and left the limo filled with silence. Rinde was breathing hard from the forcefulness of his remarks. After a few seconds, there was low laughter. The noise started almost too quietly to hear, but grew and grew until the prime minister was roaring with it.

"Oh, I do love the passion you show. It's too bad you couldn't use that to work with me, instead of trying to overthrow your rightful leader." A cloud of smoke filled Rinde's face, and he had to turn his head and hold back a cough.

"That vote was never going to pass, by the way," the prime minister said. "I knew what you were doing after your first call to a member of Parliament. My people were ahead of you, telling them to agree to your foolhardy plan. You would have fallen flat on your face in front of the entire House."

"No," Rinde said after a stunned silence. "If that were true, you wouldn't have sent goons to pull me away. It was going to work, and you're afraid."

"Maybe you're right," the prime minister said. "Maybe I felt threatened by you, and had to do whatever I could to save my position." There was a loud sucking sound, followed by another heavy cloud of smoke. "If that was true, Rinde, would this be happening?"

A display dropped down from the roof of the car, and showed the floor of the House chamber. The Minister of Foreign Affairs was at the podium, speaking to the assembled members. There was no sound from the display, but Rinde could tell from the way the minister was waving a hand in the air that he was making emphatic remarks. Every minute or so, there would be a pause while the gathered Parliament applauded.

"Right now, Wang Lei is laying out our plan to lull the Syndicate army into believing that we're not going to put up a fight. We'll make them overreach in their desire for conquest, and then send our security forces in to pick them off."

His tone was gloating, as if he had unveiled some kind of master plan that only a genius could conceive of. Rinde felt frustration, knowing that such a strategy could never work out. The people had already been beaten down by bombings, and then ads telling them the Syndicate were coming and there was nothing they could do to stop it except hope the prime minister could save them. There was little chance that same feeling of defeat had not spread to their military by now, and watching Syndicate invaders have their way with border towns wasn't helping.

108

"So, does that look like a House that was ready to oust me, Rinde? Quite the opposite, I think. They need only the slightest bit of a push, and they'll beg me to stay in office. They'll offer me a lifetime appointment, if I want it. But I don't, I just want to finish all the things I hoped to do while in office. 'I found Rome a city of bricks and left it a city of marble.'"

The door of the car suddenly opened, blinding Rinde with the light streaming in from outside. The driver reached in a hand to help him slide out of the car. As he did so, the prime minister called out. "Do what I ask. Toe the party line. Otherwise, you'll end up like Juliette."

With a slam of the door, the driver circled the car and drove away from the curb. Rinde looked around, surprised to find himself right where he had started. Crowds of people were still pushing in and out of the government building, going about their business as if nothing out of the ordinary had occurred. He was trying to figure out what the prime minister had meant with that last comment.

A bright flash of light made him look up, just as people around him began to scream and yell. High above the capital city of the Coalition, a fireball was fading away. Several seconds later, streaks of light filled the sky as debris began to burn up entering the atmosphere of the planet.

SEVENTEEN

As the shuttle passed over the border, Yumata pressed his face against the glass of the small window beside his seat. There was no visible difference between Syndicate and Coalition territory. Trees and rolling hills filled his view in every direction. Far to the south he could see a hazy blue that he felt sure was the Mediterranean.

"We're twenty minutes from the rear command tents, admiral."

"Thank you, captain. Any chance we can do a flyby over the forward edge of the advance?"

The shuttle pilot was silent, and Yumata knew he was calling in the request to his superiors. He received a quick response. "Not at this time, admiral. If the position's secure this afternoon, we might be able to give it a shot."

He pulled his face from the window, and relaxed back into the plush seat. This was one of several shuttles kept for travel by members of the various committees, and was outfitted with all the luxuries. There was even a small bedroom at the back in case an occupant should wish to arrive at their destination refreshed. After years of sparse naval quarters and offices, it felt wrong for a small group of people to receive such obvious special consideration.

Abernathy was seated several rows farther back, with his head buried in a tablet full of reports the committee was reviewing during their absence. The man kept muttering to himself as he typed hasty notes into another device.

Yumata kept the display on the back of the large seat in front of him active, watching from the shuttle's bow camera as they approached the sprawling military command structures that followed the advancing invasion. Several dozen large tents had been set up, quarters and work space for the senior officers leading from the rear. Supply trucks were lined up outside four of the largest tents, depots providing food and equipment to the soldiers pushing into Coalition territory.

As the shuttle settled to the ground with a gentle bump, Yumata rose and ran a hand down his uniform. It felt good to be properly attired once more, after days of enduring an uncomfortable business suit. The chairwoman had told him wearing a military uniform would send the wrong message to those who appeared before the committee. He held the opposite opinion, but had bowed to the necessity of conforming with the others at the table.

Air hissed as the door on the side of the shuttle lowered, forming a short ramp. Yumata strode down it with his shoulders erect and his hands tucked at the small of his back. He paused at the bottom to look around the camp. A group of officers was clustered not far away, and one stepped forward.

"Admiral Yumata, it's a pleasure to welcome you. I can't remember the last time a member of the Military Committee joined us in the field."

"General Chang." Yumata said, giving a short bow to the group. Turning, he gestured toward the youthful man in a suit that cost more than most of the officers in the camp would make in a year. "This is Morris Abernathy, a fellow committee member."

The general hurried forward to shake hands, instantly reverting to the subservient posturing that Yumata had seen far too often during his short time on the committee. He tried to imagine himself in the man's place, and couldn't picture being anything more than his usual reserved self.

"Thank for you allowing me to visit," the admiral said, pulling the general back to the reason for the trip. "How is the operation proceeding?"

The general waved his hand forward, leading the committee members toward the group of officers. "The territory we claimed yesterday is being secured, as we speak. I've already dispatched orders to advance farther at eleven hundred hours."

Once they reached the group, General Chang introduced his staff. Each of them took a step forward and offered a short bow as their name was spoken. Yumata nodded in return, making a note of each name without much hope of remembering them later. He was intrigued to see that one of the officers wore a Fleet uniform, the patches on her shoulder telling him that she led a fighter squadron.

"You have Darts assisting your attacks?" he asked the general as they strolled toward a nearby tent. The canvas walls had been rolled up to create an open air platform, with a table set for a late breakfast. Two side tables were filled with pastries and chafing dishes that contained a variety of meat and egg dishes.

"We've been using them to scout ahead," the general said. "Initially I'd expected a fast response from the Coalition military, and wanted to have the Darts on hand to attack from the air and fend off any Coalition Kestrels. There has been no resistance at all, however."

"Yes, that worries me," Yumata said, casting an eye over the offered food without interest.

"Oh, no reason to worry about that," Abernathy said, his voice filled with cheer. "I imagine over the last few decades we've allowed ourselves to turn the Coalition into more of a threat than they really are. Now we're seeing their true colors. It just goes to show that the Syndicate is right to press the attack. Without our influence, Earth can't achieve true greatness."

Yumata and the general shared a look, and he was pleased to see his exasperation with the statement mirrored in the other man's face. "General Chang, I'd like to travel to the front lines as soon as it is convenient. I'm anxious to see how our soldiers are faring."

"I'll make arrangements for an armored convoy, admiral. It should be ready within the hour, so we can complete a brief tour before the next advance commences."

The staff officers were still milling around, glancing at the food and watching Abernathy fill a plate. Yumata knew that they were waiting on the guests to serve themselves before they could step up, so he took a small plate. A cheese Danish was selected, and then he stepped over to seat himself at the table. As if a bell had been rung, the group of officers almost charged forward to get food.

General Chang took a seat across the table, folding his hands on the table as he leaned forward. "Will Mr. Abernathy be joining the inspection of the front?"

The committee member nearly choked on the large bite of sausage he had just taken. Abernathy waved a hand as he shook his head. "No, I'll be fine here while the professionals do their thing. I'm sure I can find a place to do some work."

Yumata's lip twitched with a suppressed smile. He was tempted to press for the man to join them, but he preferred to make the tour alone. "I'd like to be there during the advance, general. At least for the early stages. It will be interesting to see our ground based forces at work, after a career spent among the stars."

Chang looked uncomfortable, but finally nodded. "If we join the fourth division, there should be little chance of encountering resistance. The villages along their path today are small farming settlements."

"Excellent. I'm looking forward to being a small part of our invasion forces."

The vehicle selected to convey them along bumpy dirt roads was a heavily armored personnel carrier. Yumata could tell that the general often used it. A bank of displays had been installed against one side of the large space in the rear, so that anyone riding in the eight uncomfortable seats on the opposite wall could watch the progress of any part of the army.

"I heard mention of a seventh division before we left camp?" Yumata asked loudly over the roar of the personnel carrier's engines.

"Yes, they arrived last night. The Executive Committee has detached the Eighth from duty along the South American border, as well. We expect them tomorrow."

"I worry we may be overreaching ourselves. Devoting half our defense forces to this invasion may leave us open elsewhere."

General Chang nodded in agreement. "Initially, I shared your concerns, admiral. However, the Executive Committee feels certain that when a counterattack comes it will be focused here. They want to ensure that we have an overwhelming force to prevent it succeeding."

The whine of the carrier engines dropped a few octaves as the vehicle began to slow. Yumata could feel the jolting of the tires lessen in intensity, and breathed a sigh of relief. A body accustomed to the low gravity aboard a ship

114

wasn't as durable as it should be. It felt as if his very bones ached from the jarring he had suffered during the half hour ride.

After the APC came to an abrupt stop, the back of the vehicle dropped quickly. In a battle situation, the troops carried within could be on their feet and exiting within seconds. Often, even while the vehicle was moving. Yumata followed General Chang into a scene that was much calmer than he had expected. Hundreds of soldiers were spread out as far as he could see, clumped in squadrons of eight soldiers. Men and women from the quartermaster corps were unloading crates from nearby trucks, and runners were lined up to gather a squadron's supplies to deliver before their next push began.

"As you can see," Chang was saying as they walked into the throng, "our logistical officers have been on top of keeping the soldiers well supplied. Fresh clips for flechette rifles, charged power packs for stun pistols, enough food and water for at least two days. Our soldiers suffer no hardships as they march for the glory of the Syndicate."

They spent half an hour visiting groups of soldiers, with Yumata often stopping to speak with random members of the squads. He was pleased to see that morale was high among them. Few of them voiced any concerns about the aggressive action, which he noted with cynical detachment.

"We should return to the APC," Chang said as the soldiers around them began to rise to their feet while officers made the rounds. "The advance begins shortly."

"How far will the divisions push before they stop to consolidate territory?"

"My orders are to push as far as we can by nightfall, and then halt. If our progress is the same as the first advance, we should be twenty miles further into Coalition territory by then."

Yumata stood beside the armored carrier, watching the soldiers begin the steady march forward. The squads were spaced closely enough to always have at least one other squad in view, but wide enough for the expansive line to cover vast amounts of terrain. Here and there he could see heavily armored tanks rolling slowly on their heavy treads. They left deep ruts in the ground as they passed, often climbing small hills before dipping forward to drop down the other side. Several squads had jumped onto the mechanical beasts, saving their legs for later in the day.

The rear hatch swung closed as soon as Yumata, Chang, and their four bodyguards were back inside. The displays on the opposite wall were rotating views from cameras strapped to various officers through the divisions. Two of them were dedicated to the cameras mounted below Dart-class fighters as they zoomed past overhead to look for any surprises ahead.

For several hours, the army pushed forward into enemy territory. They faced no opposition, and even the towns and villages they passed through in this lightly populated part of the world presented no difficulties. Men, women, and children would line the streets as the soldiers walked by. Their faces were sad but resigned, and Yumata couldn't understand how they could accept an invasion so placidly.

"It's strange to see them stand there," the general said, as if reading his mind. "I've yet to see one of these Coalition people with fire in their eyes. It makes you wonder why we didn't do this years ago, and rid ourselves of the nuisance."

116

"Hm," Yumata replied noncommittally. He wasn't so sure that he hadn't seen flashes of hatred in a few faces, those near the back of the crowds. They often turned away when they noticed the cameras focused on them, melting away. "We must finish them quickly, if there is a hope to succeed. Their frigates still threaten us from above."

"When can we expect a resolution to that, admiral? I must admit that I feel the weight of those ships above me often."

"Shipments of replacement weaponry have been sent up to the *Indomitable*, and several shuttles continue to take crates up every day. I should expect Captain Guildersen to be ready for an offensive move soon."

Chang grunted. "So it's true the cruiser was heavily damaged in the battles, then?"

"She was a victim of Transport Guild ingenuity," Yumata said, surprising himself with the admiration he felt for the maneuver that had nearly crippled his ship. "We were able to shield the extent of the damage from them, or I'm sure the Coalition frigates would have pursued us with more fervor."

Once the armored personnel carrier passed through the latest town conquered without a blow, the general ordered the driver to find a spot to park. The three other vehicles in their convoy spread out around them. Soldiers verified the safety of the area and set up a defensive perimeter, reporting their status to the general.

"As you can see, admiral, we have taken nearly eight miles of ground already. It's barely midafternoon, so we are ahead of expectations."

A small table was being set up, and junior officers were setting out a late lunch for the two of them. Yumata marveled at the waste of it in the midst of a push into enemy territory. He'd have been quite happy with a simple protein bar or a pouch of nutrient slurry. Both had been frequent meals for him during his years in space, and he'd developed a fondness for them.

He and the general were sitting at the table when shouts of alarm drew their attention. A few of the soldiers standing guard were looking west and pointing at the horizon. Yumata stood and stared with raised eyebrows as the sky there filled with streaks of red light.

A major who was riding in another vehicle in the convoy hurried over. "General, there was an explosion over the Coalition capital. We're not sure what happened yet, but it looks like one of their frigates was destroyed in the blast."

Yumata strode toward the armored vehicle. "Get me a connection to the Military Committee at once." He felt a cold streak down his spine. If it had been the *Indomitable* attacking, then the war may have just been won. Without support from above, taking Coalition territory on the ground would be no more than a series of mopping up skirmishes.

EIGHTEEN

Tom looked over the two militia members he'd selected for the scouting mission. He unstrapped and tightened armor plates, and double checked the seals on their helmets. There was no need for his intense ministrations, but it was the only outlet for his nerves. This would be his first mission in command of anyone but himself, and he was strongly hoping he didn't make any mistakes.

"Okay, everyone good? Oxygen and nitrogen tanks are topped off?"

"Yes, captain," both soldiers replied. They looked so young to him, one nineteen and the other only days past his twentieth birthday. Tom had been in space aboard Guild freighters and then serving aboard the Syndicate cruiser for so long, he dreaded doing the math to find out if either had even been born yet before he left Earth.

He thought about the four ten member squads going through various stages of training. Meyers was still getting volunteers from Earth to join the new militia, but he said it was getting harder to get shuttles to the ground. The two governments on the planet were tightening their grip in response to what they saw as an illegal action by the Guild. If not for the black market locations, their supply and personnel shipments would have ground to a halt.

Tom was hoping to get enough people for a fifth squad in today's shuttles, but wasn't holding his breath. In the meantime, he had to focus on the militia that he had. This scouting trip to Armstrong would give him a better idea of the feasibility of using his soldiers to secure the other half of the Luna settlement.

After a cursory check of the stun pistols they carried, he knew he couldn't delay any longer. He led his young troops through the airlock, stepping out onto lunar dust for the first time in his life. Tom had years of experience in pressure suits outside freighters and the *Indomitable*, but this was his first time setting foot on the bare surface of any planet or moon aside from Earth.

The week spent working inside of Aldrin had allowed him to grow accustomed to the one sixth gravity of Luna, so his bouncing steps were quick and sure as he led the way around the exterior of the former Coalition dome. In the interest of security, the docking platforms had been built on the far side from the Syndicate dome, and there were no other airlocks in the structure.

Tom glanced to either side, making sure the two young soldiers were keeping up with his pace. The youngest, Milner, gave him a sardonic grin through the faceplate of his helmet. *Okay,* he thought, *let's see you keep up with this.* Putting all his weight behind the next push from the lunar dust, Tom bounced higher and farther. He continued the forceful leaps for half a dozen steps, before turning to look at the others. He had to fight back a laugh. Milner had mistimed one of the jumps and his right side was covered in fine gray dust where he had impacted the surface. Hotchkiss had done well, but was still several steps behind his captain.

"Don't get cocky," Tom said over their comm channel. "Just because you've been walking in this low gravity for a while, it's completely different when you're doing it in a bulky suit."

"Yes, captain," they said, sounding slightly dispirited.

120

Tom chuckled, and then stared as his attention was drawn to a battered freighter lifting from the docking pads now out of sight. He recognized the *Vagabond* even before he saw the name stenciled on the side. He'd only spent half a year aboard the ship, but along with Jen and Mira her crew had come to feel like family. Staying to oversee the training of the militia had been a difficult decision to make.

"Let's get moving," he said finally, turning back toward their objective. There was still a long way to go before they reached Armstrong, and he expected to survey the docking area for at least an hour before attempting an approach. He didn't want to face gunfire from Syndicate Marines as the last party had.

Tom waved forward as he rushed over the lunar surface. They'd spent more time than he'd expected watching the Armstrong docking facility, but he'd wanted to be sure before committing himself. There had been no movement at all around the pads or behind the thick windows between the various airlocks.

They passed by the metal girders of one of the docking pads, a large octagonal structure capable of holding a ship twice the size of the *Vagabond* or his old *Telemachus*. Using the thick struts kept them hidden behind cover for most of the advance. He paused before the last stretch of open ground, his eyes darting around to verify there was still no movement from the airlocks

"Go," he said quietly, and the three of them ran in loping strides. It only took twenty seconds until Tom had his back flat against the wall at the base of the docking facility, but he felt as if there were a gun pointed at him the entire time. *Just nerves*, he told himself. Milner and

Hotchkiss took up position to either side, and he could see their chests heaving under the bulky pressure suits.

A dozen steps away was the nearest airlock. With the docking tube retracted, the portal was several meters above their heads. This was something they'd planned for, though. At Tom's gesture, Hotchkiss began climbing the wall. There were plenty of protrusions and bumps in the metal skin at the base of the dome for him to use. Once he'd gotten high enough, the soldier found a position in which to comfortably brace himself.

Hotchkiss was carrying a small tech kit, a piece of hardware that was almost impossible to find outside of Marine squads or security forces special units. President Meyers had managed to procure two, but hadn't offered any details as to how. Two small leads could be pulled out from the device on retractable wires, and once clipped onto specific wires inside an access panel the kit could be used to override the security codes.

Tom watched the young militia soldier work to remove the panel and then connect the leads. The seconds felt like hours in his hyper aware state of extreme adrenaline, but the timer on the small HUD of his helmet told him it took only thirty seven seconds for the panel to be removed. Forty nine seconds later, the display on the small tech kit flashed green. Five seconds after that, the airlock door slid open.

"Go," he said again, and began climbing with Milner. Hotchkiss was easily able to swing himself over once retracting the leads and replacing the panel cover, so that he was waiting with an outstretched hand to help his companions through the airlock hatch. Tom looked for the panel to cycle the airlock, and grunted when he saw it was locked down. Hotchkiss stepped up with the tech kit again.

122

The process was faster this time, especially since he wasn't having to support himself against a sheer wall. Thirty two seconds for the panel, thirty seven for the lock override, and five for the airlock to fill with air before the inner door hissed open.

The interior of the Armstrong docking facility was eerily dark and silent. Tom had instructed the others to keep their helmets on, pausing in the airlock long enough to fill their oxygen and nitrogen packs. The three minute delay could save their lives, if things went pear shaped further into the dome. They advanced using a classic leapfrog system. Tom would rush forward a few meters while Milner and Hotchkiss covered from other positions. Then Milner would move past Tom, and Hotchkiss would advance past both. It was a slow process, but gave them a maximum amount of protection.

Tom had hoped to have the use of some nano drones, but that had been one item the Guild had so far been unable to procure. They had larger drones, the size of a grown man's palm, but Tom hadn't wanted to use valuable storage space on their suits to carry one or two. Drones of that size generated enough noise to make them almost useless for stealth scouting, anyway.

When they reached the exit from the docking facility, Tom brought the group to a halt. He had shivers down his spine as he looked back across the open space they'd just crossed. Everything was in place, perfectly neat and tidy. It looked like a facility that everyone had stepped away from mere moments before his team made entry into the dome.

"Are either of you picking anything up on the radio bands?"

"No, captain," Milner said. Hotchkiss shook his head.

"Strange." Tom knew the Syndicate military comm channels were encrypted and secure, but they still should have picked up lots of civilian chatter. He was starting to get a bad feeling about the entire situation. Taking a deep breath, he motioned the group forward. Just inside the main dome, they found cover and ducked behind it. Armstrong was almost completely dark, lit only by the light reflected from Earth shining over the rim of the dome. The top half of each dome was thick glass transparent from inside, giving the feel of open sky to the occupants below.

He dialed up his suit's auditory systems as high as they would go, and listened for a minute. He could hear noises from his two young colleagues, but there was silence from beyond their bit of cover. After dialing the systems back to normal, he checked his temperature readings. With the sun currently behind Luna, they had walked across the surface in temperatures that were more than a hundred degrees below zero. The interior of Armstrong should have been a comfortable 20°C, but his suit was reading a temperature that had already dropped double digits below zero.

"Whatever happened in here, the environmental systems have been offline for at least a day."

"Captain, I'm getting a low count on oxygen in the air," Hotchkiss said. "Something is using up what was in the dome when the systems were shut down."

"There could be people somewhere," Milner said, excitement in his voice.

"Let's not get ahead of ourselves." Tom rose to glance around for a few seconds before dropping behind their cover again. "I'm not seeing any lights at all, so it's going to be impossible to find someone if they're alive and want to hide."

He considered their situation. He could open a comm channel to the main Guild frequency, but if there were still Syndicate Marines inside the dome they would pick up on that. Their decryption programs would probably crack through within ten to fifteen seconds, letting them hear anything said on the channel. He wasn't ready to risk that just yet.

"I'm going straight up the main avenue," Tom said. "Milner, you go one street to the right. Hotchkiss, one street left. We'll shadow each other all the way to the central square. If you run into anything you're not sure about, use the broad spectrum channel to call for help."

The two young soldiers nodded, and they all pulled their weapons to make sure it would take only seconds to fire if they were confronted by an unfriendly survivor. Milner and Hotchkiss left cover at a crouching run for their side streets, and a few seconds later Tom followed.

He stepped slowly and carefully down the main thoroughfare of the dome, his eyes sweeping the space between buildings as he passed by. The street was clean and clear, as if it had been swept earlier that same day. The only thing missing were the people who should have been traveling around the dome on day-to-day business.

Milner and Hotchkiss would appear through alleys now and then, and each time he saw one he felt a lightening of the ever increasing tension. Something had gone horribly wrong in Armstrong, and finding no evidence of what that might have been was proving to be more stressful than seeing bodies strewn all over the ground.

Halfway to the central square, Hotchkiss came running down an alley to join him on the main road.

"Captain, my street is blocked ahead. A lot of rubble in the road, sir."

Not long after, Milner joined them with the same report about his street. "It looked like the façade of one of the buildings had collapsed," he reported.

Tom tried to see through the faintly lit darkness ahead. Had the buildings near the center of the dome been destroyed in some kind of attack? Or were the side streets blocked off to ensure that anyone had to continue their approach down the main thoroughfare that could be covered from multiple locations?

"Okay, we can't turn back now. Each of you hug the buildings on the side of the street, and I'll keep to the middle. That way if there's an ambush ahead we'll have a chance of getting past it."

They continued a slow advance down the wide street. It didn't take long for Tom to start seeing the evidence of similar destruction his soldiers had reported on the side streets. Blocks of rubble were spread out across the roadway, first in ones and twos and then in greater numbers. Looking up, he could see holes in the front of several buildings, and one was smashed open so that he could see two intact levels of the interior.

Tom's HUD map showed that they were only a few blocks from the central square when the road ahead was filled with chunks of gray lunar concrete and twisted metal scraps that had once been electric carts. The road was blackened in several spots, as were the stumps of walls that remained from buildings that had been destroyed with some kind of explosion.

"Jesus, captain," Milner said in awe. Tom followed the direction of his gaze and saw the faint light reflecting from Earth shining on a central square that appeared completely devastated. Where he would expect to see light glinting off windows or metal pipes running up the sides of buildings, there was nothing but blackness. He dialed up the light from his helmet, and also flipped on the high intensity beams attached to the shoulders of the suit. Milner and Hotchkiss followed his lead, and then the three were totally still for several minutes.

Revealed by the lights shining across it, they could see a crater where the central square should have been. It wasn't deep, but the metal and plastic base below the ground level of each dome had been exposed. They could even see the gray dust of the lunar surface exposed in a few small spots. The buildings around the square had been completely flattened, the debris blown back from the crater.

"My God," Tom whispered. "That had to be a massive explosion. How did we not feel it?"

"Why didn't it crack the dome?" Milner asked, looking up. "The shockwave from something like that had to be enormously powerful."

Hotchkiss was shaking his head, but his eyes never strayed from the crater. "That glass is reinforced with all kinds of bonded materials. Built to sustain small meteor strikes, so any concussive force would have been funneled back to the ground."

Tom pulled his gaze from the destruction, and looked around. There should have been bodies, or survivors calling out from help when they saw the trio walking through their dome. One thing was certain, though. He wasn't going to be able to get any information on what caused the explosion. Any video feed data from within the dome would have been stored on the servers underneath the dome's administration building. A location destroyed by whatever made the crater.

"Let's pull back," he said to the others. "Once we get back to Aldrin, we can report in and let the President decide if we should return with a larger group to comb the area." They dimmed helmet lights and turned off the shoulder beams, and began the long trek back to the docking facility airlocks. Tom walked with less caution, but still instructed the others to keep an eye on their surroundings.

Only a few blocks from the end of the thoroughfare, his attention was drawn to a flash of light from above. Thinking that survivors might have chosen to attack while their guard was down, he dropped to a crouch and raised his weapon as he looked up and all around.

Tom's hand dropped as he saw the source of the light. Milner let out a grunt of dismay, and Hotchkiss was struck silent. There was a haze of debris over part of Earth, with flashes of light appearing and disappearing quickly as chunks of it fell through the atmosphere.

"Where is that?" Milner asked.

"That's central Europe," Tom said in disbelief. "Coalition territory."

NINETEEN

Erik settled into his command chair, checking through the readouts on the main displays. He'd managed to spend a blissful hour with Dex after the meeting with President Meyers, but now he had to turn his mind back to business. There were still pages and pages of tests that would need to be completed before the fusion reactor could be safely passed.

Meyers had confided that there was already a second reactor being built in a warehouse on Luna. The pair from Berlin had brought along all the materials in their shuttle, confident that their prototype would succeed. The engineer, Amelia, had spent their short time at Aldrin checking in on the build.

"We're clear for departure," Mira said.

"Did you even leave your station while we were docked, Mira?"

"Of course I did, cap! I had to go to the head a couple of times."

Erik laughed, though deep down he felt almost certain she wasn't joking. He'd have to be sure the rest of the crew found a way to drag Mira out for some fun the next time they docked. "Take us up. About seventeen hours of tests to complete."

"Woo. Tests." Mira fake cheered, as her fingers flew across the keypad to send the commands for the *Vagabond* to lift into orbit. Within minutes, they were passing through the orbital paths of the Guild freighters that formed a protective screen around the moon.

"Let's get clear of any area that might have traffic," he said, running his fingers along a display as he looked through a map of space around Earth. "This looks like a good spot, Mira. Gives us a hundred thousand kilometer barrier between any known ship route."

Mira looked at the information he sent to her station, and he could hear the grin in her voice. "Straight up and to the left. You got it, cap." The steady vibration of the ship increased as the pilot fed more energy into the engines. "I get to see just what this girl can do with her new reactor."

Erik grunted as he was thrown back into the gel that absorbed the almost instant three G thrust. As the freighter rocketed away from Luna, he heard a loud whoop from Mira, and couldn't help but smile with his own excitement at the burst of speed.

Vagabond settled into the chosen position, high above the plane of the elliptic where few ship routes existed. Even in an age where space travel was common, human thinking tended to be very two dimensional. It was a phenomenon to be glad of at the moment, giving them a place to run through a lot of the reactor tests without having to worry about unwanted company.

"Before the next round of testing," Amelia said as she strode into the control center, "we need to shut down the reactor completely for ten to fifteen minutes."

Erik wasn't sure he liked the thought of that. "Uh, doesn't that mean all our essential systems will be shut down? Like life support?"

"Yes, but we'll have all the air and heat we need for at least half an hour."

"Okay, but what if you run into issues and can't get the reactor started that quickly? Or ever again?"

The engineer was unconcerned. "It won't be a problem, Captain Frost. I brought along our first small scale prototype. We can connect that to the ship's systems in the event of an emergency."

Erik squeezed his eyes shut and tried to contain his frustration. "So, you came onto my ship to test a reactor that could have exploded and killed us all, and brought along another reactor to increase the odds of something bad did happen?"

"The odds of something like that occurring are beyond comprehension. Do I have your permission to shut down the reactor while we reroute systems?"

"Yeah, sure. I think my will is up to date." Amelia didn't even seem to get his joke, merely turning to speak into her comms and let Fynn know they were ready to proceed.

"Damn good thing," he could hear Fynn say. "It would've taken me half an hour to reverse everything I've already done." Erik shook his head, reflecting that he should have known his old engineer would have started on the work anticipating the permission he wanted. It actually made him feel better, in a strange way. It was the way things had always been done aboard the *Vagabond*.

"Okay, Mira. We've got a little time, so let's take a break. I need coffee. You want coffee?"

"That would be divine, cap. Bring me two!"

"Seriously, if I don't see you leave the control room I'm going to start thinking you got stuck in that chair and you're just too embarrassed to admit it."

Mira laughed, swiveling the crash couch around as she unstrapped the harnesses. "Lead the way, mon Capitan, and I shall retire to yon galley for sustenance."

"Smart ass," he muttered as she followed him through the corridors. Erik stopped to look in on Isaac in the tech hub, but found that Dr. Francks was having a discussion with the tech. From the few words Erik could understand of the scientific technobabble, it sounded like they were comparing wavelengths or transmission rates of photons.

Jen was in the galley when Erik and Mira entered, already working to brew coffee using freeze dried grounds shipped from Earth. Losing supplies like those were one of the many effects Erik wasn't looking forward to if the Guild continued to face opposition from the Coalition and Syndicate. Maybe some entrepreneur would figure out a way to grow coffee plants in a hydroponics greenhouse.

"No injuries during testing so far, doc?"

"Not even a papercut," Jen said with a theatrical sigh.

"I've always wondered about that expression," Mira said as she filled a cup with brown liquid. "Why would paper cut you? It's so fragile, and bendy."

"First, I don't think bendy is a word," Erik responded, holding up fingers as he ticked of points. "Second, I've handled real paper and I can tell you from experience that it's way more dangerous than you'd expect. Third, I'd like to say that I'm quite happy that we've gone through testing without any injuries so far."

"Cap keeps expecting everything to blow up," Mira confided in a loud whisper.

"I've been half expecting it, myself." Jen straddled a bench seat at the long galley table. "Do you realize how often new technology goes wrong in the early testing phases? The fact that we haven't had at least one catastrophe is a little unsettling."

"Yes!" Erik filled his cup and then joined her at the table. "Logically, I know I should be relieved that everything's going so well. But there is a piece of my brain

132

screaming constantly that every test that passes is making it more likely for the next one to fail."

"Aw, that's just your old pre-technology fears," Mira said. "The parts of the brain that formed way, way back when people used ancient stuff like sticks and rode around on the backs of animals."

"They, uh, still do that," Erik said. "My mom worked for a club where people could pay huge fees to come in and ride around on the back of a horse a few times a month. Supposed to be for cultured people or something."

"Well, those people are weird," Jen said, sipping at the cooling coffee. "Just a bunch of rich assholes that like to pretend they're still back in the good old days when they could buy peasants and order them around."

"No argument from me. Mom always had the strangest stories from that place. She only worked there for about six months." He closed his eyes and fought back the emotion. His memories of those days were bittersweet, the last happy times he experienced before his mom found out she had a particularly nasty form of cancer for which there was still no cure.

"Well," Jen said, as if sensing it was time to change the subject, "There's still time for things to go wrong, but I'm keeping my fingers crossed they don't."

At that moment, the lights went out in the galley. An emergency beacon high in one corner provided a wan orange light, the only thing keeping them from total darkness. The noises of a functioning ship died away, leaving silence. Erik almost felt claustrophobic without the sound of the air systems and the random clicks of the mechanical parts throughout the freighter.

"Reactor is down," Amelia called from the reactor room. "Start the clock."

"Well, this is cozy," Mira said, causing Erik and Jen to laugh.

"I'm just glad they waited long enough for the coffee to be done," Jen said as she rose from the table. "I'll be in tech with Isaac, if anyone needs me. Just shout loud enough to be heard."

"And I'm heading back to control," Mira said. "I want to be there when *Vagabond* comes back up so I can make sure she's okay." Erik followed behind, pushing down the urge to watch the work in the reactor room, where he knew he'd just be in the way.

Erik was feeling anxiousness that he wasn't about to admit to when the ship's clock told him that more than thirteen minutes had elapsed since the reactor was turned off. *Amelia said ten to fifteen*, he kept reminding himself. But his mind kept replaying all the horrible possibilities; dying from lack of oxygen, dying from the extreme cold of space creeping into the ship, dying from an explosion when the reactor was restarted. Basically, dying in a lot of painful ways.

Less than a minute later, the lights nearly blinded him and the sounds of the heating systems and air vents filled his ears once more. He almost laughed when he heard a loud sigh of relief from the pilot's station.

"Power down and power up tests all passed," Amelia said over the ship comms. "Give us about ten minutes and we'll be ready to start the next round of tests. You, uh, might want to make sure you're strapped in somewhere before that starts. Unless you'd like to know how broken bones feel."

"Do you think she enjoys freaking me the hell out with stuff like that, cap?" Mira asked, once the comm system clicked off.

134

"I think she's so wrapped up in her own little world that she doesn't realize the effect of what she says." Erik had been reaching to unstrap before the announcement, and decided not to risk it. Amelia seemed like a fantastic engineer, and Fynn certainly sang her praises, but she also sometimes forgot that other people needed warning before tests started.

As if to validate his fears, every thruster on the freighter fired only seven minutes later. Erik heard a yelp of surprise from the tech hub across the corridor, and hoped Isaac and Jen had been strapped in. The ship felt as if it were trying to shake itself apart, the thrusters trying to push it in six different directions at once. When the engines were cut after thirty seconds, he was feeling a little nauseous. After fifteen years on ships, it was the first time he'd ever experienced any form of space sickness. Judging from the groan in front of him, Mira was feeling the same way.

"Next time you complain about my flying, cap, I'm going to remind you of the last half minute."

"Fair. Totally fair." He kept his eyes closed until the feeling passed, and then checked the readouts on his holo display. Hull integrity had lost two percentage points during the test, which was a surprisingly low number after that much stress on the ship. Before the refit the Guild had performed a month before, he knew the ship would likely have suffered cracked hull plates and rips in the inner hull.

Three items on the test list were marked with green boxes, and he looked at the next few items on the list. "What did I do to deserve this?"

"We need to test how the reactor handles atmospheric entry and exit," Dr. Francks said over the comms. "I'd like to do a quick pass through Earth's atmosphere at about two G's, if you don't mind, captain."

"Sure, why not," Erik said in resignation. He'd been dreading this test from the start. The *Vagabond* hadn't been through atmosphere of any kind in more than fifteen years, and he could only hope the newly strengthened hull would handle it. He gave Mira the order, and she started to set a course that would have them dip through the planet's atmosphere over the north pole.

He was pushed back into his gel-lined chair as the engines kicked in, accelerating them toward the blue and green planet that began to grow steadily on the display from the bow cam. Erik could see the edges of the Pacific Ocean to the right, with most of Asia and Europe spread out before him. The *Indomitable* was a small speck over the Syndicate capital, and he felt his hands tighten with a desire to tell Mira to change course to get in a few shots on the cruiser with the rail guns mounted to his ship.

He dragged his eyes away, instead thinking of the unchecked invasion occurring north and east of the Black Sea. President Meyers still couldn't explain why the Coalition was taking so long to mount a defense and try to push the Syndicate troops out of their territory. His eyes continued east, to where he thought Geneva was. With the planet growing larger, he was sure he could make out the growing shapes of the Coalition frigates. Three of them, all fully armed and operational. And all of them sitting there doing nothing against the Syndicate threat.

"Cap, if you don't let us keep this reactor I'm going to have to kill you." Mira was stroking her console affectionately.

"A bit better than the old nuclear reactor, huh?"

"A bit?" Mira swiveled her seat to look at him with raised eyebrows. "That's like saying real chocolate is a bit

136

better than chocolate flavored powder. It's a huge leap from one to the other."

Erik chuckled. "I'm glad you approve so far. If these tests keep passing, I'm not going to let them yank that thing out. Unless it's to give us a newer, better version of the fusion reactor."

"I knew there was a reason I liked you," Mira said with a smirk before turning back to her terminal. "Sixteen minutes to atmosphere. Course projections show that we'll be more than thirty kilometers from any other traffic."

"Great. Let's keep our fingers crossed that...."

A bright light flashed on the main holo display, and Erik snapped his eyes up. There was a fireball over Europe, and he saw another flash soon after that was more muted than the first. As the explosions died quickly in the vacuum of space, they left an afterimage on his retinas from the brightness.

"What in all the hells was that?!" Mira yelled.

"I think that was the Coalition frigates," Erik said quietly. He zoomed in on the image, seeing only debris falling through the atmosphere over central Europe. "All three of them. Just gone."

He shook himself and pulled up a few screens showing communication traffic from the planet. He was hoping for information on what had happened, but saw nothing. "Abort the test," he told the pilot. "Get us back to Luna. We need to find out what happened down there, and make sure the Guild isn't next."

TWENTY

Guildersen was staring out over the bridge, a sardonic smile across his fleshy lips as he mulled over his choices. He always chose at least one crew member from each shift to receive a punishment. It kept the rest of the cretins sharp, fear of being singled out pushing them to work harder. If it also happened to spur them into choosing a member of each shift to be sabotaged into receiving punishment so they didn't have to, then all the better.

"Lieutenant," he called out in a gleeful singsong voice. There were three of them below, but he didn't much care which of them carried out his orders. He raised a pudgy hand to point at a woman sitting near the middle of the bridge. She cringed immediately, seeming to shrink in on herself. "Take that crewwoman to the brig. One day confinement for shirking her duties."

The officers quickly surrounded the woman and roughly pulled her away from her station. She cast pleading glances at her fellow crew members, all of whom were keeping their gazes averted for fear of being picked out to join her. She cried out, pleading for her captain to change his mind. Guildersen's attention had already wandered away, as he looked at the main displays. He knew the Marines guarding the entries below would be wrapping the woman's wrists in restraints until other Marines arrived to escort her to the brig.

The view on the large displays showed Earth, several hundred kilometers below their stable orbit over Hong Kong. Supply shuttles zipped in and out of the atmosphere a handful of times each day, delivering more crates of supplies. The *Indomitable* was nearly stocked, with a dozen railguns and torpedo tube assemblies waiting in cargo bays for the useless crew members to install. Guildersen was still frustrated by the lack of progress on repairs to the cruiser. The construction and maintenance crews no longer even bothered to give excuses, now flat out telling him they refused to do the work until another officer was appointed to command of the ship.

Mutiny. It was on the lips of everyone, and Guildersen heard it whispered every time he strode the hallways. He had his opinions on how to handle the traitorous actions, but as yet the Military Committee hadn't given their approval. He knew there was an Academy class about to graduate, and he'd been promised his pick of the new officers to replace those on his staff who were not performing to his expectations. He could mold the young minds to his way of thinking, and form a streamlined command structure.

A bright flash drew his attention to the main displays once more, where he could see a glow on the horizon to the west. Guildersen hurried to the rail, leaning forward to peer at the screen at the front of the bridge. "What was that?" he barked out. "Did anyone see what just happened?"

The crew below was silent, all eyes on the displays. Even the sound of protests from the woman being dragged away for punishment had died away. None of the crew or officers moved, and Guildersen tossed his half full coffee cup at the nearest person below. "I want answers. Now!"

An ensign was splattered with hot coffee, crying out in pain. The noise and shouting from their captain spurred the rest of the bridge into action. Officers hurried to the stations they oversaw, searching for answers to pass to the command deck. Each of them knew that the last person to report in with satisfactory information could face another example of their captain's punishments.

Guildersen turned when the communications officer behind him called out incoming information. He took laborious steps to stand over the young man's shoulder, his bulk seeming to cause the lieutenant to shrink away. "Tell me you know what we just saw."

"Yes, captain. Reports are coming in from central command that the Coalition frigates have just exploded over Geneva."

"What?! All of them?" Guildersen was shocked, but also pleased at the news. Without the threat of the frigates, some of the pressure on him to get the repairs completed on the *Indomitable* would be lessened.

"Central command is reporting the skies above Geneva are now empty. Debris is falling across Coalition territory, with no sign of the frigates that had been in orbit."

"Excellent." Guildersen patted the man on the shoulder, squeezing tightly before turning to stroll back to the rail. For the first time since wresting command of the cruiser from Admiral Yumata, he felt secure in his position. Now he would have breathing space, and could implement some of the measures he'd been considering to make people do the work they should be happy to perform.

The doors of the command deck swished open as Commander Vegley hurried in. "I heard the Coalition frigates were attacked?"

"They have been destroyed," Guildersen said smugly. "No doubt our military intelligence division managed to sneak saboteurs onboard to plant explosives. They will no longer be a threat to the Syndicate or our ship."

"Wonderful news," Vegley said happily. He could almost hear the smile on her face that irritated him every time he saw it. "Will we advance to support the invasion by the ground forces now? The railguns that are functional can be used to devastating effect against enemy resistance."

Guildersen shook his head. "This ship will not move until the Executive or Military Committees tell us to move. And I will not ask for such orders until I know I have officers I can depend upon." He cast a sneering look at his XO, relishing in her grimace that he read as fear for the changes she knew were coming.

"Yes, sir," she said, stiffening and turning to face forward. Her face became an expressionless mask.

"Would you care to tell me what excuse you have today for the repairs and railgun installations not progressing, commander?"

"Same reason as always, captain. The crews refuse to follow through on your orders until they are assured of better treatment." Vegley kept her eyes forward, but he could see from the way her jaw tightened that she agreed with the sentiment.

"Perhaps it is time you read the officer's manual, commander. Do you remember the section on obeying a superior officer's orders at all time? And the punishments for officers and crew found guilty of mutiny?"

"I remember. Sir."

"Well, refresh your memory after your shift, Vegley. If my orders continue to be ignored, more heads will roll." Guildersen turned and stepped forward, pressing against the thin woman uncomfortably. The look of disgust across her face made him grin. "I assure you those punishments will start at the top, commander. I can replace every one of you, if need be, but I don't think these little treacheries will continue once a few officers are removed from the equation."

"Yes, sir." The commander never moved her eyes from a distant point at the front of the bridge. He knew the woman had a will of iron, and it was one of the things he found extremely irritating. Guildersen preferred officers who were easily cowed and brought into line. It was yet another reason he wanted to replace his senior staff with Academy graduates.

Guildersen strolled from the bridge, heading for his office off the command deck. "Tell Colonel Rozier to report to my office," he growled to the communications lieutenant as he passed the console. It was time to go beyond simple stints in the brig for those found to be ignoring his commands. He would let the Marine colonel know that his soldiers had the green light to push as hard as necessary to get the ship working the way it should be.

TWENTY ONE

Mags was leaning on the rail of the command deck, sipping a steaming cup of tea. The ship's supply of dried coffee had run out the day before, and she was trying to get whatever caffeine she could to keep the withdrawal headaches away. It was just past midnight, and only a few of the stations on the bridge below her were occupied. She could see the man at the communications section still sending the messages Admiral Holgerson had commanded be broadcast on a loop. They'd heard nothing from the Coalition fleet or government in weeks, since right before the *Waterloo* was boarded and sent on a wild course for the outer system.

"Commander?"

She turned, surprised to find Sergeant Yates standing at attention just inside the door. "Yates, it's good to see you again. How have you been?" Mags waved for the woman to be at ease.

"We've been doing a lot of training, ma'am. Captain Farrow is adamant that he'll never let a ship he serves on get boarded again."

"Call me Mags, sergeant. Especially when the admiral's not around."

"Yes ma'am. Mags. I guess you can call me Brenna, when my captain's not around." They shared a secret smile.

"So what brings you up to the command deck, Brenna? It's pretty late to be wandering the ship."

Yates stepped forward to join her at the rail, her eyes going to the large displays along the walls of the bridge showing the stars outside the ship. Mags knew from experience that you almost felt as if you were floating in space yourself if you looked at them long enough.

"Well, I guess I just wanted to make sure you were doing okay, ma'am. After all the fighting down in Engineering and then here on the bridge. That's a lot for someone who isn't a Marine to have to deal with."

Mags grunted, sipping from her cup as she thought about the words. "I've got to tell you, Brenna, it was a hell of a punch to the gut when I had time to stop and think about everything I'd seen. Especially the things I'd done." She looked down at her bioprosthetic arm, now sheathed in a fleshy substitute that looked much like the real thing. Using the new limb to smash one person's spine and crushing the throat of another had been something she never anticipated having to do, much less having the fury to do it happily.

"Do you dream about it?" the Marine asked quietly.

"I did. Every night for a week." Mags shrugged. "But since then, not once. I still find myself thinking about it from time to time, but I think I've come to peace with what I did. It was them or us, and that's a choice I'd make the same way ninety nine times out of a hundred."

Yates smiled, and nodded. "I'm glad to hear that, Mags. I had the feeling you were pretty tough skinned from the way you rushed for the bridge instead of monitoring the action from the engine room. But sometimes the toughest people can surprise you and have the hardest time with things." She turned to give a serious look. "You should still talk to someone, Mags. One of the ship's counselors, a friend, it doesn't matter who. Just someone."

Mags grinned, and raised an eyebrow. "Who do you talk to, Brenna?"

"The Marines have a dedicated counselor. I've talked to him a few times since we regained control of the ship. My squad has also spent some time sharing our thoughts about that day."

That was a surprising admission. Mags had to admit that if the Marines could talk it out, then so could she. "What are you doing around oh six hundred?"

"I'll be grabbing some chow before my next shift."

"How would you feel about meeting me in the officer's mess? You were there for most of it, so I'd feel comfortable talking through things with you."

"I'll see you there, Mags." Yates reached out to squeeze her arm reassuringly, and then turned to leave the command deck.

Returning to her quarters after two hours of venting feelings she hadn't expected to feel, Mags was drained and looking forward to crawling into her bed. The last thing she expected was to see a fidgety ensign standing outside her door with his eyes darting up and down the corridor. He brightened when he saw her, and jogged over.

"Commander, Captain Andrews has been trying to get in touch for half an hour. He needs you on the bridge, as quick as possible."

"Lead the way," she said with a sigh, pulling her comm system earpiece from the pocket she had stored it in before meeting Yates. She slid it into her ear as they entered the bridge.

"Mags," the captain said as she entered. He was hunched over one of the stations at the rear of the command deck. He waved her over urgently.

"What's happening, sir?"

"We finally got a communication."

"The fleet?" she asked, bending to look at the display a lieutenant was working at. She could see text scrolling through one small window.

"No, this is from Luna. Apparently from the Transport Guild, but we're running it through all the algorithms to make sure it came from them."

Mags watched over the lieutenant's shoulder as the man worked on the message. She read the text scrolling through the small window, and gasped. "Sir, if this is real...."

"Yes, commander. That's why I want to be very sure this message is genuine before we consider disseminating it. Especially in light of the fact that this is coming from someone other than our own command structure."

"At least we know our communications gear is working," she said lamely. It was small consolation placed next to the contents of the long message.

"Which brings us a host of new problems," Holgerson said from behind. Mags jumped at his words, not having heard the man approach. "If we're receiving messages, then why has the Admiralty not been in touch. I would have ordered those frigates to attack the Syndicate cruiser the moment they arrived back at Earth."

The scrolling message not only told them about the explosions of the three Coalition frigates over the home world, but also about the outcomes of the two brief battles during the *Indomitable*'s advance on Earth. It was cheering to see that their side had inflicted heavy casualties on the enemy, but sobering to then see an advantage squandered so badly.

"Everything checks out, sirs," the communications lieutenant said. "This message definitely originated on

146

Luna, and it has every bit of code I would expect to see from the Guild."

Holgerson harrumphed, and she could see him squeezing his elbows tightly as his arms were crossed over his chest. "Andrews, Richtaus, my quarters."

Mags shared a look with her captain as they followed the admiral from the command deck. She hadn't been inside the commanding officer's quarters since before the admiral joined the *Waterloo*, long before the boarding party had entered there. It was a short walk to the door off the command deck, and they entered a small room set up as an office. The admiral had several tablets scattered around the desk, and a holo display was hovering over it at eye level.

Holgerson circled the desk and sat behind it as Mags and Andrews pulled two small chairs forward to sit facing him. "The way I see it," the admiral said, "we have a big decision to make. I personally believe that the message from the Guild is truthful. I've dealt with President Meyers on multiple occasions, and the man strikes me as honest, if a little too ambitious. How do you both feel?"

Captain Andrews shrugged. "I can't think of any reason for them to lie about it, sir. Sure, they could be trying to drive a wedge between us and Earth for some reason, but a simple message from the Admiralty or cabinet could clear that up in moments. The fact that we've heard nothing in weeks makes me think the Guild has to be trusted."

"I agree," Mags added.

"Very well," Holgerson said. "The next question is why the Admiralty didn't send those frigates to finish the job. Once we received the resolution from the Houses giving us approval to act against the Syndicate, I made it clear to everyone what my plans were. If the *Waterloo* were lost in battle, they were to push to complete the job until we won or it appeared hopeless. Three frigates against that cruiser may have been bad odds, but it was far from hopeless."

"If I may, sir," Mags asked, getting a nod from Andrews. "It feels to me like we're being hung out to dry. Someone high in the power structure is pushing hard to make sure the Coalition response is slowed or ineffective. If the land invasion is truly happening, there's no way to explain why our security force soldiers still haven't acted four days later."

Holgerson frowned, but she could see he'd been sharing many of the same thoughts. "Let's keep this communication between the three of us for now. I'll order the lieutenant not to divulge anything he's read. I'm going to start sending requests for information out to the cabinet members. Perhaps I can get something from one of them since the Admiralty and prime minister's office aren't responding."

"What about Minister Rinova, admiral?" Andrews knew that Holgerson had been friends with the woman for years before she accepted the ministerial appointment. She would most likely have been selected as Fleet Admiral had she not been occupying a cabinet position three years ago when the choice was made.

"I've been sending messages to her office for the last several days. I even tried her home last night. There's been no response."

"What do we do about the Guild?" Mags asked after a short silence. "Do we respond and open communication with them?"

"I think we should," Andrews said, looking hopefully at the admiral.

"They've been our only source of updates, so I agree. Someone must be blocking the news feeds from reaching our ship, which can only be done from the Admiralty." Holgerson sighed, and for a few seconds Mags saw beneath the mask the man always wore on the bridge. He was exhausted, and she wondered how hard he was pushing himself in the hours he wasn't on the command deck. "I'll compose a response for Meyers, and get it sent off within the hour. Thank you for your input."

He rose, signaling the conference was at an end. Mags followed the captain back to the bridge, her brain roiling with more questions. What was going on at Earth, and why were they being kept out of the loop?

TWENTY TWO

The prisoner was crouched a step away from the door. He'd just given the signal through the air vent, and was about to start his plan for escaping. The Other was waiting just over the threshold. He could feel it wanting him to leave the room. Calling him to leave the room. To be devoured.

He laughed, a low cackle. He had his own plans, though, and the Other would find him harder prey than expected. They wouldn't be able to push him around anymore. Not when he was done.

The food tray was sitting in front of him, filled with the watery brown mess that had been pushed through the door ever since he destroyed the tray full of fresh fruits and vegetables. It smelled foul, and tasted worse, but he had eaten all of it until now. The Other was waiting, and he needed to be strong. He needed to be ready.

When the tray slammed against the cell door, the brown substance spread all over the wall. Streaks of it slid to the floor, making the room smell like a backed up sewer. But he didn't care. He wouldn't be in it much longer.

He let out a loud scream, pounding on the door. Pounding on the wall. Pounding on the floor. Incoherent screams that ripped this throat raw with the power he put behind them.

"God damn it!" a loud voice called from the other side of the door. Grinning, he heard the sound of the keypad beeping as the Marine entered the security code. Was the Other grinning, too?

As the door slid open, he pulled the long shard of plastic from his bed and held it by his thigh. The Marine took one step into the cell and gagged. "What the hell is wrong with you? You ate this shit for three days, but now you complain?"

The prisoner tried to keep from cackling as he approached the Marine. Her back was to him as she examined the streaked walls and shook her head. "You're going to clean this up, traitor, or I'll beat the ever loving shi…"

Her words were cut off by a gargle as he stabbed the long shard into her neck, through the weak spot where her chest armor and helmet met. He'd been around Marine armor for years, and knew every weakness that existed. No one could protect themselves from him.

The Marine started to slump down, but he wrapped his arms around her chest. Holding her tight against him, he pushed forward to the cell door. The Other waited.

"Come on!" he screamed. "Attack me. Now's your chance. I'm here, ready and waiting."

When nothing happened, he giggled. Had he scared the Other away with his words? Or did it lurk just on the other side of the door, waiting for him to step forward.

It was a struggle to hold up the weight of the dead Marine and her armor, but he gritted his teeth and stepped forward. Feeling his arms begin to lose their grip, he pushed the body through the doorway. Bait for the Other.

Screaming defiance, the prisoner rushed through the portal. He swung the plastic shard through the air, cutting nothing. Where was the Other? He could feel it, closer and closer. But he couldn't see it.

He saw the security console, and remembered why he was here. There was a Marine turning a corner in the opposite direction, but that had nothing to do with him. It wasn't the Other, so he didn't care.

The prisoner found a row of buttons on the console, and cackled as he pressed them all deliberately. The Other screamed out in pain with each one. "Take that!" he screamed. "And that! And that!"

He felt a nudge against his shoulder and looked down to see an inch of round metal sticking out of it. Two more Marines were rounding the corner now, all of them yelling words that didn't matter.

"Where is it?" he screamed back. "Where is the Other?"

All of the doors along the corridor were open. Did the Other escape through one of them? He saw movement behind one, turning and snarling at whatever was about to appear.

It wasn't the Other. It was a woman. *The* woman? The voice from the vent! It had to be. Marines were getting closer now, still yelling at him as he felt another nudge and saw another inch of metal sticking out of his body.

"You!" the woman spit out. She'd been smiling, but now she bared her teeth in anger. Why would she be mad? Did she know he had planned to feed her to the Other while he escaped?

"You!" she shouted again, starting to rush forward. A Marine was behind her, grabbed her around the stomach and flung her back against the wall. "You damn traitor! I should have killed you! What did you do with my brother, Richard?"

The prisoner went still. Richard? Who is Richard? Was *he* Richard? Or was that the name of the Other? He had to know. The question felt important.

152

Another inch of steel lodged in his pectoral, and this time he felt tickling. Why would Marines want to tickle him? He blinked, and when his eyes opened again he was looking at the ground. How had he gotten there?

Marines piled on top of him, pulling his arms roughly behind his back while the woman continued to shriek. "I'm going to kill you! Do you hear me, Richard? I'm going to kill you!"

As the world began to go dark around the edges, he remembered. *He* was the Other, the cruel creature that lurked in the shadows. Waiting to betray all those who he'd truly loved. His family.

TWENTY THREE

The streets of Geneva were chaotic after the obliteration of the frigates. As the larger bits of fiery wreckage fell to Earth a few dozen kilometers away, the people of the capital went wild. Fear drove them to do things they never would have considered in better circumstances. Stores were broken into as people hoarded essentials, other stores were broken into by the opportunistic who saw a chance for the fancy new gear they couldn't afford, and mayhem spread across the city like a virus.

Members of Parliament streamed from the government building within minutes, the House session abruptly canceled. Most rushed for their cars, parked many streets away, so they could run home and check on families. Others milled around with their heads craning up to look at the last of the artificial meteors falling from the sky. Rinde stood among them, the prime minister's final words echoing in his head as he watched the remains of the frigates fall from the sky.

It had been fortunate that most of the wreckage fell on unpopulated areas far from Geneva, but the city still bore significant damage. Half a dozen buildings near the city center were destroyed by impacts, while hundreds of homes and smaller businesses were levelled. With the rioting ramping up, the city's emergency services had been overwhelmed. The troops that had been slowly gathering not far from the city were called in to assist in rescue and riot suppression details. The numbers of soldiers arriving to help in the city were depressingly low, and yet citizens were being assured that every person available was being called in to help.

As the sun dropped below the horizon, Rinde stood at the window of his office high in the building. From his vantage point, he could see almost all of the city. The orange glow of fires was dotted throughout, with large swaths of abnormal darkness where buildings no longer stood to be lit up.

Uju entered the office quietly, asking if he needed anything. He'd been unable to tell her about the meeting with the prime minister and his forceful removal from the building before the House session could begin. Knowing him as well as she did, Uju hadn't asked about his absence from the session.

Rinde finally turned, seeing his sadness echoed in her eyes. A betrayed look, as if she also couldn't believe the latest failure of their government. "The prime minister did this, Uju. I don't know how, but I'm going to find out. See if any of Juliette's closest aides are still on Earth. If they are, I want to see them."

She nodded, and then stepped closer. "We don't know for sure that Minister Rinova was on the *Yorktown* when it was destroyed."

"I know it here," he replied, placing a hand over his heart. "They relented to her demands to visit the frigates only because they knew this would happen. She was a vocal opponent to the prime minister's lax handling of the war."

"It's dangerous to say things like that," she almost whispered.

"It shouldn't be. This is not the Syndicate, ruled by committees of whoever is richest and most powerful in the moment. We are the Coalition! We stand for freedom of all people in all things." His jaw tightened as he spoke, and he turned back to the window to see a ghostly reflection of himself.

Uju had flinched as he spoke, and he wondered if he had been yelling the words. He could feel the blood pounding in his head. Too much had gone wrong, and he'd done little to stop it. It was time he stepped up and took a more active role. If the members of Parliament were in the prime minister's pocket, then there was still at least one person he could speak with. "Get me a connection to Aldrin," he said as Uju was walking from the room.

He stood at the window until his aide announced over the speakerphone that she had the requested connection. Rinde walked to his desk and sat heavily in his chair as he pressed the button to activate the video screen. A rumpled and weary looking man appeared on the display. His thick brown hair was almost half gray now, and his face had more wrinkles than Rinde remembered seeing months before when they'd spoken about Guild freighters joining Coalition frigates in the war effort.

"Minister Brighton," the man said. "I'd like to offer my condolences. All of us here are shocked at what happened."

"Thank you, President Meyers. Casualties on the ground have been significant, also. The last report I saw had estimates of more than thirty thousand killed or missing."

"My God. Who could ever have believed we'd be talking about something like this? Has there been any indication of who was behind it?"

Rinde grunted. "So you also don't believe in the possibility of reactor malfunction? Or ships that were more damaged in the battles than admitted?"

His brow furrowed, Meyers shook his head. "Not for a second. Are there people saying such things?"

"Our esteemed prime minister has not spoken about it yet, but his Propaganda Minister has floated such claims to other cabinet members that I've spoken with." Rinde paused, considering telling the Guild leader about his private conversation with the prime minister. But he wanted to keep that information close for now, until he was sure he'd gleaned all he could from it.

"Several of our freighters happened to get excellent footage of the ships leading up to and after the explosion. I can send those files over, if you wish. The *Vagabond* in particular was ideally placed. Reviewing her recorded footage shows an explosion near midships on the *Yorktown*, followed a second later by similar explosions on the other two frigates."

Rinde sat up straighter. This was information he'd been trying to get since the event. Thousands of cameras on Earth and her satellites had been trained on the area, and yet everything released was grainy or out of focus. Even the orbital station claimed their constant rotation had put their cameras in a bad position to capture the detonations.

"Yes, President Meyers, I would like that very much. That would seem to rule out reactor mishaps, I think."

"Definitely," Meyers said with an emphatic nod. "Several engineers in our fleet have confirmed that the nuclear reactors were in different parts of the frigates from where the explosions occurred."

"Could it have been missiles fired from Syndicate territory?" Rinde asked, rising to his feet. He was feeling restless and could sit no longer.

"Possible, but unlikely. Our techs couldn't see any indication of a torpedo or missile fired at the ships."

Rinde started to pace, his brain churning over the new information. "President Meyers, how much can I trust you?"

Meyers laughed, genuine good humor. "Minister, how much can we trust anyone? I would just say that you know what I'm doing here on Aldrin to protect our people. So you can be assured that I'm not in anyone's good graces right now."

"Yes." Rinde returned to his chair, leaning in close to the video screen. "I have to put my faith in you, because I don't know if I can trust anyone here. After days of being denied permission to visit the frigates, Minister Rinova was last seen getting on a shuttle to visit the *Yorktown*. That was a few days ago, but she hasn't been seen since. I've tried communicating with her many times, and my connection requests get denied immediately. My fear is that she was sent up by someone high in our government, with the knowledge of what would happen."

Meyers looked stunned, but yet less surprised than Rinde had expected. "Minister, I'm going to trust you now. We've been seeing transmissions for Earth from where we think the *Waterloo* is. As far as we can tell, those messages are being received, but there hasn't been anything going out in the same direction. I think your government is purposely ignoring them."

"The *Waterloo*? I'd forgotten about her with everything else that is happening!"

"I imagine that was the hope of whoever's keeping them out of the loop."

"Fleet Admiral Holgerson is on that ship, President Meyers. If I can get a message to that ship, perhaps he can help me in my investigations. We have to find a way to stop…"

Rinde went silent as he saw a red bordered alert on another screen. The way Meyers looked away from the camera suggested he was seeing the same thing. Rinde pressed the button to play the feed.

A carefully coifed newscaster was staring solemnly at the camera as he spoke. "..received a communication ten minutes ago from a group calling themselves the Insigne. They claim to be behind all the bombings on Earth and Luna over the last six months. New York, Geneva, Monaco, both domes on Luna. And now they claim to be behind the destruction of our frigates in orbit.

"Again, this information has not been verified, but it is our duty to report that this channel has received a communication ten minutes.."

"You saw it?" Meyers asked, his eyes back on the camera as Rinde turned to him.

"Yes, but I don't understand why anyone would step forward now after not claiming responsibility for so long."

"The most important question is who this Insigne could be. They have access to information and places that run of the mill terrorists shouldn't. Minister, they managed to get onto and off Luna without leaving any trace. I've been through the logs of both docking facilities, and there's no way they could have gotten off Luna after the bombings unless it was on a government ship."

Rinde frowned. "Didn't your own freighters help remove people from Luna who wished to escape the danger? The bombers could have been among them."

"No," Meyers said, shaking his head. "The people we transported all had long records in Aldrin. Those were not the kind of people who'd just been on Earth committing terrorist acts."

"We're back at the old theory of Syndicate-sponsored terrorism, then. They'd have the resources to do what you're talking about."

"Maybe, but I'm not so sure. I'm viewing this from outside both governments, and to me it makes more sense that the Coalition is behind the bombings."

"What?" Rinde shot out of his chair again. "Why would we bomb ourselves?"

Meyers leaned back from the screen, rubbing a hand across his face. "Let me lay it out. It's an idea that really didn't make sense until I started seeing those ads your prime minister began releasing a few weeks ago.

"The first bombing came at a time when everyone's attention was on the *Indomitable*. People everywhere were growing more afraid of the Syndicate cruiser and what it could do when it reached Earth. After New York, that was forgotten for a while as people focused on the closer danger.

"The second bombing four days later, in the government capital where security has always been tightest. The deputy prime minister and several members of the cabinet killed in the blast, while the prime minister himself is conveniently unable to attend the meetings at the last minute." Meyers raised an eyebrow. "Correct me if I'm wrong, but wasn't the deputy prime minister vocally opposed to his boss's handling of the conflict up to that point?

"Next, Monaco. A neutral territory, so the Coalition and Syndicate both lost citizens in the explosions. The prime minister's wife is staying very close to the location of the bombing, but just happens to be far across town at a club when it happens. The growing discontent about the slowness of the Coalition to react to the oncoming threat disappears overnight, and the prime minister receives a large

160

swell of sympathetic support as people assume his wife was one of the main targets."

Rinde had closed his eyes, the words making far too much sense when laid out in this manner. He picked up the next thought. "Then the explosions in your Aldrin dome, first the docking pads and then the Marine outpost in the tunnel that connected you to Armstrong. The first destroys some of the freighters being armed to assist the Coalition fleet, and the second leaves the people virtually unprotected and creates panic with the dome."

"A team sent to Armstrong has confirmed that there was a massive explosion there, as well." Meyers shrugged. "We can't tell when it happened, but we're fairly certain it was at the same time as the second bomb in Aldrin since we didn't feel any other tremors. I have several militia squads prepping for a mission to check Armstrong for any survivors, but none were found during the first trip."

"My God," Rinde said quietly. "When you lay it out like that, it looks like the prime minister orchestrated all of it for his own purposes. Coupled with the fact that he's been so slow to react to the invasion of the Syndicate ground forces, one has to think that he's working with them in some way."

"That's my feeling, as well. Especially when you add in the detonations on the frigates. There's no way for a terrorist group to get bombs onto Navy ships operating on high alert." Meyers leaned in again, lowering his voice. "Unless you load up a shuttle with explosives, and then invite the Naval Minister to use it for a visit that she's been wanting to make for days."

Rinde's jaw dropped. It made perfect sense. The shuttle would have bypassed most of the security scans because it carried such an important person to the *Yorktown*.

The bomber could have been placed aboard as some functionary, and then used that same shuttle to visit the other frigates and plant explosives there.

"The prime minister was the one to tell Juliette she should use the shuttle for a trip into orbit," he said hoarsely. "This could be the proof I need to convince others that something illegal is going on here."

Meyers was nodding. "We need to get a message out to the *Waterloo*. If we can bring the Fleet Admiral in on this, it will…"

The display went dark, and Rinde stared at it in frustration. He tapped on his keypad, but that too was inactive. "Uju!" he shouted. "What happened to my system?" The door opened to admit his aide, her face looking guilty. Her brown eyes refused to meet his as she stepped into the room and held the door for two black suited men carrying stun pistols.

"Rinde Brighton, by order of the prime minister you are under arrest for sedition and treason." As one man spoke, the other roughly pulled him away from the desk and placed restraints over his wrists.

"You can't do this! I'm the Minister of Defense!"

"You're traitorous scum," the man behind him said, shoving him forward.

Uju kept her eyes on the floor as he passed by. "They forced me to do it," she said quietly, and he felt his stomach drop. He knew he'd just found the reason that the prime minister always seemed to know what he was planning.

162

Erik opened his eyes, and for a few moments struggled to remember where he was. The soft sheets covering him were not the thickly padded zippered bed he was accustomed to. As the room came into focus, he saw a lovingly decorated bedroom with a female touch. Smiling, he turned to see dark curls poking out from the sheets next to him. He rolled onto his side, wrapping an arm around the sleeping form. Dex mumbled in her sleep, and he felt her wriggle tighter against him as one of her hands wrapped over his arm.

He lay quietly, breathing in the smell of her and taking as much enjoyment as he could in the blissful moment. There was a lot of work and worry waiting for them, but it could wait a while longer as he luxuriated in the feeling of being so close to the woman he was coming to love.

Too soon, Dex stirred and stretched her body out against him. "Good morning, beautiful," he whispered, kissing her ear through the curls.

"Mmm," she moaned. "Keep doing that, and I'll bring you home more often."

She giggled as he pulled the hair aside and kissed the soft skin at the back of her neck. His hand was sliding over her stomach, travelling toward soft pleasure centers as she twisted her body to give him easier access. Her moans sounded like purrs of contentment as his lips traced her jawline.

A harsh tone sounded nearby, and Dex groaned. "Not now," she muttered, pulling Erik against her and bringing his mouth to hers for a passionate kiss as his hand continued to explore her body.

The tone sounded again, louder and more insistent.

"Gah!" she yelled, turning away to roll toward the small table beside the bed where her tablet was charging. Erik kept kissing her shoulder and back as she tapped the screen to look at the message creating the alert tone.

"It couldn't have waited just a few more minutes?" she asked in frustration.

"We can make it wait," Erik said, smiling as he continued to explore her body with his hands and mouth.

"You have no idea how much I would love to do that, sweetie." Dex pushed him away with a reluctant groan. "Meyers wants us at the Guildhall. ASAP."

She rolled out of bed and Erik admired the view as she walked toward the small bathroom to freshen up. Once she was out of sight, he checked his own tablet and found only normal messages waiting from overnight. The most important one was a status update from Fynn. The *Vagabond* had dropped him off on Aldrin and then launched again to complete the reactor testing without her captain on board.

"Us?" he called out. "I don't have a message about going to the hall."

Dex laughed, and her head poked around the doorway. "Do you think everyone doesn't know where you are right now? Meyers knew he only had to send the message to one of us."

"Oh," he said, feeling a blush spread across his face. Their relationship was far from secret, but he hadn't taken the time to wonder how obvious it would be to the people around them.

"Now, come join me in the shower and let's wash off all the sweat from last night."

"Yes, ma'am," he said with a grin, jumping out of the bed.

"No funny stuff," she admonished laughingly. A protest that didn't hold up for very long once they were in the tight space together.

Walking into the Guildhall twenty minutes later, they found the people at the desks more active than usual. Dex led the way into the president's office, where they found Meyers ensconced behind his desk. His suit was rumpled and looked as if he'd slept in it. A glance at a pillow and thin blanket on the office's couch confirmed the impression.

"I'm glad you're both here," he said as Erik closed the door. "A lot happened overnight, and only half of it was good."

Dex started for her desk on the opposite side of the room, but Meyers waved her over to sit with Erik near his desk. "The *Waterloo* finally responded to our message." Dex gasped, and Erik knew she was thinking about her sister on the frigate. "Fleet Admiral Holgerson confirmed that they've been getting no response at all from the Coalition government or the Admiralty. I told him that we think Minister Rinova was on the ships when they were obliterated, which I think came as a serious blow.

"Holgerson said the ship was boarded by Syndicate soldiers before the first battle, nine of them wearing strange black armor. The bridge was taken, but one of the officers on the command deck had the presence of mind to send the ship toward the outer system." Meyers sighed and turned to look at his second in command. "Dex, it was your sister. Natalia was the one who sent them away from the battle before the Syndicate troops could fire on the other Coalition frigates in a surprise attack. But she was killed for it."

Erik could see the growing joy fall away as Dex went white with the shock. Tears formed and began to slide down her cheeks, and he reached over to grab her hand. She clenched tightly. "She died a hero. I'll make sure our parents know that."

"Yes, she did." Meyers grimaced. "She wasn't the only one. Everyone on the bridge was killed as the Syndicate soldiers tried to force the captain and admiral to give up their command codes. Captain Andrews said he was close to giving in, but it was Ensign Avila who told him to resist."

"Ensign?" Dex whispered, sniffling and rubbing moisture from her eyes.

"She was promoted shortly after the battle over Earth," Meyers said with a wan smile. "Battlefield promotion kind of thing, but the admiral guarantees that he'll make sure it's retroactively approved and made official."

Erik felt her squeeze his hand as she smiled faintly. "Mom would have been so proud of her."

He had picked up on a different part of the information. "They killed *everyone* on the bridge? What kind of monsters do something like that?"

Meyers sighed. "It wasn't just on the bridge. A second group of soldiers invaded the Engineering department. The chief engineer was killed, and others were held hostage until the ship's Marines arrived. There was a bomb that damaged the engines, and it took them a week before they could get them back online to reverse course."

Erik tried to do all the math in his head. "They should be about a week away, then. Less if they're burning hard."

166

"That bomb did too much damage. It sounds like the explosion was meant to destroy the frigate, but bad placement prevented that much, at least. Holgerson said they're running at thirty percent of their normal power. It'll be a few weeks before they get here."

"We could have used their help. Our fleet isn't enough to go up against that cruiser without assistance. It'll be months before the new Coalition frigates are completed in their shipyard."

"That brings us around to my other news." Meyers leaned back and started tapping on his keypad. "I was speaking with the Defense Minister last night, and I think we both agree on who's behind the bombings and slow response to Syndicate aggressions." With a final command, the wall display showed the conversation between the two men the night before. Erik and Dex watched in silence, gasping in shock at the end when the screen went dark. Erik hadn't followed the same train of thought about the bombings, but it made sense to him when everything was laid out.

"The prime minister? Why would he sabotage his own government?"

"Because he's being paid," Dex said. "It's the only thing that makes sense now, if he really did help destroy the ships that could have turned the war in the Coalition's favor. The Executive Committee must have offered him great wealth to sabotage the war efforts." Her face grew grim. "That bastard is the reason my sister is dead."

"We can't prove it," Meyers cautioned. "I haven't been able to get in contact with Minister Brighton since our conversation was cut off. His aide tells me that he was called into an emergency meeting, but there's something off about the way she's acting."

"This is bad," Erik said. "If their own prime minister is working against them, the Coalition doesn't stand a chance. The Syndicate is going to take control of Earth, and then the *Indomitable* will come for the rest of us."

"We can't wait for that to happen." Meyers rose and walked around the desk to lean against an edge of it. "You remember that second reactor? It's complete and waiting to be deployed. I'd like you to get it to the *Waterloo*, Captain Frost. Get that ship back to Earth as fast as possible so we can fight back against the cruiser."

Erik looked over at Dex. Her eyes were red and tears still rolled down her cheeks, but she nodded. "Do it for Nat, Erik. She would've insisted it was the right thing to do." She smiled as she thought about her sister, fighting to do the right thing.

"Okay, I'll call the *Vagabond* back from testing. We'll push the ship as hard as she can go."

"Your freighter is already docked," Meyers said. "I asked them to return a few hours ago, after Dr. Francks reported the tests had completed. The new reactor is being loaded into your cargo bay as we speak."

Erik tried to be upset about his ship being ordered around by someone other than him, but he knew it had been done for the right reasons. He shook hands with President Meyers before leaving the office, and then walked toward the docking facility with Dex tight against him.

"I wish I could have met her," he said quietly.

"Nat would have loved you, Erik," Dex told him with a faint smile. "Almost as much as I do."

He stopped walking for a few seconds at the words, before continuing. "I love you, too, Dex. More and more every day. When I'm back, we're going to spend as much time as you need talking about Natalia. I want to know everything about her."

She pulled him down for a kiss, and had a genuine smile on her lips after she released him. "If this crap ever ends, I'm going to take you down to meet my parents. They can tell you stories about Nat and me when we were kids."

"Meeting the parents, huh? That's more stressful than facing a Syndicate cruiser with only the *Vagabond.*"

She poked him in the side as he laughed. "Be nice, or my dad will definitely be more of a threat than any ship." She poked her tongue out at him as he laughed.

They held each other for several minutes before Erik forced himself to pull away. "Stay safe," she told him, waving as he entered the airlock. He returned the wave before turning to walk through the rigid tube toward his home.

TWENTY FIVE

Admiral Yumata stared down at the surface of the table, wondering why someone would have thought cutting down the last redwood on the planet just to turn it into furniture was a good idea. Everything on his ships had always been metal or plastic, resources that were found in abundant quantities in the asteroid mines. On Earth, the committees seemed to believe that owning something made from an extinct species made them all the more special.

General Chang sat before the committee's U-shaped table, presenting a report on the status of the invasion after five days. "We've now taken more than three million square kilometers of land away from the Coalition. There are eight full divisions in the field."

The general rose and approached a holographic map showing Europe and Asia. A handheld pointer allowed him to create a glowing dot that he used to circle areas as he spoke. "I have four divisions devoted to pushing forward for five hours each day, while the other half of our forces follow behind securing what we've taken. They scour the towns and cities for any weaponry, and ensure that soldiers are not lurking to attempt an attack from our rear."

The chairwoman spoke up. "General, following this careful strategy, how long would you expect a full invasion of Europe and then Coalition-held Africa to take?"

Chang paused, considering his response. "Six to nine months, I would expect. If we continue to face no opposition, that is. Should the Coalition security forces begin to fight our advance, it would slow us significantly."

"I don't think we have to worry about that," Abernathy said with a snicker. Yumata turned to look at the man on the opposite end of the table. He saw a flash of consternation on the chairwoman's face, and knew the rash young man had spoken out of turn. They knew something about why the Coalition wasn't responding to the Syndicate advance, and Selene didn't want it aired.

"General," she said quickly. "If we asked you to push the advance to a faster pace, how much would you be comfortable with."

"I believe we could move another division to the front lines, madame chairwoman, and extend the amount of time each day that we spend advancing. That should give us a fifteen to twenty percent quicker pace."

"Would that not overextend our reach in the event of an attack?" Yumata asked. He kept his eyes on the general, feeling the chairwoman's disapproving gaze turn in his direction at speaking up out of turn.

"To a minor extent, admiral. We would continue to clear the area behind the lines, and I feel confident that there would be minimal risk of an attack from within the conquered territory. As for an attack on our front lines, we would know well in advance with another squadron of Darts scouting the terrain ahead."

"A second squadron of the fighters will be placed at your disposal," the chairwoman said, motioning to an aide sitting behind her to send the order.

"Thank you, madame chairwoman. That will give us a greater measure of security." Chang paused, licking his lips. Yumata could see that the man wasn't sure how prudent it was to ask the next question. "Would it be possible to have the *Indomitable* join the attack? If they

171

could make targeted strikes of Coalition military facilities, it would hamper their ability to fight back."

"I'm sorry, general. The *Indomitable* is needed where she is, to guard against the armed Transport Guild freighters that are clustered around Luna. Should the Guild decide to join their allies again, we must be certain that Hong Kong is defended."

Yumata almost spoke up, but saw Selene shoot a quick glance in his direction. He knew the Guild freighters were a small threat without the frigates that had made the Coalition fleet so dangerous. The reason for the explosions that destroyed the three over Earth was something he still hadn't figured out. His voiced concerns had been met with ambivalence from the other members of the committee, another instance when he felt they shared knowledge that he was not privy to.

"Yes, madame chairwoman," General Chang responded. "In that case, could a few assault shuttles be transferred to my forces? With those, I could drop squads into defended areas as we get closer to the more heavily populated areas."

"That's an excellent idea, general. I'll have four of them sent down from the cruiser." There were several seconds of silence as Selene looked to a few other members of the committee, wordlessly asking if they had questions for Chang. Yumata was amused to note that he and Abernathy were both excluded from the looks.

"Thank you for your report today, General Chang. The Military Committee commends you for excellent service to the Syndicate, and we won't keep you any longer."

Chang rose, bowing deeply to each member of the committee before turning and marching from the room. The day's attendant hurried forward to hold the door for him, and then stepped out of the chamber herself.

The chairwoman brought the meeting to a close, announcing that the next committee meeting would occur in three days' time. "Enjoy some time away from the capital. I'm sure we all have families who haven't seen us as much as they'd like." Selene remained at the table as the others stood and filed into their private hallway. As Yumata passed, she raised a hand to hold him back. "Admiral, I appreciate that you feel more cautious about the current military strategy than the rest of us, but I'd like you to restrain your comments during sessions."

"Yes, madame chairwoman." His voice was tight, as he wondered for the thousandth time why he had been asked to join the committee if they didn't want his input on anything.

She seemed to read his mind, rising from the table with a sigh. "Would you like a drink, Hiro? I have a new bottle of Agiorgitiko that was bottled two years ago during the best grape harvest in several decades."

He had no desire to drink alcohol, but accepted the invitation. Selene led the way into her plush office, waving him to a chair as she walked to the same drinks cabinet she'd used on his last visit. The wine was almost black in the green-hued bottle, and still very dark when poured into a glass. She filled two fluted glasses halfway, and then brought one over to him. Yumata accepted the wine, and sipped to be polite. There was a fruity flavor hiding behind the alcohol taste that he'd never developed a liking for. He set the glass on the small table beside his chair, never touching it again.

"What is it that the other members of the committee know, Selene?"

She laughed, a low throaty sound. "Damn Abernathy and his big mouth. Or did you have an inclination even before that? I told them you were too smart to be left in the dark for long."

He turned his placid gaze on her, waiting for an answer.

"Okay, you dragged it out of me." She took a deep drink from her glass, then swirled the remaining wine around as she contemplated the view through her large windows. "Several years ago, we managed to insert a few intelligence operatives into the Coalition government. They were low level drones, but efficient. Before long, they were receiving promotions and climbing the ranks of the civil service.

"Fourteen months ago, one of them managed to get a posting on the prime minister's staff. She watched him, searching for any weakness we could use to destabilize the Coalition government. Then, she overheard conversations and intercepted internal communications that suggested the man was tired of the cold war. He saw it much the same way we do, as something holding humanity back from progression." She laughed, draining her glass and reaching to take his. "You don't mind, do you?"

Fingering the delicate stem of the glass, she continued. "Once our agent was sure of her feelings about the prime minister, she approached him. She initially didn't let on that she was a Syndicate agent, but told him that she had friends who shared his beliefs. Give the man credit, he tried to push her away. But when she mentioned that we were on the verge of deploying overwhelming force against them, he let her speak.

"The agent took a larger gamble than she should have, and told him everything. The *Indomitable*, a planned invasion, even that we had a dozen infiltrators deep in their

174

government ranks. Had the man not already been half convinced the Coalition couldn't win if war were pressed upon them, it might have been disastrous for us. Instead, he was persuaded to work with us."

Yumata was astonished. "If you had the prime minister under your sway, why not push the attack then?"

"Admiral, the leader may be a defeatist but his people were still convinced they could win. We had to start working on them, turn that opinion in the other direction. To that end, another of our agents stepped forward. He goes by the name Theodore Poul, and is now their Propaganda Minister." Selene shook her head. "Can you believe such an absurd thing?

"Poul has been undermining the confidence of the Coalition citizens for months, though it only became overt within the last several weeks. Those silly little ads we've all seen were surprisingly effective, based on the reactions of the people in towns General Chang's soldiers have marched through."

"So, he held the frigates back from rushing to meet my ship when we were still poorly armed and immensely understaffed?"

"That he did. Helped, of course, by the fact that the person exposing your existence was nothing more than a freighter captain."

Yumata grunted. "Guildersen pushed me to make a move for months. I assume that was the Military Committee influence, trying to work through him?"

Selene smiled faintly, but shook her head. "Executive Committee. They've been wanting to move against the Coalition from the moment we learned one of our infiltrators had the prime minister's ear. The chairman of the

Intelligence Committee and I had to work hard to keep them from exposing our hand too soon."

"The bombings on Earth, Luna, and the frigates? Was that our agent's influence?"

"No!" Selene sniggered. "That was purely the prime minister's idea. We promised him a large stake in several companies once the Coalition was no more, and he's afraid that if the war carried on too long we'd just leave him out in the cold and deal with his predecessor instead. So he wanted a way to take out his strongest competition, silence vocal critics, and spur the people to re-elect him against the rules of their constitution."

"It was poorly done," Yumata said with distaste. "Killing his own people, and then destroying his frigates in such a way that anyone with half a brain would know it had to be an inside job."

"Oh, I agree. The man is a repugnant ass. Just between us, I don't expect that he'll last long once he is part of the Syndicate. He'll certainly never be given a position on a committee, though he's tried to force such a promise from us several times."

"Why then do we not have the *Indomitable* initiate targeted strikes? There's no real opposition left, and the cruiser could bring a speedy end to this fool's war."

"Hmm," Selene sighed and rose to return the two empty glasses to the drinks cabinet. "Hiro, I really shouldn't be telling you any of this. I blame the wine. But since I've started, I'll spill it all. Captain Guildersen has proven to be quite an ineffective military commander."

Yumata chuckled. "I could have told you that."

"We thought your leadership would have the ship functioning so smoothly that anyone could step in and keep it rolling along. That moron has managed to alienate every

176

senior officer and section chief on the cruiser. There are a dozen railguns sitting in the cargo bays still crated up because the crews keep finding reasons to ignore his orders to install them."

"Ah," he said, feeling a mixture of pride in his people and disappointment that the cruiser was being so poorly managed. "That is information we wouldn't want the Guild to find out."

"Exactly. So we send out maintenance crews every day to look like they're installing guns to give the impression the ship is almost fully armed."

"We should send up a replacement commander," Yumata said, wanting to say that *he* should be sent up to reclaim command.

"I've said the same thing to the Executive Committee, but Guildersen is their new golden boy and they can't see that his poor leadership is the issue. They're planning to send new officers instead, fresh graduates from the Academy in a few weeks. Guildersen has managed to convince them that replacing the senior staff will solve all his problems."

"Foolish," Yumata said with a sad shake of his head. "Young officers will do as they are told, only because they don't have the experience to know better. That will prove more disastrous in the long run."

"I tried to talk the orbital station into sending some people over to install at least a few of the railguns, but apparently Guildersen has been spewing orders at them since the moment he took command. The station commander said he'd rather resign in disgrace than help 'that ignorant baboon' with anything."

Yumata smiled. "If I'm not permitted to return to the *Indomitable*, perhaps I could make a trip to the orbital station and talk with the commander? Possibly I could find a way to convince him to assist."

Selene pursed her lips. "That's not a bad idea. Let me float it to the Executive Committee, and we'll see what they say."

"Remind them that I'm merely an ornament here, and my absence will not be missed."

She surprised him by laying a cool hand over his. "Hiro, you're desired here more than you know."

He heard the invitation in her words, and was tempted to follow through. But he hardened his resolve and pushed back the longing. Now wasn't the time to be getting involved in dalliances. With luck, he would be on a shuttle within a few days and one step closer to a goal that he had decided upon during the conversation with Selene.

TWENTY SIX

During the first weeks of his detainment, Altan was kept in isolation. His only contact with the outer world were the food trays pushed through the flap at the bottom of his cell door. He begged for news of the *Vagabond* crew or his friends for a few days, but received only silence from those outside the door. When the cell door creaked open one day, he was surprised and embarrassed to find that one of his old coworkers had come to visit. It also filled him with joy to see another human face, even if she seemed uncomfortable to be there. Two Marines stood just outside the open door with stun pistols drawn.

"Josie," he sighed in a voice croaking from disuse. "I've missed seeing you in the locker rooms between shifts."

Her eyes were on the ground, but he saw her face contort at his words. "Alt, I don't even know why I'm here. They say you were working with those Guild people to expose the existence of the *Indomitable*. How could you do that?"

Altan stepped forward, reaching out to take her hand. Both guards stiffened and raised their weapons, causing him to stop and hold his hands wide at his side. "Josie, my friends and I never really belonged here. That freighter crew certainly didn't deserve to be imprisoned and probably killed."

"But you put all of us in danger," she snapped, her eyes darting up to meet his before looking away again. He thought he saw understanding in those eyes instead of anger that matched her words.

"Maybe so," he said, confused at the conflicting signals the woman was giving off.

"We were friends, Alt, so I had to see you. I won't be back." She pulled a scratched old tablet from a pocket of her worn jumpsuit, dropping it on his bed. "You were good people for years, so our boss was able to convince the guards to let you have this. You can't access any ship's systems, but there are some old books loaded on it that I've always enjoyed."

Her eyes met his again, and this time he was sure he saw sympathy there. He wondered what she might have said if the guards hadn't been standing over her shoulder. "Thank you, Josie," he said as she turned to leave. She paused long enough to nod and then walked out the door between the Marines.

As the heavy cell door slammed shut again, Altan picked up the tablet and turned it over in his hands. It looked like an old junker that had been dropped and kicked a few times too many, but the screen was instantly responsive at his touch. The usual menu items appeared, but nearly all of them were faded and gray. Touching one brought up a message telling him "no network available". At the very end of the menu list, he found an icon of Josie's smiling face. He laughed as he touched it, feeling a rush of old memories from their times spent talking and joking between shifts or during late nights at the cruiser's entertainment spots.

Ten books came up on the screen, their covers presenting portals to the words themselves. The first was *The Count of Monte Cristo*, an old story that seemed particularly relevant given his situation. Once he finished that he read *Heart of Darkness*, then *Great Expectations*. All of them books he'd often heard of but never taken time to read.

An overlooked benefit of the tablet was that he also had an accurate clock and calendar. Knowing the day on which he was pulled from the skin of the ship and trapped in the room, he could accurately count the days of his imprisonment. By the ninetieth day, he felt as if he would spend the rest of his life in the small room.

With a desire for normalcy, he created his own routine to occupy his time. When he woke, he would jog in place for ten minutes and then do fifty pushups and fifty crunches. The activity got his adrenaline flowing and made him feel more awake through the day. After the exercise, he would read for a few hours, often pacing back and forth in the cramped room while doing so.

In the afternoons, Altan would close his eyes and relive his old life aboard the *Telemachus*. He would remember problems that he had dealt with, and run through the steps to resolve them over and over. He'd also think of good times spent with his friends on the crew, the days and nights they'd spent together in the long trips through the empty spaces of the inner system. It kept the faces of his old friends fresh in his mind, and reminded him of all that he had to live for.

At night, he would repeat the exercises. The exertion left his body feeling a need for rest, so that he could fall asleep in the constant half-light of the room. His dreams were often about his sister, childhood memories replayed in his mental cinema.

Altan had no access to the ship's network, but he could feel the ship's movements and several times had been forced into the zippered bunk that gave minimal protection in high G burns. His cell was at the front of the hallway closest to the main corridor, where one guard was posted at all times. During shift changes, the Marines would often talk for several minutes and trade gossip of what was happening on and around the ship. Pressing his ear against the metal door allowed him to hear most of the words spoken, though some were muffled or said too quietly to make out. Through them, he'd learned of the attack on the colony of Interamnia and the quick skirmishes with the Coalition frigates.

Hearing that they were now orbiting Earth was his biggest surprise. In his mind, Altan had always thought the ship would never be allowed to reach the home world if they could only warn the system of its existence. It felt like a crushing defeat to know that hadn't been the case.

He'd hoped for information about his sister, but had heard nothing. The *Vagabond* itself was only mentioned once, and from what he picked up in the conversation the freighter had managed to be part of an attack that heavily damaged the cruiser. That had been one of the rare days when he smiled.

On the morning of the day that changed everything, he was lying on his bunk reading *The Count of Monte* Cristo for the third time. He was puzzling over a section in the middle of the book, paragraphs that looked to have been corrupted since the last time he read it. Lines of code were inserted that made no sense to him, along with random words that seemed to spell out a message. *Alt.. a.. gift.. for.. an.. old.. friend.*

When the locks clicked and the door began to swing open, he smiled and swung his body around to sit up on the bed. Instead of seeing a guard with a tray of food, though, he saw two armed Marines facing the security desk at the opposite end of the hall. Altan rose and took a step forward, causing the nearest Marine to swivel. He held up his hands, and the soldier waved the weapon to tell him to stay put. There was shouting from down the hall, a shrill male voice.

"Where is the Other?!"

His brows furrowed as he frowned. The voice sounded vaguely familiar, but he couldn't figure out what the person was talking about. Other what? And why was his cell door open?

After the Marines passed by, he took a few cautious steps forward. He could see the cell across the hall, the door slightly offset from his own and wide open. Was there some kind of malfunction, allowing another prisoner to escape? The man sounded crazy as all hell from the way he was yelling. The Marines were yelling back, telling someone to step back and get on the floor. Their voices were intermingled, hard to understand with competing orders. It sounded like the hallway was utter chaos.

Then, there was another voice. "You!" It was a female voice, and it made him go still. "What did you do with my brother, Richard?"

Altan felt the air escape him. The inflections in the voice were so familiar. Hearing it felt like being back in his parent's house, listening to his mother talk about this or that while he and his sister played at her feet. It was Tuya! His sister, only steps away. Why was she still on the *Indomitable*? She should have been on the *Vagabond* when it escaped. He started to rush out to see her, but another Marine appeared from the main corridor. The woman turned her weapon toward him, and he had to force himself to keep from pushing past. He could hear scuffling from further down the hall, and knew that whatever fool started this was being restrained.

"Tuya," he croaked, trying to yell her name. It had been weeks since he spoke more than a few words, and his voice was rough. "Tuya!" he called again, louder this time but not enough to be heard over the noise of the Marines and their recaptured prisoner.

"Where is he?" the man screamed, his insane cries coming closer as the Marines propelled him away from the cells. "I know the Other is here. It can't be me. It can't!"

Altan got another shock as he saw the wild-eyed prisoner pushed struggling past his door. It was Richard, from his old crew. Had the man also been captured during the escape attempt? But no, Tuya had shouted something about being a traitor. That must mean he had turned against the freighter crews in their escape attempt. Perhaps that was why Tuya was there, as well.

"Tuya," he shouted again, louder.

The Marine outside his door took another step. "Mouth shut, prisoner."

"Altan?" a quiet voice called from the corridor. "Altan, is that you?"

"It's me! I'm here!"

A moment later he felt a stun bolt slam into his chest, and the electricity sent his muscles into spasms. He could hear Tuya call out and then groan. *Only a few doors away all this time*, was his last thought as everything went dark.

When he regained consciousness, Altan was still laying on the floor. The stun bolt had been removed, but he could still feel a trickle of dried blood on his skin. He groaned as he forced sore muscles to work, rolling over and pushing to his feet. His body was feeling abused, but his emotions were higher than they'd been in months. His sister was still on the *Indomitable*, and she was no more than a dozen steps down the corridor. He knew he should be

184

disappointed she wasn't safe somewhere far from the Syndicate cruiser, but didn't have time for that with the joy of how close he was to a sister he hadn't seen in more than a decade.

Altan sat heavily on his thin zippered mattress, then rose to pull the tablet out from under him. He racked his brain, trying to figure out a way to get in contact with her. Maybe he could find an amenable guard to pass a quick message, or ask to be moved to a cell next to hers. The small air vents set low on the wall looked to give a possible conduit for conversation.

He felt his eyes drawn to the scratched old tablet held in his hand. If the device still had the ability to connect to the ship's network, he could have used it to try and forge a transfer order. The thought made him wonder. How had the network connection been severed? Was the required hardware still in the tablet but disabled, or had it been pulled out entirely?

Searching the cell, he found a small sliver of plastic that had been pushed under his bed during one of the rare cleaning sweeps through the prison block. It was barely a quarter inch in length, but thin enough to work between the two halves of the tablet casing. His fingers were swollen and bleeding by the time he was able to pop of the back of the tablet, but the two hours of sweating and straining had been worthwhile. Laid out before him was all the miniscule wiring and circuit boards that kept the tablet working.

Checking each wire and circuit for loose connections put a strain on his eyes. It was an especially onerous task in the half-light of the cell. He had to keep twisting the tablet back and forth to get enough light on the portion he was examining.

Halfway through, he fell asleep. He woke with one arm numb underneath him and the other dangling over the edge of the bunk. The tablet had been in that hand, and dropped to the floor at some point during the night. Altan cursed himself as he scrambled to grab it up, sure that he had broken something without the protective case attached.

Amazingly, everything looked exactly as he remembered it from before falling asleep. His quick glance over the complicated workings made him notice a wire that he had overlooked. It appeared attached, but when the light flashed just right he could see that one edge of the silver connector was exposed. He pushed against it as hard as he dared, his thick finger barely able to push on the tiny wire attachment. When the small click finally sounded, he breathed a sigh of relief.

Several more hours were spent in agonizing examination of the tablet's inner workings. He found a few more connections that could be loose, but nothing more. He thought he recognized one miniature square as the chip that controlled the network connections, but that was based on knowledge that was ten years or more out of date. He grinned, thinking of the fidgety and nervous tech from the *Vagabond*'s crew. Isaac could have found the problem within minutes, and then used the tablet to tunnel into the cruiser's systems. An idea blossomed as he thought about it, remembering the lines of code he'd seen in the book just before all the commotion.

Once the back cover was snapped back into place, Altan powered the tablet up again. He held his breath for the few seconds it took to bring up the main screen, and then breathed out heavily when he saw several of the menu icons were now vivid and sharp. He tapped on one, and laughed joyfully as the settings menu appeared.

The network connection was still disabled, but he could now see the dozens of little sliding buttons that would let him enable the various protocols and communication algorithms. It might take a day or two of trial and error, but he felt confident he could find the correct combination.

Touching the first slider, his grin dropped away when a new box popped up. "Please enter administrator password" appeared, along with a line where he could type it in. Altan groaned, but knew he was one step closer. "Okay," he whispered to himself. "I can do this. It might just take a little longer than expected."

TWENTY SEVEN

"Captain Fitz, the airlock is open and squad four is inside the facility."

"Excellent," Tom said over the radio. He'd wanted to lead the first group into Armstrong himself, but had been talked out of it by the squad leaders. "I'm bringing squad one in now."

Milner was nearby, quickly running the airlock through a decompression cycle. He and Hotchkiss had been brought along for this mission even though they didn't belong to the squads participating, since they had the only other experience with what waited inside the dark Armstrong dome. Three squads were entering, and they would each be attached to one of the other squads.

Once the airlock opened, Tom waved his team in. Before stepping over the threshold himself, he raised a hand to Milner, who would be entering last with squad three. Squad two of the new Guild militia had remained behind in Aldrin, performing security duties there.

It took twenty seconds for the airlock to pressurize, an eternity when you weren't sure what you were going to find on the other side. The walls of the airlock were shielded in case of any contaminants, and the suit radios were almost cut off until one of the doors was open. Tom stepped to the front of the group, the ten soldiers unconsciously forming two lines to either side of him.

He felt himself tensing when the panel beside the inner door turned green. Air hissed as the airlock door opened, and the militia squad tightened into a crouch, those in front raising their weapons to a ready position. Tom knew he was holding his breath, as the opening slowly widened. The area in front of the docking bay was empty, and as he stepped forward he looked to his right and left. Squad four was waiting steps away from the entry into the main dome area, and the rest of the facility was deserted. It still looked just has it had days before on his first scouting trip.

"Squad one is in, area secure," he reported over the comms.

"Copy, captain. Squad three beginning entry procedure."

Tom led his squad forward, taking up position on the other side of the entry from squad four. The sergeant in charge of that team, Fuller, raised his hand in a quick salute. "No movement inside the dome so far, sir."

"Someone has to be left in here. We saw no evidence of bodies on the first scout, and someone fired at the first group to try entering the dome."

"That was weeks ago, captain. Those folks could've left on a shuttle by now, since they still have working docking pads."

Tom shook his head. "The Guild was watching all the traffic in and out of Armstrong after the events in Aldrin. They saw people leaving, but not nearly enough to account for everyone. Zero traffic a few days after that first scout attempt."

"Okay, well consider me spooked," the sergeant said. Fuller motioned to one of his soldiers, and a small hard-shell case was passed over. "Permission to deploy drones?"

Tom looked out into the darkness of Armstrong. The dome was as still and silent as his last visit. It was an eerie feeling to look at a wide area filled with streets and buildings, but see no movement at all around them. He nodded, and motioned for the member of his squad carrying a similar case. "Let's get them in the air."

By the time the whir of the drones' rotor blades was filling the air, squad three had joined them near the entry into the dome. "Should we pull out our drone?" Corporal Zavala asked.

"No, hold it in reserve. If we lose one of the others, yours will come in handy."

The squad leaders huddled around the two open cases, looking at the small displays set into the open lids that were showing the view from each drone's camera. He sent both of them down the broad central street, advancing slowly with frequent turns to get views down side streets and the top of buildings. When they reached the point where the rubble began to fill the screen, Fuller grunted. "That is a very large debris field, sir."

"Just wait," Tom murmured, as the drones continued forward. Once the wide crater came into view, everyone who could see the screens murmured in astonishment. The square in Armstrong had been twice as large as the one in Aldrin, and it was completely obliterated by whatever bomb had exploded there.

Tom sent the cameras higher and had the operators circle the crater. The debris field stretched for hundreds of meters in every direction, with buildings ripped apart or showing large holes from the shockwave.

"Jesus, captain. Can you imagine waking up to whatever caused all of this?" Zavala asked, her voice quiet with awe.

"I'd be happy to wake up at all," Tom replied.

He had the cameras go as high as they could under the dome, and then turn to give a three sixty view of everything below them. Even with all his attention riveted on the screen, he could see no evidence of movement or survivors. "Anyone else see anything promising?" Sergeant Fuller and Corporal Zavala shook their heads.

"Let's spread out and do recon," he said. "Sergeant Fuller, take squad four left while Corporal Zavala takes squad three right. Both of you circle the outer edges of the dome. If I survived whatever happened here, that's where I'd hole up."

"Far from the destruction," Fuller said in agreement, watching as the drone pilots brought the machines back to the docking facility to be reloaded into the cases.

"Milner and Hotchkiss have experience in here, so keep them close. We stayed near the central avenue last time, but they'll recognize any odd sounds or movements."

Once the two squads had filed through the entryway and begun their crouching circuit of Armstrong's outer edges, Tom turned to his own team. Squad one was filled with the first people to join the militia. Unlike the later squads that were created with young recruits, the people here were a scattering of Coalition or Syndicate veterans and men and women with a decade or more experience in other fields. They were also the hardest to command, being full of their own opinions and not afraid to voice them.

"We're heading up the central avenue. I want to check the buildings as we go. A team of four will enter and clear the buildings on either side, while two remain on watch with me in the street." One of the old veterans shifted, and Tom could see the man wanting to speak up. He motioned permission. *Get it out now, instead of trying to do it out there*, he thought.

"Captain, is it worth the risk? Anything could be waiting in those buildings, and if we find a squad of Syndicate Marines they'll tear us apart."

"If a squad of Marines was still in here, they'd have shown themselves by now. Based on the state of the dome, I have a feeling they were the first to be pulled out." He looked at the faces around him, and saw a few that seemed to share the veteran's concerns. "All the same, be careful when clearing the buildings. It only takes one frightened resident with a gun to make this a very bad day."

He picked out the two groups who would enter buildings, making sure each contained at least one military veteran and one person with the skills to get past any electronic locks that might be encountered inside. For this trip, he had issued four flechette rifles, weapons taken from the *Vagabond*'s undelivered container that had started the whole mess. He made sure each entry team carried one of those rifles, while two would stay with those in the street.

Leading the way, Tom strode into the dome and headed for the wide central street. His head felt like it was on a swivel as his eyes darted all around. Something in the silence and stillness just felt wrong to him. He would've been much more comfortable if the air had been filled with the sounds of buildings crumbling or if the empty streets were brightly lit. The cold had crept in even more since his last visit, dropping the temperature by more than twenty degrees. His suit's sensors also showed less oxygen in the air. If there *were* survivors, they had to be locked down in a safe room or living in protective pressure suits.

Progress was slow, often taking fifteen minutes or more to fully explore each building before the squad could move further down the block. Fuller and Zavala checked in over comms at least twice each hour, reporting no contact with survivors. Conversely, no bodies had been found. Tom wasn't sure which was more unnerving to him.

After two hours, the oxygen and nitrogen tanks were running low. The three squads carried spares, so Tom paused long enough for his team to change out their bottles. They were stacking the nearly empty containers in the middle of the street to be collected on the way out when he heard cracking noises.

Everyone around him went still, listening to the sharp cracks in the distance. "What the hell is that?" one woman asked.

"Gunfire," Tom said. "Fuller. Zavala. Report."

"All clear, sir," Fuller said, sounding confused. "Same as five minutes ago."

Seconds ticked by with no response from the other squad leader. "Sergeant, my team heard gunfire. Since you didn't hear anything it must have been Zavala's squad. I don't know if they were firing or being fired on."

"We haven't heard a thing," Fuller reported after a pause long enough to check with those around him.

"Continue mission. I'm taking squad one to Zavala's last reported position, and will check in once we're there."

Tom had his team pull their weapons, keeping them low but ready as they jogged through the deserted streets. Armstrong had seemed so small compared to Aldrin, but now it felt ten times larger as he rushed to reach squad three. By the time they reached the position of the corporal's last report, everyone was breathing hard and glad of the chance to stop for a few seconds. Tom had to remind himself that his team wasn't as fit as the younger squads.

He crouched down and listened. There'd been no further gunfire, but with the blood pounding in his ears and boots slapping the ground, he could have missed it during their rush from the central avenue. Half a minute passed, filled with the usual silence he'd become accustomed to in the dome.

"Zavala?" he said. "Report, corporal." He waited, but squad three's channel was filled with only a low static hum. "Spread out," he told his squad in a near whisper, even though he knew his voice wouldn't be heard outside of his helmet except on the secure comms channel. "We'll walk forward and try to find them."

Spaced out with several feet between each soldier, they moved slowly along the path the missing squad would have followed. The street that followed the outer curve of the dome was narrow, low buildings crowding them on one side with the metal wall of dome on the other. Something about the solidity of that wall was comforting.

"Captain, I have movement."

Tom felt his heart flutter at the words, and held up a hand to call the squad to a halt. "Which direction?"

"Down this alley. Next block over, I saw someone run across the gap." The soldier motioned to show that the movement had been opposite their own.

Tom divided the squad into the three groups they had used to clear buildings, and sent two teams to flanking passages as he led his group of three down the constricted alley through which movement had been seen. They were crouched down as they approached the next street, and Tom peered around the corner of the building he had his back to.

There was no sign of movement in the street running through a row of squat residential buildings. Tom was ready to call it a case of overactive nerves when he noticed a tiny crack of light in a window down the street. He blinked a few times, making sure he wasn't imagining it.

"I see it, too, captain," one of the squad reported when he motioned in the direction of the light. "Looks like someone tried to block the window and missed a spot."

"That means survivors," another said hopefully.

Tom agreed, but was cautious about next steps. If they were trying to hide their light, it meant they were afraid of someone finding them. He flashed back to an old book he'd read when he was a kid, about a group of boys being stranded on an island. Friends in the beginning, they had quickly splintered into competing groups. Could something similar have happened within Armstrong in the weeks since the bombings?

"You four, circle around to the rear of that building. I'll give you five minutes before we approach from the front."

The selected soldiers melted away, quickly crossing the street to disappear down another alley that would take them behind the building. Once the time had elapsed, Tom led the rest of the squad forward. He had four wait in the street, taking only two soldiers with him as he approached the front door. It felt odd knocking on the door, and he had to keep from chuckling at the absurdity of it. After a few minutes, he knocked again. "We can see your light," he called out over the suit's speakers. "We're from Aldrin, checking for survivors of whatever happened her. We just want to help." There was still no response from within.

One of the soldiers behind him voiced a warning. "Captain, movement down the street."

Tom turned and felt a tremor of shock at seeing three people in black pressure suits walking toward them. The figures were taking slow steps, hands held away from their bodies. He watched them, waving for his soldiers to keep their weapons lowered.

He stepped away from the door, taking several steps into the street in the direction of the newcomers. "We're with the Transport Guild. I'm Captain Tom Fitz. Please identify yourselves."

The figures stopped, with one taking a step forward. Tom couldn't see through the darkened glass of the suit helmet, but the voice that issued from the speakers was female. "I am Dr. Nelda Baat. Did you say you're with the *Guild?*"

"Yes, doctor. Aldrin suffered bombings, as well, but we weren't hit as badly as it appears Armstrong was."

"My God," the woman said, taking another step. "After what we've been through, I guess we all assumed Aldrin was suffering in the same manner. I'm glad to hear that hasn't been the case."

"Dr. Baat, we heard gunfire from this direction earlier. I had another squad searching near here, and I'm trying to find them. Have you seen them?"

The woman raised a hand to her chest. "Captain, I'm afraid your friends may be in trouble." She strode forward briskly, waving for him to follow as she and the two others with her passed by and approached the door he'd been knocking on. She pulled the glove from her left hand, placed it over a hidden panel, and then quickly covered her hand again.

As the door opened, Tom followed behind the doctor and her two companions. He took two soldiers with him, directing the others to continue searching the nearby area for any sign of squad four. Inside the house was a dark hallway. The survivors' dark suits blended in, while his squad's gray material gave them a ghostly appearance before the door closed cutting off all light.

A moment later, the hall was brightly lit by small lights inset along the ceiling. Dr. Baat reached up to remove her helmet, exposing a youthful face under a short fringe of black hair.

"The air in here is safe, and the building is heated," she said as the two others with her removed their own helmets.

Tom checked the sensor readouts from his suit, and saw she was telling the truth. It wasn't exactly warm, but much warmer than outside in the dome. He cautiously unsealed his helmet and lifted it a few centimeters. Once he breathed in air that was stale but safe, he removed it the rest of the way. "How did you manage to create an airtight space and pump in good air?"

"My friends are engineers who worked on the maintenance and upkeep of the dome. They salvaged parts from an old airlock when the dome systems couldn't be repaired."

He was amazed at the work and wanted to know more, but it would have to wait. "Why did you say our friends were in danger? Do you know what might have happened to them?"

"We're not the only group doing what we can to survive, captain." The woman opened another door, revealing a small sitting room. She motioned for him to join her, and he left the two soldiers to keep a watch near the building's door. "There's a lot that's been going on in Armstrong since the bombs, and little of it has been good." Sitting in a frayed chair, Tom motioned for her to continue.

"When the square exploded, those of us on the outer edges of the dome hurried to get to the tunnel. We thought we could find safety in Aldrin, but we found the tunnel blocked off. Everyone thought it was the beginning of retaliation from the Coalition at that point, and panic spread. Believing that more bombs would go off, people gathered as far from the center of the dome as possible."

Dr. Baat shifted in her chair. "My office was close to the square, but I happened to be visiting a clinic near the rim that day. The people who gathered there for treatment are the ones living here with me. We stuck together, and didn't leave the clinic for several days. Once a few hours passed with no more explosions, people went wild. There was rioting, fighting in the streets. It was madness.

"The Marines were no better, shooting people who were merely running to them for help. They lost most of their number in the bomb or the tunnel collapse, so the few survivors took over the docking facility. I've heard they called Earth for support, but we'll never know what really happened. All I know for sure is that three days after the bombing the facility was deserted again."

"They must have been aboard the earliest shuttles," Tom said. "There was a flurry of ship traffic around then, but the Guild was too busy with increasing unrest in Aldrin to pay very close attention."

"Well, they're cowards for leaving us like that. Hundreds of people survived, but by the end of that first week I never saw most of them again. I hope they all got off Luna in those shuttles you mention, but I fear many were victims of the groups that formed in those early days."

"Like gangs?" Tom asked. "You're the first people we've seen. There aren't even any bodies out there."

Dr. Baat nodded sadly. "Some of the dead we buried, using the rubble from collapsed buildings to make graves. Most were there one day and gone the next. I fear the others may be eating the bodies."

"Cannibalism?" Tom was horrified. He couldn't imagine stooping to such a thing.

"The hydroponics farms were no use once the dome lost power. The explosion damaged something in the reactor, and even the engineers in my group have been unable to repair it. We were lucky it wasn't in the blast zone, or both domes would be no more. As for other living people, I know of only one group besides my own. We try to avoid them at all costs. They're a savage lot, driven by some urge to take what they need instead of working with us to restore functionality to the important parts of Armstrong."

"These are the ones you think my lost squad may have encountered?"

"Yes, captain. I feel certain they detected your group not long after you entered the dome, and then most likely watched you for an opportunity to ambush some of you and take what you have."

Tom frowned, his hands clenching tightly in his lap. "Where would they have taken my squad, doctor? I have to rescue them."

"There is a collection of buildings the savages call home, not far from here. I can guide you, so you can find your soldiers. If they're still alive."

TWENTY EIGHT

Mags frowned at the screen at the front of the bridge. A small freighter was magnified, growing larger as it approached the *Waterloo*. "Didn't the message say they left Luna only a few days ago?"

"Fifty three hours," Captain Andrews said, his voice sharing her astonishment.

"Can't be the same ship," she said resolutely. "There's no way we could have covered that distance with a fully functioning engine and reactor, and Guild freighters can't afford engines as powerful as a frigate."

"I would agree with you, Mags, but..." The captain waved his hand at the screen.

"Guild freighter *Vagabond* requesting permission to dock," the communications lieutenant called out. Andrews gave the approval, his eyes not leaving the image of the small ship. Twenty minutes later, the docking tube was being extended. "Shall we go down and greet our guests?"

Mags followed the captain from the command deck, stepping into the lift that was already waiting. They rode in silence until arriving eight decks lower in the ship. The freighter was on the port side airlock, a quick trip from where they exited the lift. She rubbed at the creases on her uniform automatically, wanting to give a sharp military presentation of herself.

Captain Andrews was a step in front of her as they waited in the airlock's antechamber. She could see the freighter's outer airlock cycle open, with three people exiting into the flexible docking tube to approach the frigate. As the inner airlock opened following a short decontamination and pressurization, Mags could hear the boisterous conversation of their visitors.

"...telling you, Erik. Amelia was certain we could have dialed up the power to the engines at least ten more percent before seeing any negative effects."

"Maybe so, Fynn, but there was no reason to risk it when we still made record time."

Once the door finished opening, the three stepped into the antechamber. The one in front was a familiar face from the warning that had broadcast across the system months earlier. *Too young*, was Mags' first thought. *But older than Natalia*, was her second. The man looked youthful and full of life, no doubt ecstatic over breaking every speed record she'd ever known. To one side was an older man, his full head of hair gray in a way that told her he had been blonde in his youth. Icy blue eyes roved around the room, as if he we are cataloguing every bit of it and comparing it to the ship he had just left. On the other side was an attractive woman, short but similar in age to Mags herself. The lines around her mouth told the tale of thousands of smiles and an equal number of frowns.

"Captain Frost," Andrews said, holding out his hand to the younger man. "We didn't expect to see you so soon after President Meyers told us you were coming."

"Captain Andrews, it's a pleasure to meet you. We were watching the battle over Hong Kong, and I have to tell you I was extremely impressed with your ship's performance. Guiding her between the enemy frigates to draw their fire while the other Coalition ships concentrated on one of them? That was genius."

"Thank you, but it was more luck than strategy that saw us come out of it as well as we did."

201

Erik introduced his two crew members. "Fynn Jesperson is our engineer. He's been working with Amelia Houghton and Dr. Francks from Earth, who finished off the research on a powerful new reactor technology. And this is Dr. Jennifer Montoya, ship physician."

"This is my XO, Lieutenant Commander Mags Richtaus."

There were handshakes and spoken greetings all around, and then Andrews stepped back and waved in invitation. He and Erik Frost led the way to a conference room several decks up. "Is this fantastic new reactor the reason you could make the trip from Luna so quickly?"

"It is," Fynn chimed in, almost triumphantly. "This new fusion reactor is proving to be much more powerful than our old reactor. It also generates a purer ion stream, which allows us to funnel more through the thrusters and generate a greater amount of speed in a shorter time."

"I have to admit the results have been pretty incredible," Erik said. He spent a few minutes telling them about some of the tests the ship had been through after the new reactor was installed. Mags shivered at the thought of a few of them. She knew the people in the *Waterloo*'s Engineering department would have been just as excited as the freighter's engineer was. The man's face was practically glowing just listening to his captain recount it.

Arriving at the conference room, Captain Andrews stood aside to let their guests enter first. Mags followed behind, to find Admiral Holgerson already greeting the trio. "Please, take a seat. I apologize for not greeting you at the airlock, but there has been a lot to work through now that we're getting information again. Even if it's only from one source."

The *Vagabond* crew members took the three seats on the far side of the table, leaving those on the near side for Andrews and Mags. She settled in, turning her chair so she could see everyone at the table without much difficulty. "It's strange that we haven't even picked up any of the newsfeeds that broadcast through the shipping lanes," she said.

Erik Frost's brow was furrowed. "We got an updated feed just an hour ago. That's not making it through to your ship?"

Captain Andrews looked surprised. "I assumed we were in a dead spot, or that whoever is blocking our communication with the Coalition government was also blocking those feeds in this area."

The old engineer looked intrigued. "Oh, I think they're blocking you, just not in the way you thought. I've heard Isaac talk about something like this. There's a way for a tech with access to a ship's systems to remotely tunnel into the communications software. They can disable or enable the different protocols that let you access certain feeds."

Holgerson and Andrews looked to Mags, as if hoping that her years of experiencing working with Engineering crews would give her insights into such things. She could only shake her head and shrug. "Who is this Isaac?" Holgerson asked. "Could I put someone from my communications team in touch with him?"

"He's our tech on the *Vagabond*," Captain Frost said, pulling out his tablet and typing in a quick message. "I'll tell him to reach out and see if he can explain how to check for something like that."

"You have my gratitude." The Fleet Admiral shifted, and Mags had to raise her hand to cover a grin she couldn't suppress. She couldn't imagine he had to say such things often. "Now, I'm hoping you can elaborate on what President Meyers has told us in his video messages. I feel like he's being vague about his suspicions."

Erik nodded. "Yes, admiral, he is. President Meyers was in contact with the Defense Minister on Earth. Shortly before we were sent out from Luna, he was sharing his suspicions with Minister Brighton. The connection was cut off, and Meyers hasn't been able to get in contact since. The minister's aide keeps telling us that he's in a meeting or handling personal business, but he never returns the calls. Meyers isn't sure how much he can trust the comm systems now, even when using the Guild encryption to speak with our ships."

The freighter captain scowled, and Mags saw his jaws go tight. "A few sources in Geneva tell us that a handful of high ranking government officials have seemingly disappeared. All of them were vocal about their concerns over how the prime minister was handling the situation with the Syndicate."

Holgerson took a deep breath, and expelled it slowly. "I know Minister Brighton well. Rinde's not the sort of man to duck calls. If he no longer wished to speak with your president, he would say so." He shared a look with Andrews. "I hate to act without information from another person, but I'm not left with much choice. By shutting us out, our own government is telling us everything I need to know."

Mags turned her head, bringing her full attention to the Fleet Admiral. She'd been present during discussions with he and Captain Andrews, but she hadn't realized he was so close to what amounted to mutiny. Or did such laws even apply when your own superiors refused to speak with you to provide orders and guidance?

The Guild captain seemed to feel the same way. "I know it's a hard decision to make, admiral. I certainly don't envy your having to make it. When they won't talk, they don't really give you much choice."

"Indeed." Holgerson traced a finger over the table. "Which is part of why I'm anxious to get back to Earth as quickly as possible. Tell me about this new technology President Meyers hinted at."

"I think Ms. Houghton and Dr. Francks can give a better presentation, but if I know those two they'll be tinkering with the reactor for at least another hour. Always running more tests." Erik grinned and shook his head. "Fynn can give you the basics on it."

Mags listened to the older man speak enthusiastically about the fusion reactor. She wasn't sure how the Transport Guild had come into possession of such an improvement over the fission reactors that had been in use for decades. Everything she'd always heard said fusion reactors were too expensive to maintain, and couldn't provide the power needed without costing more than the standard nuclear reactors.

She felt herself zoning out a few times, lost in a lot of the technical jargon the Engineer spewed out as if he'd learned it with his mother's milk. Listening to him reminded her of the Chief, a man who would have enjoyed being in this meeting. He and Fynn could have spent days talking about every nuance of their ships' engines.

"...as a result, you'll see a power efficiency ratio nearly five higher than you're used to." The old man leaned back with a look of utter satisfaction. He had talked for more than half an hour, and judging from the looks on their faces her admiral and captain had understood little of it.

They both looked to her again, and she shrugged. But this time she also nodded.

"Excellent. I'll be honored to have Ms. Houghton and Dr. Francks come aboard as soon as they're ready. Captain Andrews will ensure this reactor gets transferred over."

"Uh," Erik spoke up, raising a finger. "Sorry, admiral, but there's one thing we need from you first. President Meyers has drawn up a contract. The reactor belongs to the Guild, we're letting the *Waterloo* use it for a period of time, it can't be used on any other Coalition ship, yadda yadda. Standard legal stuff." He turned his tablet and pushed it toward Holgerson, who lifted it and read through a few pages with occasional grunts.

"It's nice to see the Guild hasn't changed as much as it seemed," the admiral said, smiling to take the bite from the words. He pressed his finger against the tablet, signing the document.

"Great!" Captain Frost said. "It shouldn't take more than a few days to get the reactor hooked up. Then we can both be back at Earth in less than half of your current ETA."

"I have a few things I'd like to test while we're installing it," Fynn said, turning to his captain. "I had a couple of ideas on the trip out, and I'm fairly confident most of them will work just fine."

Mags groaned. "That is definitely an Engineer talking."

Twenty Nine

Tom followed Dr. Baat through the dimly lit street. Earth was below the solid edge of the dome on this trip, with sunrise perhaps half an hour away on the opposite side. Infrared displays for their HUDs were another item that went on his list of equipment to demand the next time he spoke with President Meyers.

The two soldiers who had gone into the house were still with him, six feet to either side. The other groups of his squad, designated team one and team two, had been sent to scout the area ahead. Tom kept trying to reach Corporal Zavala over the comms with no success. An attempt to reach anyone on squad three's channel had met with equal failure. He felt a growing unease with each minute that passed without an answer.

Sergeant Fuller had wanted to rush over as soon as he heard the news. "Captain, wait for my squad. We'll wipe these cannibal bastards out and get our people back."

"No, sergeant. Stay on mission. It looks like you're reaching the end of your half of the dome's rim, so hold when you complete the sweeps. In case I change my mind."

"Yes, sir." It was a gruff response, but Tom knew the man would follow the order. He couldn't blame him for the desire to rush in and rain hell on those who had attacked and possibly injured or killed his fellow soldiers.

Ten minutes after leaving her secure hidey hole, Dr. Baat waved for everyone to stop. "It's not far," she said in a loud whisper. "You see that building ahead on the left, with the boards sticking out of the second floor window?" Tom nodded. "That's the beginning of their territory."

He examined the building, trying to remember that this had been a typical residence or commercial building only a month earlier. The windows were all smashed out, with glass shards in the street. Tom wasn't sure if that was an alarm system - the noise of someone crunching the glass as they approached. Any group capable of ambushing a militia squad, even a unit of mostly rookie recruits, shouldn't be that careless. The boards extruding from the upstairs window looked like a haphazard collection, but when he really examined them he could see they were tightly secured together. There was a cross brace on the underside of the rough platform, connecting all the boards. It would make an ideal firing platform to fend off attackers or spring an ambush on anyone straying into your territory.

"Team one, team two. Stay vigilant out there. This place looks rough and cobbled together at first glance, but I'm thinking there's a strong tactical mind behind it."

Both teams copied, and gave quick status reports of what they'd seen so far. Team two managed to get onto a roof near the cluster of buildings with similar appearance to what Tom could see ahead. They reported having a view on most of the streets around the buildings, and could see no movement. Team one had circled to the far side, and found nothing that looked threatening.

Tom was hesitant to just charge in and search for Zavala's squad, but he also wasn't sure if he wanted to give warning that he was approaching by trying to talk with them. The choice was made for him when a head appeared through a gaping window low in the building he was examining. It appeared to be a man, but it was hard to tell behind the large mask that covered the entire face. The person's hair was left exposed, hacked short and uneven. A bony arm was visible, supporting the person against the side of the building they leaned out from.

"You should shoot while you have the chance," Dr. Baat said. "I guarantee they wouldn't be so civilized."

"We don't fire on unarmed civilians," Tom said. He slid his stun pistol into the holster and raised his hand away as he took cautious steps forward. "Hello. I'm Captain Tom Fitz with the Guild Militia. We came over from Aldrin to check for survivors and find out what happened here."

The masked figure only stared. Tom was about to speak again when a voice spoke from another direction. "What do you want here, Captain Fitz of the Guild Militia?"

He looked around for the source of the voice, but could see no one. The way sound bounced around, it could have come from anywhere. "Some of my people were attacked, a little over an hour ago. I'm looking for them."

"And Dr. Baat," the voice spoke the name with obvious hatred, "told you that we're savages capable of doing such a thing."

"Something like that," the woman called out drily. "I know your voice, Cullen. You might as well show yourself."

A thin figure swung through the upstairs window into a crouch on the wooden platform. The way the wood planks barely moved as the person's weight settled confirmed Tom's assumptions about it being a sturdy structure. The person was covered in a skintight biosuit, scant protection in the punishing cold of the damaged dome. The helmet over their head was smaller than the ones Tom and Dr. Baat wore, and appeared to be designed for lab work instead of extra atmospheric conditions.

"Nelda, such a pleasure to see you again," the newcomer said with dripping sarcasm.

"Captain, this is Cullen Montgomery. He was once a Marine, discharged for conduct unbecoming." She was smirking as she said it, as if exposing a secret.

"Lance Corporal Cullen Montgomery at your service," the man said with a facetious salute. "Dr. Baat likes to think that being drummed out of the service makes me an undesirable, but you'd be surprised how many disagree with her."

Tom took another step. "I don't care what you used to be. What I care about at this moment are my soldiers. Are they safe?"

"How would I know?" Cullen asked with a shrug.

"I know you have them," Dr. Baat said. "There are only our two groups left in Armstrong, Cullen. You can't pretend that some other boogeyman attacked them."

"Boogeyman?" The thin man twisted his body, looking all around. "The only thing I see here that could be described that way is you, Nelda. Did she bother to mention what kind of doctor she is, Captain Fitz?"

Tom glanced back at the woman, noting her rigid posture. "No, and I didn't ask. All I want is to find my people." He was getting tired of the bickering between the two. Over the comms, he gave Sergeant Fuller approval to begin approaching his current position.

"She's a corpse doctor," Cullen said in a loud singsong voice. "Slicing open bodies, pulling organs from within. Sounds like the kind of doctor who'd know which parts of the dead were tasty tasty, hm?"

"You're a filthy liar, Cullen. We all know it's your group that's been eating the dead. Ran out of rations from all those buildings you broke into, didn't you?"

Tom was backing away now, as Dr. Baat was stepping closer to the man crouching above. He didn't really

210

know either of these people, and while the discharged Marine sounded a little off his rocker the man also had the presence of mind to create a perimeter that looked rough and tumble while being sound. He couldn't reconcile that sort of thinking with the way Dr. Baat characterized him.

At the same time, he had been inside of the doctor's home. He'd seen at least two of the people she lived with, and none of them had given him an uneasy feeling. All in all, he was starting to regret entering Armstrong at all.

"What's going on, sir?" one of the soldiers standing off to the side asked. "Which one should we be watching?"

"Both," he said. Reactivating his external speakers, he spoke loudly. "Look, I don't care what kind of squabble the two of you have. Someone needs to tell me where my missing squad is right now, or we'll take both of you into custody and search every inch of this dome."

A wheezing laugh was his only response, as the man above shook his head in merriment. "You can search my little kingdom all you want, militia man. The only people in these buildings are those too afraid to live out in the dark with no protection from *them*."

His outstretched hand was pointing at Dr. Baat, who had never taken her attention from him. "No one has any reason to be afraid of me," she said in a tight voice.

"We all know what happens when the black suits come in the dark," Cullen said, his voice quiet. "Few escape them, and those who do are too frightened to leave our homes again."

Tom gave orders, and his two soldiers hurried forward to restrain Dr. Baat. He raised his weapon and fired at the man crouched above, the stun bolt penetrating the thin biosuit with ease. "Team one, team two, advance and clear these buildings. Stun only, unless someone uses lethal force against you. Sergeant Fuller, come pick up the doctor and use her handprint to access the secure building."

Dr. Baat was struggling against the soldiers holding her. "What is the meaning of this, captain? I've done nothing but try to help you."

"I'm sorry, doctor, but I don't have time to sort out this mess. We're going to secure all of you, and figure it out once I find my squad."

Tom turned away, ignoring her continuing protests. He saw movement further down the street, lights on the helmet of one of his squad as they swept the area. While he waited, he tried contacting Zavala on the comms again. There was still only a low static hum.

Sergeant Fuller arrived several minutes later, his men running through the streets. He took possession of the struggling doctor, pulling her along as they retreated down the street to the woman's building. Tom sketched the layout of the few rooms he'd seen, and warned that there were at least two others inside.

With both squads working to find Corporal Zavala and squad three, Tom was impatiently pacing in the street. He wanted to be part of the search, but also wanted to be close to both teams so he could quickly join whichever found something.

He noticed the first figure still hunched inside the lower window of the building, almost jumping when he saw the masked face that he'd forgotten about. The mask turned to follow every step he took, and he crouched down to present a less imposing figure. Now that he was closer, he could see that this looked more like an adolescent than an adult.

"He's just stunned," he said, pointing at Cullen above. "He'll be fine once that wears off."

The mask moved up and back down again slowly, but the person still didn't move away from the cover of the wall beside the window. They were wearing a biosuit, as well.

"Are you cold?" Tom asked. "When we get you to the docking facility, I'm sure we can find some pressure suits that will provide more warmth."

At the mention of the facility, the figure jerked back until only half of the mask was visible in the window. He wondered if something had happened to this person there. Perhaps they had tried to evacuate Armstrong and received rough treatment from the Marines guarding the docks to ensure their own withdrawal.

"My daughter," a voice croaked from above. Tom turned in surprise to see Cullen looking down from the platform. The man had to have a hell of a constitution to be recovering from the effects of the stun bolt already. "Her name is Kira."

The masked person looked up, and then disappeared. Tom could hear the sound of running and then footsteps climbing a stair, before they reappeared above him to crouch over Cullen. He could see hands reach out to grab tightly at the downed man, and felt a twinge of sympathy.

"I apologize for the stun bolt," he started.

"No," Cullen replied sharply. "It was the right thing. I would have done it sooner."

"How many people will we find in these buildings, Cullen? Are there any surprises I should warn my squad about?"

"Only two. Me and Kira."

Tom was stunned. "What do you mean? Dr. Baat said your group was large."

"In the beginning, we were more than forty. I knew the Marines weren't going to do anything for us after retreating to the docks, so I gathered as many as I could convince. The rioting was already starting, and we needed to make a safe place."

He tried to raise an arm, pointing at the building the platform extended from. "This was our home. My wife, Kira, and me. After the Marines, I never wanted to go back to Earth, so we settled here. It was different, but a new adventure." The masked girl nodded at his side.

"All of us stuck together to stay safe. It seemed to work, for a while. The night after the docking facility was found to be empty, two of our group disappeared. They'd been out looking for food and supplies, but they never came back. So the next night, I organized a search. Five groups of two, all of us looking at the places we knew the missing pair had expected to go. Two of those groups didn't return.

"After that, we knew that someone was out there taking our people. The dome was dark, and growing colder by the hour. People we had met and spoken with in the early days after the bomb either stopped talking or also disappeared. We stopped sending out groups to look for supplies, and instead cut our rations to make what we had last. But people still disappeared. They would step outside to look up at Earth, cursing them for leaving us this way. Or to have a quick patrol of our neighborhood. Never seen again."

Tom was quiet, trying to imagine living through something like that. Having your friends and family vanish without a trace, right after you've survived the largest attack in Luna history. If it were him, he would have been very angry.

214

"A week after the first disappearance, my wife decided we needed more food. We were starving, and a few of our number had raided the meagre pantry to gorge themselves on what kept all of us alive. I had no choice but to agree. There'd been no indication that help was coming, and we felt certain that Aldrin must have suffered a similar fate. She decided to take four of our group, and promised to stay together." The masked girl was slumped down now, her body shaking in what Tom was sure were sobs.

"I'll never know if they were taken together or if she broke her word and split the group, but they never returned. Only seventeen of us remained." Cullen groaned as he raised himself, and then rolled to drop to the street below. Tom stepped back, but the man only slumped into a lotus position as the masked girl dropped behind him.

"The next day Dr. Baat appeared. We'd known there was another group not too far away, but never managed to make contact with them. Finding out it was a building full of doctors and engineers gave our group such hope. Nelda was known to a few of our group, and they said we could trust her. The doctor offered to give us food, and to help those who were weakened from lack of food. Two of our oldest, those were, and four others went with them back to Dr. Baat's home."

"Let me guess," Tom said. "You never saw any of them again?"

"We saw one. Mark. He brought back a dozen plastic jars filled with a meat paste, and said the others would come back later in the day after the doctor could treat our sick. When those five hadn't returned the next morning, Mark led myself and a few others to Dr. Baat's building. She told us our friends had left a few hours after Mark. That she watched them walk away down the street.

"Fool that I was, I took her word. She offered help in looking for them, and we went off in groups of three. Two members of my group with one of hers, combing the area to find any trace of our missing. I never saw any of them again, and I still don't know why Nelda left me alone to return with the certainty that her group was behind it all. Maybe she felt powerful, like a god sparing an ant."

Tom was trying to reach Sergeant Fuller, but receiving no answer over the comms. His teams searching through the surrounding buildings told him that they'd found only empty homes so far, abandoned for days. He ordered them back to his position as Cullen continued his dark tale.

"I knew then who had taken our people, but I didn't know why. I learned that too late. Two days ago, Dr. Baat showed up. She stood right here and taunted me. Did I want to see my wife again? Of course I did! Kira and I were all that were left by then. I begged her to let me see Mary, offered to trade myself if she'd release my wife. The evil bitch laughed, dropped a small sack, and walked away. When I opened it, I found more of the meat paste. And laying on top of it was the old silver ring my wife had never taken from her finger."

"My God," Tom whispered. He urgently tried to reach Fuller again.

"I'm sure she told you a lot of stories about my group, captain. Probably said that we ate people to stay alive. Which is technically true, since we ate meat paste. It's the only reason I'm still alive." Cullen wrapped an arm around his daughter. "My wife is the only reason we're still alive."

The Marines were gathering around, ten soldiers making him feel safer even as he felt an itch at the back of his neck. It was all too easy to imagine himself being

216

stalked through the dome, and he wondered if someone had been watching when he'd done the first scout with Milner and Hotchkiss.

"Five of you stay and keep these people safe. I want them to get out of here, no matter what it takes. The rest of you, with me. We're going to Dr. Baat's place to help squad four search." Tom didn't want to alarm his squad by telling them he'd now lost communication with both of the other squads.

The trip back took half as long, with everyone jogging at a fast pace. He had to keep himself from breaking into a full sprint in his desire to get to the doctor's building. Upon arrival, they found three soldiers standing outside. Milner was surprised to see them, especially with their quick approach. "What's going on, captain?"

"We need to get into that building, Milner. Please tell me Fuller made you keep it open."

"No, but one of the squad was left behind on the other…"

"God damn it! Milner, crack that door for me. I don't have time to explain, but it's imperative that we breach this building."

"Yes, sir!" The young soldier quickly turned and pulled out the tech kit he'd used to get them all through the airlocks in the docking facility. Tom tried to hide his mounting fears as he waited. Seconds felt like minutes, which felt like hours. Sweat was sliding between his shoulder blades, creating a dreadful itch that made him want to strip out of the pressure suit.

The lock on the door was stronger than that on the airlocks, which told Tom he should have paid more attention and wondered why a simple house in a lunar dome would need such high security. It took Milner two and a half minutes to crack the security, an eternity when he thought about what could be happening inside.

As the door slid open, Tom was first into the building. The Marine that should have been waiting there was nowhere to be seen. Tom's stun pistol was holstered, the flechette rifle grasped tightly in hands ready to find a target. The hallway just inside the door was clear, and he poked the rifle into the sitting room where he'd heard Nelda Baat's crafted fiction. The next room turned out to be a small kitchen and pantry.

At the end of the hall were stairs leading up and down. He tried Fuller and Zavala on the radios again, but received the same low static hum. It was a sound that was beginning to drive him insane every time he heard it. There were eight Marines behind him now, those from outside having followed his group in. He sent four upstairs, keeping an active radio channel open with all of them, and then led the other four downstairs. Milner had positioned himself to be in the group following Tom.

They went quickly down the stairs, all caution gone as he worried about arriving seconds too late to save his squads. The noise of their feet on the concrete stairs was deafening, even through his helmet's noise filters. A small landing after five steps was the ideal place to stop and scout, but he ignored the impulse and continued down the steps after a quick turn.

The basement carved into the base of the dome was small and cramped, with corners that the faint light from his helmet couldn't reach. With a verbal command, the lights on the shoulders of his suit flared up. The room was filled with light, revealing huddled figures in the far corner. "Fuller? Zavala?"

One of the figures raised her head, black eyes defiantly staring back at him. "Captain Fitz?"

"You don't know how happy I am to see you, corporal. Is this all of your squad?" He did a quick count without waiting for an answer, and sighed with relief to get ten. A couple of them looked to be sporting wounds, but were stable.

"Sir, these people... they're not very good people."

Tom had to fight back a laugh. "Yes, corporal. I've discovered that the hard way." He motioned for those with him to help the members of squad four. "Zavala and her team have been found in the basement. What have you discovered upstairs?"

There was silence, and then a faint voice. "You need to see this, captain."

After checking to be sure the rescued squad would be alright, he pounded up the stairs as fast as he could. Once he reached the second floor, a soldier from squad one motioned down a hallway that had three doors. The first was a small washroom, with a black pressure suit hung from a hook and a helmet on the shelf above. The second room was an office that had been hastily turned into a bedroom, with a bare mattress placed on the floor. He grinned to see Dr. Baat and a disheveled man sitting on it, with a few people from Fuller's squad flanking them.

The expressions he could see through the soldiers' helmets killed his smile. One of them flicked their eyes in the direction of the room he hadn't yet seen, and shook her head. Tom turned that way and forced himself to walk to the end of the hall. Milner stepped out of the room as he approached, refusing to meet his eyes.

"What happened?" he asked. Peering around the doorway, he could see shelves filled with plastic jars. Seven full shelves, but only half a shelf with jars that contained a reddish substance that he assumed to be the meat paste Cullen had spoken of. On the floor between the shelves and a large bed was a prone form. A large knife had been shoved into the suit, right below the lip on the back of the helmet. The blow had severed Sergeant Fuller's spine and hopefully killed him just as quickly.

"They were surprised by the occupant," Milner said. "When we got up here, the squad were beating on him. If I'd known what was in here, I don't think I would have made them stop."

"No, I'm not sure I would have either," Tom said quietly. He knelt to say a quick prayer for the dead militia soldier. "Make a stretcher, we're taking Fuller with us. And the two prisoners. Any idea where the third person went?"

Milner shook his head. "They won't say anything, either."

"We'll get it out of them back in Aldrin." He called the group watching over Cullen and Kira, telling them to rendezvous outside the house. He was getting out of Armstrong, and it would take a lot of convincing to ever get him back in the cursed dome again.

THIRTY

The shuttle lifted from the roof of the tall building that held the various committee chambers, and Yumata relaxed into the cushioned seat with a faint smile. It had taken longer than he'd expected, but he was finally on the way to the Syndicate's orbital station. His mission from the Executive Committee was to ensure cooperation for the needed repairs and railgun installations on the *Indomitable*. They had given him one week, but he didn't expect to need more than half that time to complete his personal objectives.

"You'll like it on the station, Hiro. It takes a while to adjust to the zero gravity, but they make sure it's a comfortable adjustment."

That voice belonged to the one hitch in his plans. He'd been shackled to Morris Abernathy yet again, and was more than half sure that Selene kept sending the man with him as much to get the nuisance out of her hair as to keep an eye on him to make sure he behaved as a member of the Military Committee was expected to.

Yumata closed his eyes and blocked out the voice that kept on about the comforts aboard the station. The little prick seemed obsessed with telling everyone he was important in the most roundabout ways. *He wouldn't last a week on a frigate,* Yumata thought, bringing another faint smile to his lips as he imagined it.

The trip to the station orbiting four hundred miles above Earth was blessedly short, and their pilot had made the journey many times. It took only a single attempt to connect with the station's docking tube. An admirable feat when factoring in the slow horizontal spin of the station, a complication that was unique to the orbital stations.

Unstrapped, Yumata floated through the shuttle toward the small airlock. He couldn't stop the chuckle that arose on seeing Abernathy fumbling with his own straps. The man had spent ten minutes talking about how skilled he was in zero gravity because of his two previous trips to the station, and then proved how much of a blowhard he was within seconds of arriving.

A sharp salute was presented as he neared the shuttle's pilot, a gesture he returned. Turning to the right, he entered the small airlock. It was large enough to comfortably hold two, but he took the opportunity to begin the cycle and lock Abernathy out until he was in the station. Air hissed through the chamber as the pressure equalized with that in the tube, and within seconds the outer door opened.

On the other side, the process was repeated. The station's airlock also scanned him for any dangerous pathogens, and flashed green after half a minute. Floating through the open inner door, he was greeted by a man in late middle age. His brown hair was cut close to the scalp, something Yumata appreciated very quickly with his own not too long hair floating into his face more often than he liked.

"Admiral Yumata, welcome to Orbital Station A32."

"Thank you for having me, Commander Singh."

The station commander craned his head to look through the airlock windows, cursing through a false smile. "I see Mr. Abernathy is joining us, as well."

"Mm, unfortunately." They shared a laugh, watching the younger man twist and push himself from wall to wall in the airlock. He hadn't adapted to the weightlessness, or didn't understand just how much momentum a small push could give an object. "I'm sure we can find something to keep him busy while we settle in for the real work."

The station commander winked. "I already warned the quartermaster that I was going to fob any committee members off on her. They love going over lists, and telling my people how they should be doing a job that we've done for years."

Yumata nodded once, slowly so as not to give his floating body momentum in an undesired direction. "They certainly do love that."

They watched as Abernathy completed the pressurization and scan cycle. The airlock door opened, and he presented his wide politician's smile as he pushed off far too strongly and shot through the antechamber. Commander Singh gently restrained him, and then greeted the new arrival.

"Now, if you'll both follow me I'll show you to the quarters we've set aside for your use during your visit." With a gentle push, a move made obvious in the hopes that Abernathy would observe and copy it, the station commander floated into the round hallway beyond. Yumata followed, leaving his companion to trail behind as he could.

The station was a large oval shape with two deep levels. The "bottom" always faced the planet below while the "top" was oriented to view the stars. More than a hundred people lived and worked on the station, most cycling through for six to nine months before returning to the planet below. Only a few, like Commander Singh, had the dedication to commit to long service aboard the station, knowing that the longer they stayed the less likely it would be for their bodies to allow them to return home. The loss of bone density and muscle mass became crippling after extended periods without gravity.

Commander Singh traveled a corridor that followed the outer edge of the station. He talked as he led the way, pointing out labs and explaining what experiments were being conducted in each. Yumata wasn't surprised to find that most of them related to the planned voyages beyond the asteroid belt in coming years. The Syndicate was eager to expand its reach. The planets and moons offered countless opportunities for settlement and extraction of valuable minerals and ores.

The first room he stopped at was a small but carefully arranged space. There was a small window on the floor that looked down on the planet, and the zippered sack that would serve as a bed to hold the occupant securely against the wall was positioned to easily watch the view. A zero gravity toilet and sink were behind a small partition in a far corner.

"This room is for Mr. Abernathy," Singh said, once the man had caught up with the other two. "I've ensured that the room's display has a direct connection with Earth. Our quartermaster will be by in about half an hour so you can go over supply lists and requisitions. We'd love to have your guidance on a few things."

"It'll be my pleasure to assist in any way I can, commander. I think that with my input, your station will be running much more efficiently by the time we leave." Abernathy was grinning with obvious pleasure, full of his own importance.

Once he entered the room and the door closed, Singh led Yumata onward. "I've put you in a room closer to the control center, admiral. I anticipate seeing a lot of you there."

"Will I be able to communicate with the *Indomitable* from there?"

"Yes, sir. We can also arrange a direct connection from your room, but that requires routing through satellites and might take a few hours to get all the approvals needed." Singh sounded apologetic, but Yumata assured him it was perfectly acceptable.

"I doubt I'll need it, commander."

"I just hope Captain Guildersen will listen to you, admiral."

Yumata chuckled. "Not an easy man to work with, is he?"

"That would be a hell of an understatement. When the Military Committee asked me to coordinate assistance, I contacted the *Indomitable*. Captain Guildersen came on the line immediately and demanded that I send twenty people in the shuttle he was sending over. He said, and I quote him here, 'Have them pack their things, I'll get the approval to transfer them to my command.' Can you believe that?"

"Yes, unfortunately I can. Guildersen has never been one to give much thought to others. It has always been an enigma to me that he managed to ingratiate himself with members of the Executive Committee."

Singh raised a hand to a bulkhead, halting his momentum. "This is your cabin, admiral. My people will see to it that your bags are delivered shortly."

Yumata pulled himself into the cabin, virtually the same as the one given to Abernathy. "I'm ready to see the control center, commander. If you have time to show me."

Singh bowed, holding an arm out in invitation. "It's only a few meters away." Together, they floated through the corridor for a short distance. The commander keyed in his access code, and the door slid open to reveal a gray room with high walls that took up both decks. Above the door they entered was another that gave access to the second level of the station. The floors and wall were metal with a dull sheen, while the consoles and chairs were made from a plastic of similar color. At the front of the room, the floor and ceiling were one large window, broken only by thin metal supports separating thick glass panels that were a meter square.

Two other people were in the room, tapping at screens in front of them as they completed tasks. Singh floated over to one, and grabbed hold of her console to steady himself. "This is Lieutenant Peters, our day shift controller. The kid is Ensign Soter."

Yumata returned their salutes, his gaze continually drawn to the view through the panoramic windows. "It's an amazing sight, isn't it, sir?" Singh asked. "The station design called for this to be in every room, but the builders wouldn't do it. Too high a chance of damaging the structural integrity. At least if something happens in this room, it can be sealed off from the rest of the station with the touch of a button."

"It is indeed an astounding view. I have seen Earth like this so many times, but always on displays showing what a camera sees. There's something special about seeing it with my own eyes."

They were silent for a few minutes, until Yumata shook himself and turned away from the windows. "Is there a station I may use, commander? I will begin contacting the *Indomitable* and talk with some of the officers who served with me for years."

"Of course, admiral. You can use the command station here."

Several hours later, Yumata pushed himself away from the console. He'd managed to speak with a few officers on the cruiser, and all shared the same frustrations with the ship's new captain. As they spoke, he listened patiently and felt greater satisfaction with each complaint. It had been only a few weeks since Guildersen forced his way into command of the *Indomitable*, and already the crew was on the verge of a mutiny.

He'd managed to talk the most incendiary down, not wanting their ire to cause a schism within the ship just yet. If he was going to get revenge and resume his rightful place, matters had to carefully controlled and orchestrated. Surprisingly, the colonel in charge of the Marine squads on the cruiser had suggested a similar plan to the one he was already following. Guildersen had been so overbearing and brutish in the few meetings they'd had, the colonel was adamant he would never work with the man.

Checking the time, he saw that it was half an hour past when he'd been expected to contact Selene with status updates. He turned and saw that the shift in the control room had changed while he was working. A different lieutenant said at the station near the middle of the room, and she looked up when she felt his eyes on her. "Can I help you, admiral?"

"Yes, lieutenant. I need a connection with the Military Committee chairwoman. How do I get a channel opened?"

"That station is approved for all channels, sir. The commander made sure of it before you arrived."

"Ah. Excellent." He turned back and cycled through the menus until he found what he needed. The wait for a connection was short, but the aide who answered his call told him the chairwoman was occupied with another meeting. Sighing with impatience, Yumata had to endure the annoying music that played over the line while he waited. He still remembered when silent holds had been tested during his boyhood. Even those who most hated hold music had thought the line went dead when there was no sound, and would keep calling back. The experiment lasted two months.

"Hiro," a voice finally spoke, recalling him from his thoughts. "You missed the scheduled update."

"I apologize, Selene. I lost track of time, but I assure you it won't happen again."

The chairwoman gave him a stern look on the screen. "Make sure of it. I just spoke with Mr. Abernathy, and I would hate for his to be the only reports getting to the Military Committee. It wouldn't do good things for your tenure."

Yumata smiled faintly. "Well, I don't have much to report for today as it is. I've spoken with several people onboard the *Indomitable*, and done what I can to calm the troubled waters. Guildersen has agreed to speak with me in the morning, and I'll try to get Commander Singh to join us."

Selene pursed her lips as she examined him. "What do you put the odds at, Hiro? I don't have to tell you the Executive Committee is pushing hard to get the cruiser up to full strength. Our ground forces are still advancing easily, but there are signs of resistance beginning to coalesce. It seems that quite a few of their military leaders have decided to ignore the prime minister's orders to maintain a defensive line around Geneva."

"That took far too long," he said with a sad shake of his head. "I'd like to think our own troops would have seen the wisdom of bucking orders sooner. As to a timeline, I would hope something can be worked out tomorrow. If not, it may be necessary for me to go aboard the cruiser with Commander Singh."

"Hiro, you know you'll never get the approval for that. The Executive Committee wouldn't allow it."

"Then perhaps they shall have to fight their war without support from above," he told her in a solemn tone.

"Do what you can," Selene said with a heavy sigh. "And make sure you report on time tomorrow."

The screen went black, and Yumata leaned back with a smile. If the Coalition had truly found their spine, then perhaps his plans could be put into motion sooner than expected.

THIRTY ONE

Erik couldn't believe how quickly the new reactor had been installed on the *Waterloo*. Fynn had spent more than twenty hours on board the frigate, working alongside Amelia and the ensign in charge of the ship's Engineering department. By the end of that time, they'd been ready for a series of quick tests to verify the connections were secure and the reactor was working with the engines.

Fleet Admiral Holgerson had been quite pleased, commending the engineers for their diligent work and excellent results in so short a time. After a few more hours for both crews to wrap up any business with each other, Erik and his friends had transferred back into the *Vagabond*. Isaac was babbling away about the program upgrades he had worked up with the frigate's tech department. Apparently, they'd used the results of the freighter's tests with the new reactor to improve functionality and make use of the greater power supply.

"Lieutenant Hays thinks her team can even find a way to tie that power into the weapons systems. Eject railgun rounds at greater velocities, overcharge torpedoes before firing them at enemy ships. That kind of thing."

"It's theoretical at the moment," Amelia said, with a look in her eyes that told him she was seriously considering the ways to make it work. "I'd like to get in contact with her and discuss it further, if you'll provide me her contact information."

"Of course!" Isaac was ecstatic that the ideas could become reality. "I also heard Dr. Francks was getting ideas from the *Waterloo*'s engineering crew."

"Yes," Fynn said as they all crammed into the freighter's airlock. "It was amazing to watch how fast his reluctance to stay aboard the frigate turned to excitement. If they're not careful, he'll be trying some of those ideas before we even start the burn for Earth."

Erik shook his head as the three walked the opposite direction from the airlock, still talking about the abstract uses for the energy provided by the fusion reactors. He could imagine how happy Robert would have been to share those ideas, and work toward making them reality. The researcher may not have survived Interamnia, but his name would live on. Already, people were calling it the Silva Reactor in his honor.

The one thing no one had dwelled on much was the fuel needed for the reactor. Deuterium was a readily available isotope of hydrogen, one of the most common elements in the observable universe. As such, it was currently relatively easy and cheap to get hold of. He could see that changing as the demand increased and companies realized they could make a larger profit from the sale of it. His running costs had dropped precipitously after changing out the reactor, so he enjoyed it while he could.

Settling into his command chair, he pulled up the holo displays and waited for the docking tube to be retracted into the frigate. Mira was already at her station, unsurprisingly. He'd seen her a few times on the frigate, visiting the bridge or chatting with other pilots in the crew mess. Seeing her enjoy time outside of the freighter had been reassuring.

"Ready to race the *Waterloo* back to Earth?"

"Cap, you know I'm always ready for something like that. There's no chance we can keep up if they give her all she's got, but I'll make them earn it."

Erik was about to reply when the communications system alerted him. He accepted the connection, and saw the frigate's smirking XO on the screen. "Captain Frost, Captain Andrews wanted me to extend our gratitude for the Guild's generous loan of the Silva Reactor. Also, we're about to test this baby out, so you might want to get clear."

"It's our pleasure, commander. I hope it helps you put a few dents in the Syndicate's new toy."

"We're certainly going to try, and we're counting on Guild assistance in that."

"You'll have it, ma'am." He glanced over at Mira and saw a hand signal. "We've given you a ten kilometer clearance. I'm looking forward to seeing how well your frigate performs."

The woman grinned widely just before the connection went dark. On the main displays, he watched the frigate's engines flare up. For a reason the engineers hadn't explained in a way that he could understand, the new reactor gave the engines a purplish glow around the normal blue of the ion thrusters. Erik felt sure it had something to do with the ions being produced by different elements, or possibly because of the increased number of ions passing through the nozzle screens. Whatever the cause, it was pretty as hell to look at.

"Cap, if you give them too much of a lead I'm going to pout."

He laughed. "Punch it, Mira." With a wild yell, she pushed her fingers forward on her console and he felt the *Vagabond*'s engines push them forward. The gel wrapped around him as he was pushed into the crash couch, and he watched the numbers on his display climb up past six G's. The frigate slid by and fell behind them, her captain choosing to slowly ramp up the power to the thrusters. After

232

days of testing and the flight out to rendezvous with the frigate, Mira had no such hesitation.

Two hours later, the *Waterloo* was several thousand kilometers behind the freighter, but cutting that gap increasingly. Erik was impressed to see the frigate performing so well, and so soon. Admiral Holgerson had seemed a careful sort, though from talking with some of the crew he learned the man had relaxed greatly since his early days on the ship. Even the ship's snarky XO had looked at her admiral with respect a few times when they were in the same room.

"Cap, I've got the Guild on the line for you."

He checked the communications system and saw the connection had been established several minutes earlier. "Send it through. I hope you had a nice chat with Dex."

"The nicest," Mira said with an audible grin. "She was making sure you behaved on the *Waterloo*."

When the woman's mocha skin and brown curls appeared, she stuck her tongue out at his stern frown. "I knew I could trust Mira to keep you in line, mi amor."

"Uh huh. And how long have you two been conspiring against me like that?"

Dex only laughed and blew him a kiss. "So, everything went well with the frigate?"

"It went great," Erik said. "All the engineers were happy to play with the new toy, and I had a chance to get acquainted with most of the ship's officers. I have to say, Dex, if the *Waterloo* had been involved in those battles, I don't think the *Indomitable* would have made it to Earth."

"Impressed with them, are you? Even the Fleet Admiral? Meyers said he's a bit of a stick in the mud." Her eyes sparkled with amusement as the use of the old expression.

233

"Enemy soldiers boarding his ship followed by abandonment by his own government seems to have given him a different perspective."

"Yeah, that'll do it," Dex said soberly. "Speaking of, did he happen to mention his plans for when you're back at Earth and he can get in contact with Parliament or the Admiralty again?"

Erik narrowed his eyes, examining the woman on the screen. "You and President Meyers are up to something."

She gave him a look of wide-eyed innocence. "Little old me?"

"Uh huh. Now I'm sure the wheels are turning in that gorgeous head of yours. I won't pry, but warn me before something happens that might affect my ship."

"Erik, you know I'd never do anything to put you in danger. Anything Meyers and I might have in the works is for the good of the system." Her expression brightened. "Which reminds me, we've heard back from two of the mining colonies. Davida and Hygeia are on board to join forces with the Guild."

"That's great news!" Mira called out. "Not that I'm eavesdropping. I just happened to hear that one sentence."

Erik laughed and shook his head. "It *is* great news. What about the other three colonies?"

"No word yet, but we're hoping to hear from them before you reach Earth. We don't need the backing of all five, but it would make things much easier." She looked off screen and shook her head at someone out of his view.

"One last update for you. Tom made it back from Armstrong." She told him about the scouting groups and the survivors they encountered. "Can you believe that? Eating people?"

He shuddered. "I've heard about things like that on Earth. People will do some crazy things to survive, but it's been less than a month since the bombings. It seems like there should have been enough food and supplies to support the low number of survivors left behind."

"We're sending in two squads again this afternoon, along with some people from Aldrin that have experience working on dome systems. Meyers is hoping we can get the air exchangers and heating systems working again, and then clear the tunnel to restore access."

"What will happen to those people Tom brought back to Aldrin?"

"Cullen and his daughter have been given a place to live. Tom's trying to talk him into helping train the new militia recruits, since he has experience as a Marine. The other two are being held while a psychologist works with them to determine if they're even sane."

Erik leaned back and closed his eyes. "I hope more survivors are found. I know we can't be sure how many people were killed in the blast, or how many the Syndicate took back to Earth, but finding only four people alive in a dome that held more than a thousand? *That's* insane."

"Five people," Dex said. "One of Dr. Baat's associates is still out there, remember. We don't even know if that's a man or woman, since Tom never saw them out of the pressure suit. That's information we're hoping the psychologist can get out of the two we have." She looked off screen again. "I have to get to a meeting. Get back here as quick as you can."

"You know it," Erik said, as the screen went dark.

"Cannibals. Gross." Mira swiveled her chair around to face him. "I bet the entertainment vids that inevitably get made will turn them into cannibal zombies. Double gross."

"And there'll be dozens of them, roaming around the dome eating bodies and chasing survivors." Erik thought about it for a few seconds. "I'd actually enjoy watching that."

"Oh, totally. I didn't say I wouldn't enjoy it." Mira turned back to her station. "By the way, the *Waterloo* has been waiting to speak with you."

"What? How long? Why didn't you say something?"

"Five minutes or so, and I just did."

Erik growled in frustration and he hurriedly brought up the communication menu and activated the call. The screen was empty, but he could see two people standing against the command deck railing a dozen steps away. He was about to call out to get their attention when a face appeared as a young man rolled in front of the camera. "Captain Frost?"

"Yes, that's me."

The man turned and spoke to someone off screen. Seconds later he left the chair and was replaced by the frigate's XO. "Captain Frost," Mags said with a tight smile. "Good of you to make time for me."

"Sorry, commander. I was speaking with the Guild, and my pilot decided not to tell me you were waiting."

Mags chuckled. "I guess we all have someone we report to." She glanced back at the two men standing at the rail behind her. "I just wanted to let you know that the new reactor is performing admirably. Our engineers confirm they haven't encountered any errors yet. Power generation is magnitudes greater than before."

"I'm glad to hear that. Mira shows the *Vagabond* as forty four hours from arrival at Luna. I'm betting your frigate is going to be there a bit faster."

236

"A tiny bit," Mags said with a laugh. "If our projections are correct, we should be at Earth in just over forty hours." Her smile turned wolfish. "I'm sure it's going to be quite a shock when we appear far ahead of schedule."

THIRTY TWO

Beyond the small heavily tinted window, rain fell on the depressing factory. Smoke rose from chimneys scattered around the industrial complex, almost blending in with the curtain of water falling from angry skies. Lights were shining all over, lighting up an afternoon that was almost dark as night in the storm. It had been hours since he woke to the sound of thunder and the flashes of lightning through the only window he had.

Rinde sat at a small table, cheaply made from plywood covered with a thin plastic sheet printed to give the appearance of thick wooden planks. There was only one chair at the table, an old relic that creaked every time he sat. He constantly felt as if it was going to fall apart beneath him, with the way it would wobble and shift precipitously at every movement. A chipped plastic plate sat before him, holding a thin circle of chewy bread with only a few bites taken out of it. Made with only flour, water, and a bit of salt, the bread gave his body calories for energy but not much else.

His cramped room was larger than a prison cell, but not by much. A thin bed was shoved into one corner, a closet that contained a toilet and shower head in the other. Two cabinets contained a collection of broken and chipped plates and bowls, with dented old silverware in the single drawer. The small food storage device was refilled every night while he slept, the back opening to allow one of the soldiers constantly roaming the halls to insert a small bottle of milk, the daily ration of flour, and one multivitamin pill.

The sink was tiny and the water stained a light brown, but his refusal to drink it hadn't lasted very long.

The table completed the room's furniture, placed so that the occupant could sit and stare out at the bleak view. Rinde often wondered how many people had sat there before him, and how many would sit there when he was gone. In all his years serving in Parliament and then on the cabinet, he'd never known places like this existed. Work camp, the guards called it when they shoved him through the doors on the first day. A place for political dissidents and troublemakers to be tucked away. Out of sight, out of mind.

It was hard for him to believe that millions of Coalition citizens lived in places like this every day. Unable to afford anything better, stuffed into small apartments in towering buildings that allowed thirty or forty million to share a city. He'd seen poverty in Africa as a child, but the wide open spaces there outside of the large cities were a stark contrast to the clustered industrial estates spread across Europe, Asia, and the Americas. If nothing else, his current situation was making him understand how overloaded their planet truly was. For some reason, their desire to expand to the stars and relieve the pressure had died out over the last several decades as resources were focused on maintaining a status quo between the two globe spanning superpowers.

He'd spent the day before confined to the room, but expected a guard at any moment to take him for his first shift in one of the factories. There had been only a two minute "orientation" as he was pushed and shoved through hallways, but they had been clear that he was expected to work. "If you don't work, there's no reason to keep feeding you." That was the wording used.

Rinde thought of Uju, the woman who'd worked with him for so many years. He still couldn't understand how the prime minister or his people had turned her into a spy, but he knew that she wouldn't have been able to say no. If she had tried, he wasn't sure she'd have even lived to see a place like the one he was in now. She would have had no value at all for them, and he would have just walked in to find a new aide one day. His hope was that Uju was still okay, and hadn't been disposed of anyway once he was no longer around.

Loud sounds alerted him to a key being shoved into the first of the heavy locks that secured his door. Rinde carried his glass and plate to the small kitchen, and placed them in the sink. He considered throwing away the bread, but knew he might want it when he returned. If there had been any containers, he would have placed it in the food storage. Instead, he pulled out another plate and flipped it over to lie on top of the partially eaten bread, hoping that would be enough to keep it for the day.

The door was pushed open on rusty hinges, and he winced at the sound that sent shivers down his spine. "Brighton," the guard at the door called. "Time for your shift." Rinde stepped into the hallway, pausing to let the guard lock the door. He was surprised when the door was left wide open, but then realized he had no possessions to steal.

He was led through seemingly miles of twisting and turning corridors. Up and down in elevators. By the end, he was so lost that finding his tiny room in the warren of doors would be impossible. Stepping into a large chamber filled with people, he was shocked at how silent it was. There wasn't even a whisper of conversation as people stepped into neoprene suits that covered them from neck to toes. The guard ushered Rinde to a locker, pointed at the number, told him to memorize it, and then told him to get dressed. When he pulled down on the metal latch and opened the door, the scent of neoprene filled his nostrils and made him sneeze.

By the time he'd pulled and tugged the suit up to cover the threadbare clothes they issued him the day before, hundreds of others were already lined up at doors on the far side of the room. "If you're not in line when the buzzer sounds, you'll be punished," the guard told him emotionlessly. Rinde hurried to join the nearest queue, stepping into place only seconds before the sound that signaled the doors were opening. He looked around at the people near him, noticing a lack of expression across most faces. Some were old, some were young, but most were in that middle range where you couldn't decide on an exact age just by looking at them. All of them shuffled forward listlessly, following those in front as the lines moved deeper into the factory complex.

The next chamber was a massive room spreading out in all directions. Rinde could see that it was some sort of station, a place where you could find transport to the section you were assigned to work in. The guard pushed him toward a desk just inside the doors where a bored woman sat with her chin resting in her hand. "Another new one?" she asked the guard, ignoring him completely.

"A new pain in my ass every day," the guard said, scowling at Rinde.

The woman behind the desk typed at her console for a few minutes, a grin spreading across her face at the end. "The furnace needs another body." She turned her eyes to him for the first time, looking him up and down. "He looks like he could last a few weeks down there."

The guard only shrugged. "Not my problem, once I get him where he's going."

After a few more keystrokes, the woman waved for the guard's palm-sized tablet. He stepped forward and waved it over a scanner on top of the desk, and a loud ping verified that the assignment details had been transferred. She put her chin back in her hand as the guard shoved Rinde toward a dull red sign a few hundred meters away.

The few dozen people standing near that sign looked exhausted already. Some were swaying on their feet, as if holding themselves up by sheer will. Rinde wouldn't have been surprised if one or two had dropped dead while he looked at them, as frail as they seemed to be. For the first time, he was truly worried about the situation he found himself in.

At first he had been certain he could withstand whatever torture they attempted, that his principles would not be broken. For those first few hours after he was dragged from his office, sitting in the back of a dark car with two soldiers up front that refused to speak, he'd even been furious. How could they expect to arrest the Minister of Defense and get away with it? The other cabinet members would demand an explanation. They would call for his release, and fight the injustice behind it.

But he'd known it wouldn't happen. Had they complained when he was excluded from meetings? No, because they were told that the prime minister had a reason to exclude him. He doubted that anyone would even know he'd disappeared until days or weeks had passed. Most of his contact had been with people off planet or in the far reaches of Coalition territory. The kinds of people who had little clout with the leadership behind his detainment.

After the car stopped and he'd been shown into a room of featureless gray, he'd been unconcerned. Hours passed as he sat in that room, with no sign of another person.

Even banging on the door and demanding a trip to the bathroom had elicited no response. *Psychological tricks,* he'd thought, finally resorting to using a small trash can as a toilet.

When two soldiers did finally enter the room, they never spoke. They only shoved him down a hallway into a dented old shuttle with blacked out windows. A few other people already occupied most of the handful of hard seats, looking as disheveled and dirty as he felt. The soldiers pushed him down into a seat, strapped him in, and enabled the security lock on the restraints. Rinde wondered at that, but thought they were merely transporting him to another place for whatever interrogation was planned.

Seconds after he felt the shuttle's thrusters push them from the ground, a light mist filled the cabin. He could remember faintly wondering what it was, and then nothing until he woke up and found himself being pulled from the shuttle. He was groggy and his head felt like it was stuffed with cotton as they walked through the twisting hallways, barking rules and regulations at him that he only half heard.

His memories were interrupted by a loud grating noise as a maglev train car appeared. The old system was not being maintained as well as it should have been, and Rinde felt apprehensive about entering that scratched and battered car. A shove between his shoulder blades reminded him that he had no choice, and he filed in with the other wretches who had been waiting at the red sign. They all kept their distance as well as they could in the tight confines, heads down so they weren't tempted to make eye contact with the guard that glared around with his lip raised in disgust.

The trip wasn't long, and they arrived at their destination in less than ten minutes. For the last half of the trip, the car had grown warmer every second. When it squealed to a stop, Rinde felt as if he had already sweated through this ragged clothing. The neoprene suit was chafing his skin, and he was only hotter because of the now uncomfortable weight of it.

Exiting onto a platform made of grated mesh plates, he was roughly guided to a corridor beside a small room where more guards sat in climate controlled comfort staring at monitors. His guard knocked on the clear plastic window, and held up the small tablet showing Rinde's assignment to the section. One of the guards in the room nodded, and waved for them to follow the line of people shuffling through a small scanner. Rinde was pushed under the scanner, waiting for a second as it looked for any weapons or contraband materials, and then shoved deeper into the complex. Beyond the scanners, he found a small room with tiny lockers. The guard told him to find his number, which confused him until he remembered the large locker before the train station.

Inside the locker he found a small rebreather. It fit his mouth, with two thumb-sized projections to either side that would filter the air he breathed. He wasn't familiar with equipment like this, but thought he remembered seeing articles about the filters only being good for a few hours. There were no extra filters in the locker, and when he turned to ask about them the guard only snarled and pointed to the next door.

Rinde had thought the heat was intense before, but as soon as the heavy steel doors opened, a blast of superheated air washed over him. He almost reached up to make sure his eyebrows hadn't been burned off, before remembering the thick gloves that kept him from feeling anything at all. None of the others around him reacted at all, telling him it was a feeling he'd have to grow accustomed to.

The next room was the furnace. Great cauldrons were filled with molten metals, heated from below by ovens that he knew must reach nearly a thousand degrees or more. Rinde turned to look to his guard for direction, but the man had disappeared. He was left to figure out the work on his own, or so he thought until a baton slammed against his right thigh.

"Get to work, maggot!" A man was glaring at him through the thick visor of a shiny suit. Rinde knew the guard wasn't feeling much of the heat from within that protection.

"Where?" He asked. "What do I do?"

The baton was held out, pointing toward the shambling group of suffering wretches he'd shared the train car with. "Do what they do, and learn quickly. No one leaves until your quota is met."

It took more than thirteen hours to complete the work needed for the excessive quotas. By the end, Rinde could barely stand. They were permitted a break every hour to drink a bottle of water, but he felt as if he sweated that out again within five minutes. The boots of his suit were so full of liquid that he could almost imagine he was wading through a shallow river.

As he shuffled along with the others, anxious to leave the forge and return to cooler air and the relative comfort of his cramped room, another man banged against his shoulder with every step. Rinde looked up to croak out a plea to stop, but closed his mouth when he saw the man holding a finger over his lips. "I'm Rawls. Hang tough. The Guild is coming."

Before Rinde could work up a reply, the man had melted away in the small crowd. He searched in the locker room, on the platform, in the train car, and in the room where he finally peeled off the neoprene suit.   There was no sign of the man who'd called himself Rawls. He could only wonder at the man's words. How could the Guild know where he was, and what did it mean that they were coming?

THIRTY THREE

After more than two days of digging out rubble, the transit tunnel between the domes had been almost completely cleared. Tom was on his third inspection of the work for the day, stopping to give praise to the people who had devoted time to the job. These men and women were researchers, scientists, and former government workers. For them to dedicate themselves to manual labor in the interests of helping anyone still hiding in Armstrong was proof to him of the spirit of compassion in humanity.

Dexterity Avila had joined him on this inspection, and was as effusive with praise as he was. "I can't believe so much has been done in such a short time."

"These people have been filled with worry and anxiety for weeks. We've given them something to do to work those feelings out, and also gave them a sense of accomplishment. People may be selfish sometimes, ma'am, but give them a chance and they'll prove they care about their neighbors just as much."

"I only wish the people on Earth were in the spirit to prove that. They're so busy fighting each other, they still haven't bothered to ask what's going on up here. Luna is a forgotten backwater, as far as the news programs and politicians are concerned."

Tom stopped walking, and leaned against a pile of the larger rubble. "I saw the latest reports. The Syndicate has taken half of Europe now."

"Only several hundred kilometers from Geneva," Dex said. "The security forces are finally fighting back, though. That's slowed the advance."

"We'll see if it's enough. If they bring in the *Indomitable* to provide orbital support, I don't know that it will matter how many soldiers the Coalition throws into the defense."

"Yes." Dex frowned. "We still can't figure out why that cruiser hasn't moved. Surely any damage from the battles with the Coalition fleet is repaired by now."

"Overconfidence, maybe. The general of the ground forces could feel he doesn't need the Fleet taking credit for the win." Tom pushed off and resumed his walk through the tunnel, the sounds of repairs filling the air as they entered an area where the steel plates securing the tunnel walls and roof were being reinforced. "What's the latest update on Armstrong? I'd like to get these people working on that last bit of obstruction, and have this tunnel fully cleared."

"Integrity of the dome is confirmed, so the engineering teams are going to run the first tests on the reactor repairs tonight. If that goes well, they'll move on to testing the life support systems. We've already covered the exposed lunar surface, and begun the process to clear any particles from the air. With luck, we'll be ready to turn on the lights tomorrow morning. Figuratively and literally."

"Lights will be good," Tom laughed. "My squads are not enjoying combing the buildings in darkness, especially after the incident with Dr. Baat. They're seeing monsters around every corner."

"Captain, has President Meyers shared his plans with you? For Armstrong, I mean."

"No, ma'am. I just know he wants to move some people over there to start rebuilding."

"That's part of the goal. The president has many contacts on Earth, and we have quite a large number of

248

people that will hopefully be joining us soon. We need to have Armstrong ready for them when they arrive."

Tom frowned, wondering if they were taking in refugees from the war zones now. "If the dome's systems can be restored, I can get Armstrong cleared faster. Then we can start working to prep buildings for new occupants before we clear the debris at the center of the dome."

Dex sighed. "It may take years for Armstrong's square to be rebuilt. Especially since we're going to have to put a lot of our resources into the militia and our fleet of freighters, for the inevitable day when Earth decides they want Luna back."

"Get me the people, and we'll train them," Tom promised. They had looped around now and were headed back to Aldrin dome. "The *Vagabond* should be back soon?"

"Not soon enough for Mira's liking," Dex said with a smile that he shared. "She's pushing as hard as Erik will let her, but the *Waterloo* is still hours ahead of them. Tomorrow afternoon is the current ETA for the frigate."

"I'm looking forward to the light show," Tom said, trying to make it sound like a joke. He had spent an hour sharing drinks with the squad leaders the night before, and those with experience aboard ships had been certain the Coalition frigate wouldn't stand a chance if they tried to go up against the larger Syndicate cruiser. Five hundred to one were the odds being offered by an enterprising gambler.

Once their inspection tour was complete, Dex parted ways to return to the Guildhall. Tom watched her walk away, calling out greetings to people she passed. He marveled at her ability to remember names of people she'd probably spoken to only once or twice before. It was amazing to see the woman transforming into a politician before his eyes.

"Captain Fitz," someone called out, and he turned to see one of the construction team leaders waving him over. "I think we found some of the bomb fragments, sir."

Tom hurried over and bent to examine the tiny bits of warped metal shards. One woman was pushing them around with a bit of steel rebar from the debris, flipping one piece over as he watched. No larger than his thumbnail, the newly exposed side had writing on it. Gray letters on a cobalt background. Tom scooped up the fragment, sliding it into a pocket.

"Gather all of it that you can find," he told the people gathered around. "Don't touch it, but get it into bags so we can have it examined." He stood back as they combed the area, his arms crossed and lips tightly compressed. If the bit of metal in his pocket was what he thought, things were about to get much more complicated.

A few hours later, he left one of the dome's laboratories carrying a small box filled with the bomb's remnants. The report on their composition and most probable explosive materials was on his tablet, kept away from any network location where it could be vulnerable if someone with the right skills wanted to poke around. The Guildhall was his destination, and he'd already placed a call to Dex asking for an urgent meeting with Meyers.

The guards on the door saluted as he approached, a fist over heart gesture that he had put in place instead of the traditional fingers to brow. It would minimize any unwanted momentum in zero or low gravity, and also kept hands closer to weapons. He returned the salute, passing through the doorway into a long hall stuffed full of desks and people. Sometimes, he wondered if someone showed up every night with a couple more to cram into whatever space was available.

Dex was waiting outside the president's office, and raised her eyebrows inquisitively as he approached. He held up the box in answer, but didn't speak until they were both inside and the door was closed. President Meyers looked up from his terminal, and rose to greet the leader of his militia.

"Captain, good to see you again. Dex said you have something important you wanted to discuss?"

"Yes, sir. Something I don't think other people should hear about."

Meyers nodded, and pressed a few buttons on his desk. "The office is secure. What's going on, Tom?"

In response, he set the box on the desk and popped open the lid to show them what was inside. "One of the teams clearing rubble found this material. I've had it tested, and it's confirmed that this was the casing of the bomb that exploded in the tunnel."

Meyers leaned over and looked at the shards, turning a questioning look on Tom. "We knew there had to be a bomb. It's nice to see we found it, but I'm not sure why it's so important."

Tom pulled the small bit of metal from his pocket, laying it gently on the desk next to the box. The letters were face up, and he heard a gasp from Dex as she read what was there. -ARI- in large letters on the top line, -DNAN- in smaller letters below it. Combined with the coloring, there was only one thing it could be.

"Coalition Marine ordnance," he said. "This wasn't just any bomb, sir. I've seen devices like this before, they're used by Marine strike forces for boarding enemy ships or assaulting positions on the ground. They've rarely been used in the last few decades, but every ship in the Navy has a few crates full of them. There are probably some in warehouses on Earth, as well. But you'll never find it anywhere else."

"My God," Meyers said, dropping into his chair. "I'd already been sure Geneva was behind the bombings, but this is proof."

"It's not just that," Tom said, pulling out his tablet and swiping through a few pages until he found the report he wanted. "They found traces of DNA on some of the fragments. On the *inside* of the casing."

Meyers pulled the tablet closer, reading over the text. "We got a match?"

"Yes, sir. We still have the Coalition databases from the server in the administration building. One marker is from a corporal, her last known posting was in Cartagena. Based on her service record, she's in the quartermaster corps. I'm thinking she handled the device when it was being stored somewhere." He paused, and put a finger on the tablet. "The other result belongs to a man named Theodore Poul. I've never heard of him, but apparently he's got some position on the cabinet now."

"Minister of Propaganda," Dex said. She was shaking her head, but her eyes were bright. "It fits with your theory, sir. This is exactly the kind of proof we needed. There's no way he could say he'd come into contact with the explosives in any other way."

"We need to keep this information confined to just the three of us," Meyers said, looking at the two standing near his desk. "Who ran the tests? I'll need to make sure we lock them down until we have the chance to reveal our findings."

"I requested the highest security," Tom assured him. "The tech who ran the tests didn't have clearance to see the results. They were sent directly to my tablet."

"That was good thinking, Captain Fitz. I'm glad to see I chose the right man for the job. Dex told you that we're expecting an influx of newcomers fairly soon?"

"Something like that."

"I can't give you exact numbers at the moment, but I'd plan for around a thousand. If everything goes exactly to plan, it could be closer to fifteen hundred."

Tom whistled. "That's a lot of extra mouths to feed, sir. How soon are we expecting them?"

Meyers looked toward Dex, and she tapped her nails on the desk as she spoke. "We received word from one of our people a few minutes before you arrived, captain. Thirty six hours, forty eight at the most. Sooner than I'd been expecting, so we'll need your construction teams to work fast to prepare places for them once you're able to enter Armstrong."

"I've put a rush on the engineers," Meyers added. "We should have results from their testing by zero three hundred tomorrow."

"I'll have my squads increase the pace of their sweeps," Tom said. "As soon as these new people arrive, we'll have a place ready for them."

Thirty Four

"Colonel Rozier, are you telling me that you refuse to follow my explicit orders?"

"That is correct, captain. Your orders go against the military code of conduct, and as such I am honor bound to refuse them."

Guildersen stared at the Marine commander, his eyes wide from disbelief at the man's impudence. It was bad enough that fewer than a dozen of the harsh punishments he'd ordered had been followed through. To now stand in front of the ship's commanding officer and flat out say you weren't going to follow his orders? That was the barest form of mutiny.

He pressed a button on his desk, and the doors of his office slid open as the two guards on the door entered in response. A full squad had been dedicated to the rotating duty cycle, and he'd spent his time wisely in buttering them up. He handed out favors to the Marines, and offered them perks their fellow soldiers could only dream of. In return, they were invested in making sure he maintained his position. That was the only kind of loyalty he'd ever trust.

"Take the colonel into custody. He's relieved of his command."

Rozier stiffened at the words, his lip twisting in disgust. "You don't have the authority for that, Guildersen. My Marines may be attached to your ship, but we follow your commands as a courtesy only. I report to my general, and he's the only one who can tell me to step down."

Guildersen chuckled, folding his hands over his mountainous stomach. "That may be how things work on the planet, colonel, but on this ship I am God. There is no one higher, and only the Executive Committee can tell me what I can or can't do." He waved his fingers, and the door guards stepped forward to restrain the colonel. He couldn't resist the rolling laughter that welled up from within as he watched the proud Marine officer struggle while being forcefully pulled from the office. Perhaps after a few days in a cell, the man would come around. If not, it would be no loss to send one more person through an airlock.

"Now," he said quietly, "to deal with my so-called first officer." He pressed another button on his desk.

"Vegley," the sharp reply was almost instantaneous.

"Commander, come into my office. Now." Guildersen's lip curled as he pictured the snarling expression the woman would wear after being so perfunctorily called before him. Especially when she was standing near other senior officers on the command deck, all of whom would have heard his casual disregard of her rank and authority.

Vegley entered several minutes later. Quick enough to follow his command, but long enough for everyone on the command deck to see that she wasn't rushing to obey him at the drop of his hat. It was the sort of move Guildersen himself would have pulled. Had pulled, in fact, many times during his tenure under Admiral Yumata.

"What can I do for you, captain?"

He considered her for half a minute, knowing that the stretched out silence made her feel uncomfortable. Colonel Rozier had failed to dig up dirt on his XO, but in light of the man's recent refusal to follow orders he now had to consider that the two officers had been in collusion against him. Guildersen made a mental note to talk to the sergeant of his personal guards, to have them work on finding something that would allow him to rid himself of the troublesome commander.

"I've received the latest reports, Vegley. Not only are the construction crews still not working on the needed repairs to our weapons and defense systems, I now see several capacitor issues appearing across the ship. What excuse do you have for something so critical not being repaired?"

Her eyes were focused a foot above his head. "Captain, we only had a few people on board trained in those systems. You tossed them all through an airlock several days ago."

Guildersen sniffed, narrowing his eyes and glaring at the woman. "If they earned that punishment, then they were useless simpletons anyway. Get me more people to do the work, commander. This is the last time I'll tell you how to do your job. Do you understand me, Vegley?"

"Sir, the only people Earth will send are the new officer school graduates next week. I've requested replacements for the people you've *murdered* many times, but they tell me to coordinate with the orbital station."

He chose to ignore her blatant attempt to get a rise from him, contenting himself with a serene smile and a leer. "And you are too incompetent to contact the orbital station and requisition the personnel we need. Yet another failure on your record, Vegley. I wish that I could feel surprised." He raised a hand and waggled his fingers. "Get back to the bridge. Maybe you can find one or two things you're capable of handling without my help."

Vegley was fuming as she turned and stomped from the room, putting him in a great mood as he typed in the commands to initiate a connection to the Syndicate's orbital station. Guildersen knew that his old commander was aboard, and grimaced again as he thought of the video call he'd reluctantly agreed to the next morning. He couldn't understand why Yumata had been allowed to leave Earth at all. His contacts on the Executive Committee had assured him many times that the admiral was corralled and would pose no difficulties going forward.

Commander Singh's face appeared on the screen after a short wait. The man looked harassed and tired, just the mood Guildersen had been hoping for. He wasted no time on pleasantries. "Commander Singh, I'm still waiting on those people I ordered you to send over. Now I need more. You will have fifty people packed and waiting tomorrow at noon System Standard Time. A shuttle will be sent over to collect them."

The station's commander opened his mouth, but Guildersen killed the connection. He didn't care if the man were about to protest or agree to his demands. All that mattered is that he needed people, and he would have them. One way or another. He typed up a quick note to his guard squad's sergeant, ordering six of the Marines to go to the station on the shuttle. They would ensure cooperation. Perhaps he'd even order Singh brought over. It would be a wonderful example of the reach of his power if the man faced one of the harshest punishments.

His pleasant musings were interrupted by a chirping communication from the command deck. "What is it, lieutenant?"

"Captain, sensors just picked up a ship approaching. They're about an hour out from Earth, and the readings are showing it to be a frigate."

"What?!" Guildersen sat up, his fingers gripping the edges of his desk in alarm. "Where did a frigate come from?"

257

"Visible markings seem to match up to the *Waterloo*, sir. A Coalition frigate, the one boarded by our Ghost Squad before the first fleet battle."

Guildersen ground his teeth in frustration. It had been less than a week since the destruction of what he thought were the last Coalition vessels, and now a new one shows up to surprise him. Would there ever be an end to the constant obstacles in his path? "Watch that ship closely, lieutenant. I want to know where they're headed, and when they'll arrive."

His only hope was that the *Waterloo* had been damaged by Lieutenant Davis's team. If the *Indomitable* had the advantage, he would order the attack and remove the ship before they had an opportunity to repair and recognize his own inferior status.

His other hope was that Davis hadn't managed to somehow wrest control of the ship, and was bringing it back to hand over to the Syndicate. Such a coup would reflect glory only on Yumata, a situation Guildersen didn't need to deal with at such a crucial time in his process of taking full control of the ship.

THIRTY FIVE

The *Waterloo* was five hours from Earth when they began receiving messages from the Admiralty. The first tried to pretend the weeks of silence hadn't occurred, welcoming the frigate back to the home world. When Fleet Admiral Holgerson responded, demanding to know why his standing orders to fight the Syndicate cruiser at any opportunity hadn't been followed, the tone of the messages changed.

The Admiralty began giving orders for them to divert their course. Too high a chance that the boarders were still in control of the ship, according to the sallow faced old man on the screen now wearing a Fleet Admiral's uniform. The sight of him caused Holgerson to go red with rage, and his knuckles were starkly white as he gripped the rail of the command deck with all his strength.

"They replaced me!" he hissed out. "With that coward who always had his nose buried in a minister's ass, of all people." Mags realized at that moment that everything they'd heard from Captain Frost and in messages from President Meyers was true. The leadership of the Coalition had lost their way. From the looks Captain Andrews had shared with her, he was feeling the same way.

When the frigate didn't change course or slow her approach, the messages from Earth became more threatening. The prime minister himself appeared on screen, demanding that the *Waterloo* change course and divert to Mars until the crisis on Earth was resolved and they could spare the time to deal with the people aboard the ship. He also referenced the boarding party, which Mags found interesting. They had sent messages about the Syndicate intruders, but those messages had been bounced back as undeliverable.

An hour from the planet, Holgerson called Andrews and Mags into his office. "We have a decision to make, and I don't want to do that without all of us being in agreement."

Captain Andrews held up a hand. "We both know what you're going to say, admiral, and there's no need. We agree." Mags nodded.

Holgerson looked at both of them for several seconds. "If we do this, it's officially a mutiny. It would be done for the right reasons, but that doesn't change the fact that we'll be breaking every rule in the book."

"It'll be entirely justified," Mags said through a smirk. "No offense, sir, but the crew of the ship have been in support of it for the last few hours."

Andrews snorted, turning to look at her. "Leave it to the XO to know the mood of the ship within minutes. If Mags is getting that information, admiral, then we can be sure it's the prevalent opinion."

"Very well, adjust our course and I'll make the announcement soon. Commander Richtaus, I'd like you to work with the docking bay to prepare shuttles for anyone who chooses not to join us."

Once the meeting was concluded, Mags traversed the ship to the docking bay. As she entered the small control room, she marveled that two people could stare at all those screens and make sense of what was going on. The lieutenant standing behind them turned at the sound of the door, and stiffened as he raised a hand in a salute. Mags laughed at the mug of coffee being held in the raised hand, and quickly returned the salute.

"Commander, what can we do for you today?"

"Lieutenant Simon, we need some shuttles prepared. I don't think we'll need many, but better prep half a dozen just to be safe." She strolled over to the wide windows at the side of the room, looking out over the vast docking bay. It was quiet at the moment, only a dozen or so people walking to their next tasks.

"What kind of journey should I prep the ships for?" Simon asked shrewdly.

Mags felt one side of her mouth twitch. "Planet and back, though I'm not sure if the return will happen."

There was a sound of pent up air releasing from lungs. "The admiral decided to join the Guild forces, didn't he?" She turned to arch an eyebrow at the lieutenant. "We've known it was coming for the last several days," he explained.

She turned back to the window, watching as a stream of crew members appeared in response to the orders sent down from the control room. A shuttle receiving upkeep maintenance on the wide deck was moved to make room, and cranes began to fill the bay with noise as more shuttles were removed from sturdy racks along the walls. Within fifteen minutes, four of them were already on the deck and had maintenance crews swarming over them.

The ship's comms chimed, and all action below ceased as everyone stopped what they were doing to look up. "*Waterloo*, this is Fleet Admiral Holgerson. I'm sure word of our situation has trickled down to all of you over the last few weeks. Over the last several hours, it has been made harshly clear to me that the Coalition has lost the desire to fight back against Syndicate aggression.

"We have been ordered by the Admiralty and the prime minister to divert to Mars, where we are to enter orbit and await orders. Ostensibly, they claim to be unsure if we're still under the control of Syndicate boarders. As a result, I have come to a decision that we must go against orders and continue along a new course for Luna. Once there, were will enter orbit alongside the Guild freighters.

"I anticipate initiating battle with the *Indomitable* within hours of our arrival. However, I know that not all of you will agree with my decision in what is effectively a mutiny. Therefore, shuttles are being readied now to take you to Earth if you wish to leave us. We'll enter orbit around Luna in twenty two minutes, and the first shuttles will depart within sixty seconds of that."

The comms chimed again, signaling an abrupt end to the announcement. Mags was pleased to see the people on the deck below return to work with visible reluctance. She hoped it was a sign that they didn't think the shuttles would be in great demand. She felt a presence at her side and glanced over to see Lieutenant Simon standing next to her. "The admiral is doing the right thing, commander. We've all seen the reports about the Syndicate invasion, and we know opposition is only being raised now because soldiers are disobeying their commanders. Everyone I know shares that same feeling, the desire to fight for our homes even if those in power have decided not to do so for some inexplicable reason."

Mags wrapped a hand around his arm in mute thanks for the show of support. "I think most of us have family down there, lieutenant. I have a brother, several nieces and nephews. I don't know how they're going to feel about what I do, but I'm not going to sit back and wait at Mars while I hope they make it through okay. I'm going to fight. For them, and for me."

"Yes, ma'am," he said, surprising her with the snap of a quick salute. He gave her a boyish grin before turning away to stand behind the two crew members monitoring the cameras and communications.

Minutes ticked by, seeming to go slower as they got closer to Luna. Once they arrived, Captain Andrews announced it over the comms and Mags started a mental countdown. The first shuttle was prepped and ready to depart in exactly sixty seconds. The air in the control room was thick with the tension, as the four occupants waited to see how many would want to leave the ship.

Her mental countdown was only seconds away from elapsing, when a few people entered the docking bay doors. She stopped breathing, watching them look around uncertainly as they approached the shuttles. The mechanics and other crew on the deck were loitering around the walls, watching as carefully as she was while the people approached the nearest shuttle. The door on the side lowered, and the pilot stepped forward. He looked up at the control room as the two people rushed aboard the shuttle, and shrugged.

"We'll wait until the shuttle is full," Mags said, hoping that it wouldn't happen.

Five minutes later, only seven people were aboard the shuttle and it had been more than a minute since the last of them arrived. She reported in to the bridge, and got a happy grunt from Holgerson in reply. "Send them down, commander, and then stow the shuttles we won't have to use."

"Yes, admiral." As the connection ended, she turned a wide grin on Simon. "You heard the man, lieutenant. Get those people on the way, and button things up in here."

She had turned to leave when Simon called for her attention. "The pilot, commander. He doesn't want to leave, and frankly we're all a bit convinced that once that shuttle is on Earth it's not coming back again."

"Ah. Give me roster of the passengers." She stepped over to one of the control room consoles, looking over the shoulder of a crew woman as she brought up the seven names on a screen. Mags examined their postings, and pointed at one of them. "That one has experience as copilot on supply shuttles before he joined the Navy. He can pilot the shuttle with the computer's assistance."

"Yes, ma'am," Lieutenant Simon said happily. "We'll get them on the way as quick as we can."

Mags was feeling elated on the journey back to the bridge. She'd expected the majority of the ship to share her feelings about the decision to partner with the Guild, but seeing only seven out of hundreds wanting to leave the frigate was a roaring acclamation of approval.

Back on the command deck, Andrews was standing at the rail staring at the planet rising over the small bulk of Luna. She joined him, sharing the silent contemplation for several minutes. "I've spent perhaps two months of the last twenty years on Earth," the captain said wistfully, "and yet it always feels like home when I look at it. How long do you think humanity will experience that, as we expand to other stars?"

"I grew up in Ottawa," she said with a grin. "Want to guess what my dad still says when people ask where he's from? Germany, every single time. It's been six generations since my family left Dresden, and yet he still proudly says he's German." She snorted a laugh. "Hell, I find myself doing the same thing."

Andrews nodded in understanding. "But Germany is a ninety minute shuttle ride away. Will our great grandchildren be calling themselves Earthers when that

264

planet is light years away? They'll probably never even visit our solar system in their lifetimes, unless we figure out how to build faster than light drives."

"They may well call themselves Martians or Lunans, the way things are going," Holgerson said from behind. Mags bit her lip to keep from crying out in surprise, once again wondering how the man could be so quiet on his feet. "I'm taking my shuttle down to Aldrin, captain. Maintain orbit until you hear from me. Commander, you're coming with me."

She looked at him in surprise. "Are you sure, sir? I'm not what most people would call diplomatic."

"No, but I need your bluntness," the admiral said through a chuckle.

Finding herself retracing steps back to the docking bay, Mags was filled with questions about what was waiting in the dome. She'd seen stories in their newly restored newsfeeds about unrest after the bombings, but hadn't paid attention to many since she was looking for more information about Earth. The admiral's shuttle was on the deck and waiting, his pilot standing at erect attention beside the short ramp. She followed him, and found a richly appointed interior. There were only half a dozen seats, but they were built for maximum comfort. Displays were built into trays that could swivel up to any position the viewer found comfortable.

Admiral Holgerson waved her to a seat near the one he selected, and they were soon departing the *Waterloo* for the short flight to the surface of Luna. Mags pulled up the external feeds on her seat's display, watching as the gray dust of the moon grew closer. She could see scars in the surface where docking platforms had been destroyed in the bombs, beside two new docking pads and a half completed third. The shuttle was directed to the first, a smaller one that had been built hastily to restore access to the dome without having to get into pressure suits and walk the surface.

Once through the airlocks, they were greeted by a man she recognized from the frequent videos they'd received over the last few weeks. President Meyers was effusive with his welcome, shaking hands vigorously before introducing them to the beautiful woman standing at his side. "Dexterity Avila has been my right hand through all the hardships and struggle. She officially became vice president of the Guild a few weeks ago."

As they walked through the streets of Aldrin, Mags was surprised to see people scurrying around. It was clear the dome was operating as usual, and from the smiles he received it was also clear the people here appreciated everything Meyers and his Guild had done to help them. When they reached the central square, she half expected to be led into the administration building. However, it was dark and the doors were blocked with yellow tape.

"We haven't fully cut ties with the Coalition yet," Dexterity said, noticing the direction of her gaze. "Until we do, the dome's administration building remains untouched."

"The Guild has taken over everything else," Mags said. "Why not run things from there?"

Dexterity eyed the building, and Mags thought she could see a hint of disgust in the other woman's eyes. "The Guildhall serves our purposes, for now."

Curious faces looked up from dozens of desks as they entered the Guildhall, gazes filled with hopeful inquisitiveness. Mags was tempted to ask what that was about, but kept her mouth shut as they were led into the office at the end of the building. Meyers motioned for them to take seats around a small table that looked as if it had been

266

brought in just for this meeting. There were only four chairs at the round table, and it's placement in the room meant it would be in the way of everyday flow.

"So," President Meyers said, "how did you like the fusion reactor technology?"

"It's quite impressive," Holgerson acknowledged. "Our engineers and technical teams seem to come up with new ideas for the increased power every day."

Meyers laughed, sharing a look with Dexterity. "The crews of our freighters are doing the same thing. Most are impractical with current technology, but they promise great things for our future."

"Indeed. I've approved research into several proposals." Holgerson leaned forward, clasping his hands on the table. "What did you have to share that couldn't be said on a video feed, President Meyers?"

Mags and the admiral listened in shock to the story of the bomb fragments, and looked at the small remnant and the letters on it. Holgerson seemed to deflate as the story was related, and she saw his eyes go dull as the evidence of Coalition complicity was placed on the table. "So that's it," he said, barely above a whisper.

"That could have come from anywhere," Mags said, trying to lend him strength. "Some enlisted in a warehouse could have taken one or two explosives from a crate and sold it to anyone."

Holgerson only shook his head. "They're closely monitored. The Marines keep a record of every one, checking them monthly to maintain control of their supply. If this was removed from a ship or warehouse, there would have to be records of it."

"Then we find the record, and we know who took it," Mags reasoned.

Meyers shrugged. "You could do that to find out who else is complicit, but finding Minister Poul's DNA inside the casing tells us he's involved somehow. He couldn't have placed any explosives on Luna, since we have no records of his travel here, but he was in every location on Earth that was hit."

"Okay," Mags said, frowning at the bits of metal on the table. "Where does that leave us? We know that at least part of the government is working against Coalition interests, possibly collaborating with the Syndicate."

"Probably," Dexterity said quietly.

"My point is, how do we go about stopping them and then pushing the Syndicate back to where they belong?"

Meyers was grinning, his facing growing more animated as she talked. "Let me tell you about something I have in the works on Earth, and share my thoughts for what we can do up here."

THIRTY SIX

After nearly a full day of patiently inputting password guesses, Altan finally remembered the lines of code he had seen in *Count of Monte Cristo*. Wondering if they might help him he navigated the menu to find and click on the picture of Josie's smiling face, noticing that she now appeared to be winking. As soon as he tapped the icon, the screen of the tablet went black and lines of white code began to scroll across it.

Several minutes later, the tablet rebooted. *It's about time, Alt* appeared on the screen as a greeting before the icons showed up. A new icon was visible, in the middle of the first screen. The picture was an old world padlock, with the hasp open. Altan considered it for a few moments before tapping the screen. The only thing that displayed was a chuck of code several pages long. He didn't understand much of it, but from what he could glean it appeared to be transfer instructions.

Navigating the cruiser's operating system had been relatively easy, since he had years of experience working with parts of it. He was surprised to find that he'd learned more from listening to Mira complain about her work on the bridge than expected. She'd often moaned about the clunky programs she had to work around whenever they had her review log entries or AI flags. That knowledge allowed him to find the system container where bridge crew often stored copies of files until those reviews were completed.

Then he had to wait and watch. As soon as he saw a chunk of data marked complete, he knew he'd have no more than half a minute to open it, insert quick changes, and save his work before the person on the bridge copied it back into the operating system structure again. His first several attempts took too long, resulting in increasing frustration as he failed.

Tuya was so close! Altan would stand at his door for long stretches, his head leaning against the cool metal surface, imagining the moment of stepping into the hallway and seeing his sister again. It had been twelve years since he left home, eight years since he'd last seen her face over video link. He felt like he'd watched his sister grow up on the screen. Her face and body had changed in subtle ways every time he was able to talk with her for an hour or so, telling stories of his latest adventures aboard a Guild freighter.

A soft beep was his notification that a file structure had been placed within the system container, drawing him away from the door to return to his bed and tablet. This was the fifth time watching the screen update with the changes made to the chunk of coding, and it would be his fourth attempt at inserting the code from the new icon.

As soon as the completion flag was inserted, his fingers flew across his tablet screen. He could feel his body tensing up as he urged the connection to move faster. The lines of code he needed to insert into the data chunk were already copied so that he only need to paste them once he found the specific section it needed to be placed in. Altan could feel the seconds ticking by as sweat dripped down his face and his fingers started to cramp.

Thirty seconds.

The file would be moved out soon, cancelling any unsaved changes. He finally found the correct location in the strings of code, and scrambled to bring up the menu.

Thirty three seconds.

Altan couldn't believe the file was still there. He pressed the button to paste in the new code, and watched as the progress bar steadily filled in.

Thirty seven seconds.

Copy complete! He swiped his finger on the screen frantically to find the end of the data chunk. Doing so, he loudly cursed whatever idiot had decided the option to save changes should be at the bottom. It had to be some middle management type who never worked with the protocols they created.

Forty one seconds.

He finally made it to the end, and stabbed his finger down to press the button that would save the data file changes. His lungs were working as if he'd just spent ten minutes running around his small room, and he was drenched with stress sweat. But the smile that spread across his face was radiant. All his work had been worthwhile, and the code would begin to spread through the cruiser's systems.

Altan tried reading to pass the time, but his mind refused to concentrate on the words and he often found himself reading the same line three or four times. He was too amped up to sleep, so he rolled off the bed and ran his body through a series of exercises. He ran in place, dropped to the ground for push ups, anything he could think of to burn off the energy.

Within an hour, the adrenaline had left his system and he was feeling washed out and exhausted. He splashed himself with water to wash away the sweat, and changed into the new white prisoner jumpsuit that had been pushed through the door slot with his last meal. Feeling refreshed, he flopped down on his uncomfortable bed and waited for the results of his work.

He didn't have to wait long. No more than a few hours after he slumped onto the bed, the door of his cell slid open and a Marine guard stepped in. "On your feet, prisoner. You're being transferred."

"What's going on?" Altan asked, feigning surprise. "Where are you taking me?"

"No questions." The Marine stepped closer and wrapped his arm in a strong grip, pulling him from the room he'd been confined in for half a year. Several other Marines were in the short hallway beyond, where three other doors were open. Altan tried to hide his interest as he watched the door he'd last seen Tuya in from the corner of his eyes, keeping his face turned away in case the Marines were watching him.

His sister was not the first prisoner he saw, however. A disheveled man near the end of the hall on the same side as his cell was hurled out of a door, slamming against the opposite wall. "What the hell, Mika?" the prisoner yelled out. He staggered to his feet and turned aggressively to face the Marine exiting his room. "I'm supposed to be released tomorrow. Why the hell am I getting transferred?"

"Orders," the Marine said gruffly, seemingly as unhappy about it as the prisoner. "All occupants of this cell block are being transferred, and that's all I know."

Altan bit his lip, inwardly cursing himself for not searching out a roster of the cells. He'd assumed it would still be only Tuya and himself, after Richard had been removed during the short breakout attempt. He groaned when another unknown face exited a room, a youngish woman still wearing the uniform of the ship's crew. From her red-rimmed eyes and hands holding her head, he guessed she must have been picked a few hours before to sleep off whatever alcohol or drugs she'd put into her system.

272

"I don't remember asking for a wakeup call," the woman groused, slumping against the wall on unsteady feet. "Anyone got a hit of zoom? Hair of the dog, yeah?"

The man and woman were pushed toward the end of the hall, where they joined Altan in getting restraints strapped around their wrists. Once that was done, one of the Marines kept a weapon trained on them while three others advanced on the cell he'd last seen Tuya in. He couldn't help but grin as the sight of how seriously they were treating her as a threat.

His smile slipped when the diminutive woman with features so similar to his own was pushed roughly from the room. Her prison jumpsuit had no sleeves, and he could see angry red scars lacing her arms. Altan remembered the *Vagabond* crew telling him that Tuya had gotten implants, and knew that what he was seeing were the remnants of surgery to remove them. Not very long ago based on the look of them. He was impressed and proud that she was handling herself so well. Based on the stories he'd always heard, once the implants were removed a person was left with very little muscle mass.

Angry eyes swept the hallway, and slid across him before changing course and coming back to lock on his face. He offered a faint smile, and saw hope infuse her face. "Altan," she breathed, barely audible across the distance. He nodded once, then raised a hand to scratch his nose while making a motion to keep quiet. Tuya understood immediately, but her eyes remained on his face as the four prisoners were pushed into the hallways and told to walk.

Their progress was slow, all the more so since they could only move as fast as the hungover woman. She seemed to stumble every few steps and tripped several times a minute. Eventually, two Marines locked their hands around her arms and almost carried her along as they picked up the pace. The entire time, the man complained that he was supposed to be released. His comments were always directed at the Marine named Mika, and Altan wondered if they might not have been partners on patrols.

Altan wondered what location had been specified in his inserted code, and hoped it hadn't caught the attention of some officer who would question the transfers. He could feel himself tensing up as they got closer and closer, but at the same time he was enjoying being so near his sister again. Their arms bumped now and then, and a quick glance showed his joyful smile mirrored on her face. He hoped he had a chance to get to know his sister again.

THIRTY SEVEN

"Selene, I have to get aboard the *Indomitable*. It's the only way I can get the repair and installation process moving."

"Hiro, you know how the Executive Committee feels about that. They won't allow you anywhere near that ship, and Guildersen refuses to work with you if you did get there."

Yumata sighed and shook his head. "The *Waterloo* has returned and seemingly thrown in her lot with the Guild. If they decide to send all those ships to attack the *Indomitable*, they have a greater chance of victory than I'm comfortable with. Not to mention the frigate arrived much sooner than it should have, so there's no telling what kind of technology they've stumbled on to make that possible. Tell the Executive Committee they can either let me get aboard my cruiser, or watch it fall from orbit along with any hope to command the skies."

The chairwoman looked at him, her shrewd eyes seeming to see through his plans. "I'll speak with them, and see what I can arrange. Continue working with the officers on the ship from the station. The last of the resupply shipments should be delivered within a few hours, thanks to your work convincing them to at least unload those shuttles."

He bowed slightly before the connection was ended. Commander Singh was waiting just out of view of the camera, and chuckled as the screen went black. "I think you might just get that permission, admiral."

"The *Waterloo*'s unforeseen arrival is providing more of a goad than anything I could do, certainly."

"If you get approval soon, at least you won't have to wait too long. We have a resupply shuttle docking at the station in a few hours, and their next stop is the cruiser. You could hitch a ride with them."

Yumata raised a brow at the news. "Could you give me the contact information for the shuttle's captain? I'd like to ask him to bring a few things along that I'll need once I'm on the *Indomitable*."

Singh laughed again, pulling out his tablet to send over the info. "I feel sorry for anyone who tries to give you orders, sir. You have a force of will that I've seen in few officers."

"One must set their sights on a goal, and work to achieve it." Yumata pulled up the pilot's details, and composed a message. The list of items he requested was a dozen lines, but most would be easy for a supply ship to procure. Within minutes he received acknowledgement of the request, and shortly afterwards a confirmation that the items would be included.

He unstrapped from the chair in the control room, and pushed off to float toward the exit. "I shall be in my room preparing my bag, commander. Alert me immediately if any messages come in."

"Of course, admiral."

Yumata's trip to his room was a short one, and there were few items not already stowed in his tightly packed bag. Once those items were added, he positioned himself to look through the small window in the floor. He watched Earth rotate below him as the station sped through her high orbit, soaking in the view.

Half an hour later, Selene's face was on the display of his room. "The Executive Committee has approved a short visit, Hiro. You're not going to like the condition, though." She smiled with relish.

"Abernathy," he said through a deep sigh.

"He has to go along, and he'll have operational control of the ship. When Morris says it's time to go, you leave with no questions asked. Do you agree to the terms?"

He wasn't happy with the idea of having the other committee member tagging along, but knew he had to accept it. His only other option was his old plan, to sneak aboard the next ship to dock with the station and force the pilot to take him to the *Indomitable*. Then he would have been counting on officers he'd known for years to circumvent the rules and bring him aboard.

"I agree. A supply shuttle will be docking with the station in less than two hours. Commander Singh suggested using it to transfer to the cruiser, and I concur with the idea."

"Very well. Morris won't like it, but remind him it's a short trip. You'll have to use a shuttle from the cruiser for your return, and he can be more comfortable then." The chairwoman paused for a few seconds, and her eyes narrowed as she continued. "If you're holding any ideas of trying to undermine Captain Guildersen, Hiro, put them out of your head. The Executive Committee made it clear that if there are any problems, they will blame you. Your seat on the Military Committee is at stake."

Yumata smiled, trying to be reassuring. "I understand, Selene."

Abernathy tried to contact him minutes later, but he ignored the connection request and resumed his contemplation of the planet as he let his mind drift through his plans. He was searching for any weak points, or any reason his ideas were incorrect. It was the same thoughts that had occupied his mind for many days, and he could find nothing in them that gave him pause.

Commander Singh let him know when the supply shuttle was on final approach with the station. Yumata was surprised that the man came to his door in person instead of relaying the message over comms. Singh merely held out his hand, squeezed as they shook, and nodded. "It was a pleasure getting to watch you work, admiral. I know that were you in charge, the *Indomitable* would truly be a force to be reckoned with." The man seemed to consider his thoughts for a moment before continuing. "Captain Guildersen is sending a shuttle tomorrow to collect half of the station's crew, forcing them onto his ship. I'd greatly appreciate it if you could talk him down from that, sir."

"I will do my best, commander. I don't think you'll have to worry about your crew being taken from you." Yumata studied him, feeling that the commander had guessed at his plans quite accurately. "It has been a pleasure to see you run this station. Had the Syndicate committees possessed the forethought to place weapons here, I know you would have shown your quality in battle."

As he floated through the corridors, returning to the airlock he'd used several days earlier to board the station, he added the lack of armaments on the station to the growing list of deficiencies he'd seen during his brief stint as a part of the government. Serving aboard frigates, and then overseeing construction of the *Indomitable*, he'd always been under the impression that the various committees operated much like a ship's command structure. Finding out differently had been a crushing disappointment.

It was another disappointment to see Abernathy already waiting in the airlock antechamber. "Yumata, where the hell have you been? I've been calling you for the last hour and a half."

"*Admiral* Yumata." He turned a stony gaze on the younger man. Abernathy had the grace to blush, but wouldn't back down on his demand. "I was busy running through various tactical scenarios."

"Tactical? We're going on a ship to slap the captain's hand and tell him to play nice. You don't need tactics for that."

"Thinking such as that is the reason you committee members fail to get anything done," Yumata said coldly. He was saved from expanding on the thought as the airlock door cycled open to admit a rumpled man.

The shuttle pilot zeroed in on the uniform and saluted the admiral crisply. "Sir, it's a pleasure to have you join me for the quick jaunt over to the cruiser. The items you requested are onboard."

"Excellent. This is Morris Abernathy. He will be joining us."

"Yes, sir, I've got two jump seats prepped and waiting. If you fellas would like to follow me, we'll get ourselves stowed away. It shouldn't take more than ten minutes for the cargo systems to unload the station's crates."

Yumata could sense Abernathy's displeasure throughout the process of entering the supply shuttle. The ship was large enough to almost be called a freighter, transporting up to a quarter million tons of cargo per trip. It was satisfying to watch the young committee member's distaste at the sparse accommodations provided for their trip. The jump seats were no more than narrow crash couches with a few inches of gel.

"Unload is complete, and we're clear to blast off," the pilot said from a few meters in front of their seats. "Hang on, and enjoy the ride!"

The shuttle's engines flared within seconds of releasing from the shuttles docking tube, pushing Yumata back in his seat as he felt the pressure grow on his body. The thin gel provided minimal protection, and he knew that ships such as these could reach eight or nine G's in quick bursts to reach their next destination in the shortest amount of time. He tried to smile at the look of fear on Abernathy's face, but the force against his face prevented the muscles from moving.

Fifteen seconds later the engines cut out, and they returned to weightlessness as it flipped. Abernathy had started to laugh in relief just as the engines flared again to slow the shuttle's approach to the cruiser. It was a shorter burn this time, only ten seconds, but Yumata could see blood trickle from Abernathy's mouth once the engines died again. The man had bitten his tongue when his open jaw snapped shut, a mistake even a novice traveler should have known not to make.

"We've arrived at the *Indomitable*," the pilot announced. "Give me a few minutes to get her settled on the deck, and I'll crack the door so you can get to business."

Once the shuttle door was opened, Yumata briskly descended the steps and looked around the docking bay they had landed in. He instantly recognized it as Bay Two, one of the largest open spaces on the cruiser. There was enough room for two Guild freighters to land and still have space for the motorized carts that pulled material from one point to another.

He was home again.

280

The furnaces were burning more intensely on Rinde's third day working in the factory. Or his body was wearing down and couldn't handle the heat. He wasn't sure which, and didn't have the energy to care. After a fourteen hour shift the day before, he'd gotten no more than six hours of sleep on his threadbare cot before the archaic computer system in his room was screeching an alarm and telling him to wake up.

He understood now why those couple of dozen people waiting for the train on his first day had seemed so old and exhausted. The guards didn't seem to care if they worked someone to death. One man who appeared to be in his sixties collapsed in the middle of the previous day, and the guards clustered around the poor wretch. They shouted abuse, shoved at him with the toes of their heavy boots, and finally resorted to kicking and using their batons. When Rinde entered the furnaces for his third shift, the body was still there.

As one of the newest workers, Rinde was given the jobs that required the most strength. He spent half his day shoving heavy carts filled with ores between different parts of the factory. The other half of his day was occupied with a large wire brush that he used to scrape any drops of smelted metals that fell to the floor around the superheated cauldrons. Those scrapings would be added to the next container filled with chunks of ore that needed to be smelted. His back was feeling so tortured that he could barely push himself into an upright position. Every time he had to get on his knees, he worried that he wouldn't be able to get to his feet again. The muscles in his body screamed for relief that he couldn't give them.

The neoprene suit had proved to be more of a torture device than safety measure. The constant sheen of sweat on his skin meant that his exposed areas rubbed against the interior of the suit with every movement. His skin was scraped raw in many spots, and his feet were wrinkled and blistered from constantly being soaked in his sweat. They itched constantly, and that morning several strips of skin from his soles had peeled off. He didn't need to see a doctor to know that wasn't a good sign. Not that they were allowed to see a doctor for anything in the factory.

Rinde was halfway across the floor with the latest container load of ores when another worker bumped into him. It was light contact, but his body was so tired that he nearly fell to the floor. The other worker grabbed hold of his arm to support him, and leaned in. Familiar eyes looked at him above the rebreather.

"When it happens, run for the door."

The man turned and walked away quickly, before Rinde could ask what he meant. He felt confident the man had been Rawls, the one who spoke of the Guild on his first day. A guard was approaching, giving Rinde no time to consider it further. He twisted himself back into position and heaved on the container to get the rusty wheels turning again.

He'd just emptied the cart into the hopper that fed materials to the furnace cauldron when a scream erupted from across the factory floor. Rinde turned his head to watch in dismay as one of the massive cauldrons was tipped over. Glowing molten metal splashed out onto the guards underneath, clustered around another worker that had collapsed and couldn't get back up. One of the silver suited guards was splashed with a large glob of molten ore, yelling as the thousand degree lump burned through his protective suit. The other guards raised their heads, and started to run as quickly as they could. It wasn't fast enough, as the cauldron fell to its side. Those not crushed under the immense weight were killed by the flood of glowing orange metallic liquid that engulfed them.

A shove to his shoulder brought Rinde's attention back to his immediate area. Workers were shuffling as fast as they could for the doors they exited at the end of a shift. Some few were able to trot, while others could barely walk and were being supported as they tried to escape. Rinde grabbed one person near him who looked close to toppling over, wrapping an arm around the woman's back to help her hurry for the exit doors.

Rawls was standing near the doors, his eyes darting around to examine every person approaching. Rinde saw the man's focus settle on him just as loud sirens began to blare high above. Rawls hurried over, helping to shepherd the woman from the furnace. "We don't have much time," the man shouted over the sirens.

"For what?" Rinde asked, but his voice was drowned out as they passed onto the mesh platform where the workers met the train at the end of their shifts. The sirens were louder here, and a voice was speaking over the intercom. He tried to make out the words, but the speakers were so old and of such poor quality that the voice was no more than a constant squawking noise.

A train car was waiting near the platform. The doors were open, and a man stood nearby waving people in. Rinde and Rawls propelled the woman forward, entering the crowded car among the last of the escaping workers. When the doors closed, the sirens were muffled and he could hear dozens of voices talking over each other.

"What's going on?" he asked Rawls, leaning close to speak into the man's ear.

"You're being rescued. Well, everyone in the factory is being rescued." Rawls had a large grin on his face, the rebreather removed from his mouth and tossed to the floor.

Rinde followed suit with his apparatus. New filters had never been provided, so he'd often wondered why he bothered with it at all. "Who's rescuing us? How?"

"The Guild has been working on this for weeks," Rawls said with a shrug. "I can't give you all the details. You'll have to ask someone higher in the organization for that. All I can say is that we've been getting ourselves arrested on charges we knew would likely land us here, guaranteeing the organization we needed to make this happen."

"But what's the plan? How are we escaping?"

Rawls shrugged again, causing Rinde to grind his teeth in frustration. "I'm not high enough in the pecking order to know things like that. I was told what time it would happen, and instructed to be sure you made it out no matter what else happened."

The train continued on it's journey, taking longer than it usually did when the workers were dropped off at the large platform tor return to their rooms. For the first time, Rinde cursed the lack of windows in the car. He wanted nothing more at that moment than to see where they were heading, and find out what may be waiting for them there.

Twenty minutes after leaving the furnaces, the wheels of the train car squealed as it slowed. When the doors finally opened, the occupants were greeted by the site of a gray and rainy landscape. The ground was covered in concrete for hundreds of meters, leading to a wall in the distance that was topped by twisted wires. Rinde felt sure there would be thousands of sharp points covering that wire, discouraging any attempts to scale the wall.

The man who had ushered workers into the car stepped out onto the tarmac, waving for everyone to follow. Rawls approached him and spoke quietly for a few seconds, and then set about helping to form the workers into a rough line away from the maglev tracks. Their train car sped away, leaving a few dozen people standing in the rain staring at empty concrete.

"This is an escape plan?" Rinde whispered. He looked around, seeing only the imposing wall in one direction and the smoking stacks of the factory in another. Soon, another train car screeched to a stop. The doors opened, and twenty or thirty people exited the car. The newcomers were dressed in blue jumpsuits, sleeves and torsos covered in grease stains. They looked at Rinde's group apprehensively, eyeing the neoprene suits and soot covered faces. Five minutes later another train car arrived, disgorging more factory workers.

Rawls pushed through the growing crowd, everyone standing close enough to rub shoulders. "When our transport arrives, you're the first one aboard. Orders from the top."

"Transport?" Rinde looked around again. "What kind of transport?" Rawls smirked and pointed up. Rinde cast his eyes to the cloudy sky, and saw a growing brightness behind the clouds. Seconds later, they billowed as a battered ship pushed through them to land on the bare concrete. Landing struts extended mere moments before the ship settled on the ground.

The engines maintained a dull roar as two large doors on the nose of the ship swiveled open to expose a large cargo bay that was nearly empty. A wide ramp extended, and Rinde felt himself being pushed forward before it even touched the concrete. Rawls hustled him onto the ship, with the other workers streaming behind them to find safety aboard the freighter.

A man was waiting at the top of the ramp. He was young, with short blonde hair and blue eyes that seemed to take in everything around him. He smiled and raised a hand as Rinde stopped a few feet away. "Minister Brighton, it's a pleasure to see you. President Meyers is going to be very happy to hear that you made it out."

"I'm not a minister any longer," Rinde said, returning the handshake. "What ship is this, please?"

"Oh! Sorry about that, I got ahead of myself in the excitement of being part of a prison break. I'm Captain Erik Frost, and this is the *Vagabond*. Let me show you to the quarters I've had prepared for you, and you can freshen up. Once we get these people loaded up, we'll be launching for Luna."

Rawls waved as Rinde looked back, seeing what appeared to be half a hundred people crowding into the cargo bay. Behind them, he could see yet another train car arriving to deliver more factory workers. "This can't be everyone confined here, captain. The factory has to have thousands of forced laborers."

"One thousand four hundred and nineteen according to the documents I've seen. Don't worry, sir, we'll get as many of them as we can. Two more freighters are beginning descent soon, and there are others queued up behind them." The young captain's jaw rippled as he the muscles clenched. "We're prepared for any attempt to resist our rescues."

Three armored soldiers squeezed by at that moment, headed for the cargo bay doors. Rinde turned to watch them, fascinated by the light gray armor with red accents. He thought the design over their chests was an arm drawing back a bow, but he couldn't be certain from the quick glimpse.

"We have thirty militia soldiers, ten on each of the first three ships," Captain Frost told him as they stopped before a cabin door. "More than enough to hold off any guards that try to prevent our rescues." With a few taps on the screen beside it, the door slid open to reveal a spotless room with a bed, storage closet, and small washroom. "President Meyers provided a suit for you, sir. It's in the closet. If you need anything, you can contact the control room on your display. I left some water and a protein bar on the desk here. Galley is on the other side of the ship if you need more, and we'll be handing out food and drink to everyone in the cargo bay as soon as we're off the ground."

Rinde stepped inside the room, marveling at how comfortable it felt. It was half the size of the small room he had spent the last several days living in, but felt like a palace in comparison. "Thank you, Captain Frost."

"Just call me Erik," the young man said with a friendly smile. "We'll be travelling at low speeds since the people in the bay can't strap in, so we should be at Luna in about three hours."

The door closed, leaving Rinde alone. The fact of his escape from the factory was starting to become reality, and he raised his hands to wipe away tears. Feeling the rough gloves reminded him of the uncomfortable neoprene and he pushed the suit off his body with disgust. He could feel a vibration under his feet as he stepped into the small washroom and pressed a button to start the shower. It gave him joy to know the freighter was leaving the factory, even if it meant he was leaving Earth.

Clean and refreshed, he ate the protein bar with relish. It tasted wonderful in comparison to the tasteless compressed brown nutrient bars he was forced to eat when he couldn't make the boring bread in his room's tiny kitchen. Drinking the cool water, he opened the cabin's small closet and looked at the suit provided. It was black, with a crisp white linen shirt. Classic colors and cut, which he appreciated. The material was soft between his fingers, heavy enough to provide warmth in the cooler environment of a space ship and the Luna domes.

He didn't want to wrinkle the suit, so he left it in the closet and tied a towel around his waist before lying on the soft bunk. With a sigh, he closed his eyes and enjoyed the first true relaxation he'd been able to experience in weeks. He could feel sleep trying to pull him down, but the thought of the dozens of workers crammed into the cargo bay made him open his eyes and sit up. It was true he was no longer a minister, or part of the Coalition government, but he still felt a strong desire to care for the people.

It was quick work to dress in the suit, and he took a moment to examine his reflection in the mirrored surface of the powered down display. He was thinner than he had been, from the stress of trying to figure out what was going on with his government and then his time working in the furnaces. At the same time, he looked stronger. In body and in spirit. He had suffered hardship, and through that experience he felt closer to the people who toiled in similar labors every day on Earth to feed themselves and their families.

Finding his way back to the cargo bay was easier than expected. Rinde turned the wrong way out of his cabin, but he found the corridor to be an oval that led him to his destination via a longer route. He passed by a reactor room and the galley, paused a moment near the door marked as the control center, and then entered the cargo bay on the opposite side of the chamber from where he had left it.

The workers were huddled together in groups, tending to cluster with those they were acquainted with from shifts within the factory. Rinde could understand that need for the comfort of something familiar in strange surroundings. A few heads turned to look as he entered the bay, noticing his suit and turning away. Rawls sauntered over with a sly grin. "Don't you look good all fancied up? A little familiar, too. I guess it's true that you were high in the government before you ended up in the factory."

"I was, until I questioned the prime minister's way of doing things. Now I'm no more or less than anyone else in this cargo bay." Rinde saw a woman in a teal jumpsuit weaving through the groups, carrying a box from which she pulled protein bars and pouches of water. "It's good to see these people being treated well. Do you know what is waiting for us on Luna?"

"Sanctuary," Rawls said simply. "A place where we won't be forced to work in harsh conditions just because we say something the government doesn't like."

"Hm." Rinde hoped the Guild would prove to be more enlightened than the Coalition had become. He wouldn't give up on setting things on a better path on Earth, but he knew there would be a lot of work ahead before that could happen.

As soon as the freighter was safely settled on the Luna docking pad, Rinde was one of the first to enter Aldrin through the airlocks. It would take half an hour to get all the rescued factory workers off the ship, and he could see impatience in Captain Frost's eyes. A desire to get back to the planet and scoop more people to take them to safety.

President Meyers was waiting in the docking facility with a relieved expression, hurrying forward with a hand outstretched. "Rinde! You don't know how good it is to see your face again."

"No more than it is to see yours, my friend. I thank you with all my heart for your help in releasing us from that horrible place."

"If I'd known such a thing as the factory existed, I wouldn't have waited as long as I did." Meyers examined him, one hand tightly clenched on his shoulder. "How do you feel, Rinde? Are you strong enough to help me start a revolution?"

ACKNOWLEDGEMENTS

I would like to thank my friends and family, who have been so supportive of my venture into authorship. On days that I'm feeling down, my friends help to keep me focused on what's important – telling the story.

I'd also like to thank Christopher Doll again for the awesome cover art on this series. He is a joy to work with, and his creations are beautiful to look at.

Tim has been a dreamer since he was a small boy, and is finally putting all his wild imaginings onto paper. During the day, he is an IT support technician for a nationwide bank. At night, he bangs away on his keyboard and often obsesses over the proper word to express an idea or feeling.

He can be found online at www.timrangnow.com, along with all the latest news on his upcoming books and works in progress.

Vagabond *March 2020*

Indomitable *May 2020*

Waterloo *July 2020*

Resolute *coming August 2020*